The Decider

A Dangerous Gift

Kami,
  thank you for always being so
supportive and loving! I always
enjoy the moments we get to just
sit and chat!
  Have a blessed day!
            Always, Mychaiel
                    Schupbach-
                        Nowell

The Decider

A Dangerous Gift

Mycheille Norvell

A. Joyful House Publishing & Design LLC

2020

Depoe Bay, Oregon

This book is a work of fiction. Names, characters, places, and incidents are the product of the author's imagination or are used fictitiously. Any resemblance to actual events, locales, or persons, living or dead, is coincidental.

A. Joyful House Publishing
& Design LLC
2020

A.   Joyful House Publishing & Design LLC

PO Box 75, Depoe Bay, OR 97341

Description: First Edition 2020/ Book 1

Summary: 16-year-old Kaydence "Kayd" Harrow has been on the run with her brother Galen for 4 years. Her brother has the gift of Prophecy, and it leads them towards the Green-Eyed Man, with whom will someday overthrow the tyrant acting as their president. The world has changed, it is darker, meaner, and when Kayd discovers she too is Gifted—and with the most dangerous gift—everything she knows will change forever.

Identifiers: ISBN – 9798573475042

Acknowledgements

Inspiration: My amazing mom, Sandra; my darling daughter, Abby; my sister, Stephanie; my brother, Robert; my sister-in-law Dominique; my dad, Bob; my best friend Natasha; and the many others in my life who tirelessly share their love, their confidence, and their unwavering belief in me and my abilities. You are all so incredible, and I'm beyond blessed to have you all in my life, and rooting for me in my corner. Thank you!

My Team: Without you all, this would have been a much different version of my story! Thank you! And I want to thank my amazing Illustrator/ Cover Designer, DMarieHull. You are an amazing artist, and I'm honored that you would lend your own skills and your talent to this project. Much love! To my brother that threw ideas back and forth with me, helping me create backstories I never would have considered, and guided me forward in marketing plans. And, to my sister, who is a constant cheerleader for me in my books!

You are all amazing! Thank you!

~ <u>Title Page</u> ~

The Decider

A Dangerous Gift

Prologue

I can hear Mommy washing dishes in the next room singing some little song. I sit on Daddy's lap as he pulls out one of the big books I'm not usually allowed to read. Galen is crying in his nursery—he woke up, I guess.

"Kaydy, the world wasn't always like it is now. Once, it was different." When Daddy talks, he always sounds like he's talking about the greatest things in the world. He always shares his excitement with me. Adults don't usually seem excited about things with kids, but he does. "This book is special, it's by one of my favorite writers, but it's all true." He says seriously like he expects me to really commit it all to memory.

"'Rome wasn't built in a day,' they used to say." Daddy begins as he starts to read from the book. I make out a few of the words on the page, but I'm too tired to focus on reading, so I let Daddy's beautiful, low voice lull me as he reads. "This was to say that everything takes work, and that anything worth having doesn't just happen without time and effort. But what if anything could've been built in a day? What if all good things happened as soon as you wished them? Well, after the Discovery of the Gifted, this became a reality. Men and women began developing special abilities from birth, and at first it seemed not to discriminate, almost every child was born with these Gifts."

Mommy lets out a long sigh, "Really Grant? You have to read *that* of all things to a five-year-old girl?"

"It's our history, darling. It's important." He calls back with a small smile before he looks back down at me, and then he continues.

"With these Gifts came the long-awaited peace. Cities were being built in a single day with a combination of the Speakers, who could convince any person of the importance of a project, giving them the will to continue; the Emotys, who could change a bad attitude into a positive one instantly; the Creators, who could turn wood or bricks into buildings with a few simple movements of their hands and the right materials at their disposal; and the Healers who quickly turned any wound into new flesh. There were others too, like the Prophets who could see into the future—it was rumored the older ones could actually change the future if they were strong enough. Also, there were the Growers who could make any seed grow anywhere, even in the desert. Within a few years, all war ceased, and death from old age seemed to be the only way someone might pass."

I sat up a little straighter now. This was like a fairytale, and it was way more interesting than the newscasts on the TV that we usually watched this time of night. I know I've heard the men on the TV talk about Gifted people... but they aren't nice about them. In Daddy's book, though, the Gifted people sound beautiful.

"But, after five hundred years, the Gifts began to change, and new abilities began to form that became known as the Dangerous Ones." Daddy hesitated, his tone slightly darker, and I felt a shiver

move down my spine. *"These included Freezers, who could stop you in your spot with a single look in the eye; the new Speakers, who, from a single touch, could know all of your secrets and would sell them to the highest bidder; the Shockies, who, like their name, could shock you with more than just a spark or a bolt of lightning; and the Colossals, who were stronger than anyone should be, who tore apart the cities that had been so beautifully created.*

"And quickly all things lovely and good were forced into ruins. War consumed the world until those who were not Gifted began killing those who were in hopes of destroying the threat. By the year 2892, almost all the Gifted had been wiped out. New leaders were put in place, going back to the Old Days of Presidents and Democracy from before the Peace, and for a while it seemed the world might be pieced back together.

"Grant—that is enough! She doesn't need to hear this!" my mom said, moving to the edge of Daddy's study, glaring in at him with worry. Mommy worried a lot.

Daddy waves her off, "Honey, it's just a story. Kaydence can handle it."

Mommy sighs with uncertainty, holding my little brother Galen against her hip as she continues soothing him. I think he already fell back to sleep against her shoulder though. "She'll learn about it in school. She doesn't have to hear this biased version from that crackpot author." She says, shaking her head.

Daddy sighs, "Joseph Hensley has some good points, dear. Now stop fretting. I'll make sure she goes to bed." He urges. Mommy lets out a long sigh before disappearing around the corner. Daddy chuckles, "Let's get back to it, huh?" he asks. I nod. My eyes are wide, but I want to hear more.

"*Cities and homes were built up again, going back to that old saying, 'Rome wasn't built in a day,' and no city was built in a day ever again. By the year 3042 more Gifted children were born, though scarcely, and President Pierce, the thirty-seventh president since the end of the Peace, suggested that it was time to allow Gifted children to live, aside from the Dangerous Ones. But 35 years later, when President Reece came into power, everything changed.*"

Daddy suddenly sounded mad, but that was strange... Daddy never got mad. He was always so calm. I noticed him clench his fist, but he didn't say anything about it. He just continued.

"*The Presidency became a dictatorship, though Reece made the people believe that he was the only hope in the fight against the Gifted. Soldiers were put in place on every block in every town to 'protect' the people, but instead they were informers to what would soon be referred to as the Authority. Reece quickly started keeping the Dangerous Ones as his hidden army, making sure that no one would challenge his leadership, and no one did. Those who were Gifted began hiding, faking their own deaths, or trying to seem normal to escape persecution.*

"There was only one form of the Gifted that President Reece has not yet caught—possibly the most dangerous, and most mysterious of all the Gifted—the Deciders. Little is known about them, because as soon as one was found early on, they were one of the first to be killed... or captured. The only thing known about the Deciders is simply a rumor that they could decide whether someone was worthy to live or die. And President Reece will do anything to find one, even if it means killing those whom he swore he would protect."

"Oh my God, Grant!" my mother's voice was like a shriek. I jumped in Daddy's lap. Mommy hurried in, scooping me up into her thin arms, "That's enough! I don't want you reading this nonsense to her again!" I barely glanced at the cover of the book as she swept me away. It said: *Conspiracy of the Gifted.* And then she pulled me up the stairs.

I looked up at her in confusion, "But wasn't that stuff real, Mommy?" I asked with curiosity.

Her expression turned tense, "The Gifted aren't good, sweetie. The Gifted are evil... Daddy and I just don't agree on that." She replies softly before dropping me on my bed and tucking me in.

Mommy went to read me a little fairytale, but I couldn't stop thinking about the book Daddy read to me. For some reason I wanted to know more about the Gifted people Daddy talked about. I liked thinking they were good... maybe Mommy was wrong?

Chapter 1: Gifted
(11 years later)

My head rests against my 12-year-old brother's shoulder, and though he is probably the boniest person on the planet, he makes a surprisingly comfortable pillow, at least when you are used to sleeping on rocks. The smell of rotting flesh and burning newspapers overwhelms my nostrils and my eyes burst open as I begin searching the horizon for our attackers, but I see nothing. I find myself standing without knowing how I got to my feet so quickly. My brother's eyes flutter sleepily as he looks at me in confusion,

"Kayd... what's wrong?" he asks, his voice slipping between the voice of a young boy and the manly octave that it is trying to transform into.

I raise my hand to silence him, and he understands instantly. No more words are spoken until my hand drops and my body relaxes again. I roll my shoulders to loosen my tight muscles from another restless sleep. I pick up my black backpack and pile the few possessions we still carry back inside, "We need to get moving again..."

"But Kayd! Why can't we just sleep a little longer?" he replies in his whiny tone, and I suddenly recognize that he is still the boy I remember from when we were little kids. I smile at the memory of the small boy with perpetual bedhead, and a blue bowtie that he never wanted to take off his neck even when he was in pajamas. His blonde hair always shined in the sun, and his bright blue eyes always seemed to glow in the dark with the pleasant light of youth and innocence. I often miss the little boy, but every so often I see him once more in my brother's still-blue eyes—they still hold that innocence, even though mine have long since lost such naivety.

I sometimes wonder if he remembers me back then too, long red pigtails and a ruffled dress that usually was covered in dirt from playing where I wasn't supposed to be. I often forget that I was also little once since it feels like so much longer ago than it actually is. I'm 16 now, but I feel even older since we left home.

"Galen, you know we can't stay out in the open like this when sunrise is only an hour away." I say more harshly than I mean to, but the cruel dreams came again, and I don't know how to separate those emotions from my reality. He nods grumpily and forces himself to his feet.

We start trudging towards the denser part of the forest again. He doesn't smell what I smell, nor does he see what I see, and luckily for him he never will.

My body has changed since then when I was 12 and still felt like childhood would last forever instead of only seconds. I was beginning to form the shape of the woman I would someday become, even if that woman will be forever imprisoned for her crimes.

But why would a young girl of 16 possibly be imprisoned?

Because I saved someone who I was not supposed to save… but what else could I have done? I couldn't let them kill him, the boy that was so sweet, so bold. I knew exactly what I was doing when I saved him, though I didn't know what it would mean then.

Galen is Prophetic, sharing with his family a treasonous vision in which our dictator would be removed, and that a young man with green eyes would free our world from the confinement we have suffered. Such a simple vision, it could've just been a dream, but in our society such dreams are forbidden. Prophets are not praised but extinguished as soon as they are found. Even at 12, I knew that my brother was going to die, yet it was something I could not allow. At 12 I forced myself to become an adult to protect him. At 12… I promised my father that I would shield my sweet brother from all harm even if it meant dying to protect him.

I watched the Soldiers with fire in their hands as they threw the torches into my home with my parents barred inside, and began circling the house with flames created from books and old newspapers. I had forced Galen into a tree stump to hide as I went back to my home and watched my world burn. He didn't know what was happening—always stuck in some other world where everything was good and nothing bad could happen.

My heart breaks at the memory and I shake my head as I try to hide the trickling tears that occasionally escaped. Galen was not allowed to see these pesky emotions, because then he would ask questions I couldn't answer. He would say,

'Kayd, why can't we go home yet?'

'Kayd why are you crying'

'Kayd... why can't we stop?'

These questions are not allowed because I don't know the answer, which is why I cry.

"Kayd... where are we going?" He asks me quietly, knowing that he would get in trouble by me if anyone heard us.

My father had prepared me for the day I'd have to leave, but we always assumed it would be well after I had become a young woman, not a pre-teen. How funny the hunting practice and the lessons about being like a ghost had seemed—Ninja Lessons, I called them—though now I use them daily. I had thought they were games for make-believe, but now I see they are the only way of survival.

"This week we are going to Westin Falls, it's about a three day walk from here, I think." I tell him as I consult my map. We had been blessed to not meet another human in almost a year. The last time we met someone, we were nearly given over to the Authority immediately.

We walk silently over the moss-covered ground as the birds sing happily in the trees, reminding me of a kinder time. The dark sky turns a gentle gray-blue, ushering in the dawn of a new day. I take in a deep breath knowing that Galen and I are possibly only moments from being caught.

My usual strategy was for us to stay in the thickest trees so no one would recognize our movements as anything other than animals.

When we first left home over four years ago, we used to walk during the night and sleep during the day. I had thought this made more sense, but the problem was that people tend to notice when people are running past their windows, or odd rustlings in the trees in the dark. We were almost caught at least three times in our first month because of this.

I didn't really know where we were going in the end, except that we were supposed to keep moving. My dad had given me a map when I was a little girl and had just begun my training just in case my brother and I had to go out into the woods. He outlined special paths I was supposed to take while Galen and I hid from the Authority.

While we walked in near silence, I would often get lost in my haunting memories. Every day I found I was drifting too far into that unknown abyss of my mind. I would be gone in my thoughts for so long that, by the time I came back to reality, Galen and I had walked for a few hours. The nightmares were entering my daydreams now, and, no matter how hard I tried to get away from them, they hung onto me with an iron grasp.

I've been trying to keep my foothold in the now when my mind starts drifting, and for the most part I'm getting better, but I still get lost sometimes. I think it's because deep down, I missed that simple life. I missed being the little girl who could play with friends, and sit on her Daddy's lap, and go to her parent's room at night when she was scared. I wanted to be that little girl. But I wasn't anymore...

I was the 16-year-old fugitive forced to run possibly for her entire life.

I really didn't know where we were supposed to go besides the neatly laid-out lines my father had sketched for me at least four years ago. Eventually we would have to stop, but nowhere ever seemed safe enough. We used to stay at our checkpoints for a few weeks... until we found that we were being followed. The longer you stay somewhere, the easier it was for people to find you.

I honestly didn't understand why anyone would still be looking for us. Galen was a Prophet, not a Speaker who could make you do anything he wanted with a touch and a command. He wasn't doing anyone any harm, so why were they still following us?

I laughed angrily at the thought and Galen jumped, "Did you see something Kayd?" he asks, and I stop suddenly, looking back at him with surprise.

How long had I been out of it this time? I look at my watch: Only an hour. It was getting better... barely though.

"Sorry, just lost in thought." I say quietly as I urge him forward.

"Kayd... wait." He replies with fear tainting his innocent voice.

I yield instantly to his warning. Though Galen couldn't control when his visions appeared, I never took them for granted just in case they were meant for our near future. I move forward quickly as he faints in my arms.

This happened sometimes, but usually he woke up within a few minutes. I wait the usual five minutes for him to stir, but there was no movement. So, I wait ten, twenty, forty minutes... he isn't waking up anytime soon.

The sun was breaking over the mountains in the morning sky, signaling it was around 7:00, and my watch agreed. We couldn't stay where we were—it was too open, even for a forest. I felt my paranoia set in, as every sound around me seemed to sound human instead of those made from birds or small animals that weren't a threat.

I put my elbows under Galen's armpits and braced my hands on the front of his shoulders, pulling him backwards towards a small rock enclosure. I waited another two hours before Galen awoke, his mind a haze of blurred people and confusing actions.

He rubs his eyes slowly and I hand him a bottle of water. He gulps it down in a minute and wipes his lips before he speaks, "It was the Green-eyed Man again." He said tiredly, "He was younger this time though. I'm not sure when it was... maybe now? Maybe a few years from now?" he sighed, it was his turn to drift into his thoughts, but his were important.

"What happened this time?"

He opens his eyes and looked at me with care, "You were with him actually." I felt my shoulders fall... it was just a dream. He did this sometimes: mixed his visions with his dreams. I, of course, would not meet the man who was going to be leader of our world, "You were, Kayd!" he urged, almost angry at my unbelief.

I nod as I put his water bottle back in my black bag, trying to think of where we could fill it up next, "Of course I was, Galen." I say with more sarcasm than I intended. He tries standing, probably to stomp away in a childish tantrum, "Galen sit down. Don't be mad, okay? It's just you have had dreams like this before, where you saw Emma with him, remember?"

His angry expression wilted at the memory. He knew I was right since obviously his friend Emma could never meet the Green-eyed man since she was dead. The girl was given to the Soldiers when she was found out to be Gifted. They said she was dangerous, but she was just a Grower—someone who could turn any seed into easily grown food—but they killed her all the same.

"This was different though, Kayd…" he whispered hopefully, his eyes pleading like he *needed* me to believe it.

I sighed as I sat back beside him and put my arm around his shoulders, so he felt comfortable again, "Okay, tell me about it."

I tried to be patient and kind as he told me his newest 'vision', though I still believed it was just a dream. Only in a dream would I, the awkward redheaded girl, be running through the forest with our future Leader. He said that we were sitting by a waterfall, and I had my toes dipped in the water as the man and I spoke, though Galen couldn't tell what we were talking about.

When Galen was done, I kissed his forehead, "Well I guess you never know, right?" he nodded as if this was the affirmation he needed, even though it was my way of kindly saying, *"That's never going to happen."*

Galen often was incredibly worn out after his visions, and since this one kept him under for a few hours, I figured he would want a little time to recuperate. It wasn't often that he said no when I offered a rest, and today was no different. He decided to take a short nap, and I kept guard, not that it was really necessary.

I was just getting comfortable when Galen shot up with his eyes wide open. He stared at me as if making sure I wasn't a figment of his imagination. He quickly stood up and packed everything back into my backpack.

"What are you doing?" I asked in confusion, "I thought you wanted to rest? You've only been asleep for like 15 minutes."

He smiled too excitedly, "I just want to get moving. I think Westin Falls is closer than you thought." He pulled me to my feet and practically dragged me through the forest at first. After a while he started slowing down, probably realizing that we were not going to get to the waterfall today. And as we slowed, my mind started drifting again. I thought back to the day we left.

Honestly, when I first vowed that I would leave with Galen, I hadn't known what would happen. I thought we could come home after a few days when the Soldiers had given up... not realizing that they don't give up. Not knowing that my parents would be burned in a fire meant for my brother and me... because of his Gift, and because I saved him. I still could hear my mother screaming out my name from inside the house, the horrid smell of my happy memories being erased.

After the Soldiers left, I ran back to my home, forcing Galen into a log hidden from view, not caring if I was caught. I pushed through the dying flames that still grew with the occasional wind that fanned it. I walked through the rubble, still remembering the white walls with picture frames angled up the stairs, and flowers strewn throughout the room. Now all that was left were ashes and the frame of my once beautiful home.

I remembered how the tears blurred my vision, and suddenly those tears were in my eyes again, and I realized Galen was trying to get my attention. I looked around, feeling the confusion as I reminded myself of where I was... *when* I was. "Kayd!" he said in a loud whisper.

I was on the soft ground. I could feel the hidden branches stabbing me through the layer of moss. I looked up at Galen. His face was red, almost swollen looking. I rubbed my eyes, "I'm sorry, Galen, I guess I was the one who needed that rest." I said with a small smile, thinking that was the solution to his red face, and fearful tone.

He looked behind me and then into my eyes. I felt my body go stiff as I looked down at my hands—they were tied tightly together with rope. How had someone tied me up? I hadn't been sleeping... I had been walking, hadn't I? I often got lost in my thoughts, but not lost so far that someone could catch us that easily.

I looked around, trying to catch sight of our attackers, and I was instantly taken aback when I looked into the eyes of the man closest to us—a man with bright green eyes.

Chapter 2: Trusting

He was the most handsome man I had ever seen. I tried to hide my awe of him and show strength instead, but I was dizzy, and I still didn't understand what was happening. "What should we do with them, Leon?" said an older man who was probably over 40 years old.

The handsome man looked over to us, and suddenly I saw his features more clearly: a strong chin, with slightly angled cheeks guiding up to his remarkable green eyes. Green eyes! Suddenly the reference meant something to me.

I looked to my brother with a gaze I hoped he would understand, and he nodded with a slightly fearful gaze. I wanted to hold him because I knew what that look meant to him: this was not what he expected the hero from his vision to be like—a raider with a group of thugs.

I looked back to the handsome man who I assumed to be Leon, and he was looking me in the eye. I thought I could see warmth in them. He smiled, and without meaning to, so did I.

"Kids don't just hide out on their own, Kent. They were probably running from something." He said to the older man. Leon's voice was so kind—soft, though commanding at the same time. I couldn't be sure of his age, but I had to assume he was at least 20.

"Who says they are alone?" growled Kent, his hands flinging in the air. "Their parents could be hiding in the trees, waiting to jump us!" Kent had a surprisingly high-pitched voice to come from such a burly man, standing at about 6'3.

I tried to scoot towards my brother, and he put his head on my shoulder as soon as I came within reach. I lifted my bound hands, wrapping my arms around Galen and held him close.

"If they are running, it means the Soldiers are not far behind!" said a man that looked like he was in his mid-twenties.

"Thomas, you know the Soldiers don't come into the forests—they aren't *that* stupid," said Leon as he rubbed his temples.

"We need to find out if they are alone!" shouted Kent.

"Why does it matter really? If they are alone or not, you will still try stealing the few things these kids have," said Leon harshly. Kent glared at Leon and grumbled.

"They might be spies, Leon! You know the Authority has been using their *experiments* on unsuspecting rebels."

Leon laughed, "And where did you hear that, Kent?"

I liked his laugh... it reminded me of a happier time. I felt myself drifting back into my past again, but I shook my head and tried to stay in the present.

Kent huffed with frustration, "I hear things too, Leon!"

Leon patted him on the back, "Of course, Kent." He calmed his laughter and waved the men away from us. "Go back to camp, and I'll figure out what to do with the kids."

As I heard the distant footsteps of the other men, I watched Leon's feet as they approached us. I quickly turned my eyes down at my brother's shaking form in my arms, "It's ok, Galen... I won't let them hurt you." I whispered in his ear.

He nodded, but it didn't stop his shaking. I had always wondered if Galen's visions were real, but as I allowed my gaze to drift towards those dazzling green eyes staring down at me, I knew I would never doubt him again.

Leon stopped in front of me and bent down next to us, putting all his weight on the balls of his feet, "Would it be ok if I cut those ropes?" he said softly, and I dared to meet his gaze.

Close up, he looked even kinder than I had thought before. I trust him. Averting my gaze quickly, I nodded and pulled my arms from around my brother and let him cut my binding. I then cut the ropes on Galen's wrists and he instantly grabbed around my waist, making him appear at least five years younger than he was.

Leon took a deep breath, "How long?" he said knowingly, his eyes filled with compassion.

I looked around the canopy of trees around us, fearing that some distant spy would hear my secret and instantly know who Galen and I were, but I shrugged my shoulders like it was nothing, "Four years..."

Leon's eyes grew in shock and he sat down beside us, "I've never heard of kids so young hiding for so long." He said in a quiet, awed voice. "Why haven't you gone home by now?"

I looked down at Galen carefully and then back to Leon, "Our home was destroyed by the Soldiers…" I reply simply, hoping my tone offers him a warning.

"What about your parents." He said in a tender, tentative voice.

Galen looked up at me then, wanting to know that answer too. "Um… they told us to run… and I think they got away too." I said for Galen's benefit.

Leon looked at Galen who smiled softly and tucked his head back at my shoulder, and Leon nodded meaningfully, his lips pursed in understanding.

"I'm sure they did." He said kindly. "What Gift do you have?" he asked me, and I almost laughed. I wasn't the special one, but I realized he was serious.

"We don't even know you… and besides, why do you assume either of us have a Gift?"

He smiled carefully, "Kids don't run away unless someone does."

"I have a Gift!" Galen said, suddenly excited. I slapped my hand over his mouth. Leon laughed a little,

"Galen!" I whispered angrily.

"But Kayd, it's h—" I shook my head angrily at him and he stopped his words, but not before giving me a smug smile that said: "I told you so!"

"So, Kayd and Galen?" Leon butted in, and I was relieved to have him speak.

"It's Kaydence…" I managed to say quickly, trying to sound cold but I'm not sure it worked out that way.

"Well, I'm Leon Hensley." I instantly recognized the name… he was the son of the former Vice President. I almost choked on my next breath, he laughed, "I gather you remember me?"

How could I forget? I remember watching the interviews with my dad on Sunday afternoons. Jonathan Hensley, Leon's father, was the country's favorite even though he wasn't technically the president. He was considered the Father of the Rebels. He believed in celebrating your differences, and your Gifts if you were lucky enough to have one.

Sadly, President Paul Reese had made it clear to the country that such lies were not to be spread. Reese quickly catapulted Hensley from office, and made sure he never had any power again. I remember my dad used to say that President Reese was afraid of Hensley's followers.

But I remembered one interview in particular when I was 10… the one where I began my crush on the young Leon Hensley. He came in and stood at the door just when his dad beckoned him in, "Come on in, Leon! Don't be shy. This is my son, America." He said to his then 12-year-old son as he happily patted him on the back. Leon smiled bashfully, "Leon has been blessed with one of these Gifts as well…"

"Dad... *don't.*" Leon said almost ashamedly, clenching his fists.

Jonathan laughed, "It's time you stop letting it shame you, Leon. Everyone else like you needs to know it's not something to be afraid of."

I never did find out what his Gift was, but it was the fact that he seemed so nice, so normal, that I had liked him. And looking at him now, four years later, I liked him even more. "I remember you." I offer simply.

I was a little surprised that it hadn't hit me earlier that this man, with his emerald green eyes, had never come to mind when my brother had divulged his vision.

"I'm sorry about my companions earlier." He began as he stood up and wiped the leaves and dirt from his gray jeans. "Even though we are all Gifted, they get a little bit skeptical of the young who are Gifted since the President has been experimenting on them and making them the perfect spies to infiltrate the Rebel camps. Kids under 16 are the only ones who they use because most people won't hurt children." He said almost darkly, staring in the direction of his companions, "But I won't let anyone hurt you."

He smiled as he held out his hand for me to stand too. I just stared at it for a moment, remembering quickly that I really shouldn't trust a stranger, no matter how kind they appear. But Galen quickly took Leon's hand instead and stood.

"Leon..." I said quietly and he looked at me with brightness in his eyes, "This may sound really stupid... but how did you guys catch us? I mean... I was distracted, but I don't get it."

He laughed, "I told you, my companions all are Gifted. One of them, Kent, froze you guys to your spot while Joe came and tied your hands. Don't worry, it wasn't just because you were distracted." It had been so long since I had had a conversation with someone besides my brother, but I couldn't help but feel like Leon was awfully nice compared to how people were supposed to be to fugitives from the law. His kindness reminded me of my parents, and I suddenly didn't like it.

"Well my brother and I need to get moving... we can't really stop." My voice was harsh, and I just hoped my expression matched it.

He considered Galen and I, "Kaydence, you don't have to run anymore. My friends and I can protect you both. Those of us who are Gifted have to stick together."

"Come on Kayd, you know we can trust him. Remember my..." I put my hand over his mouth again and shook my head.

"Leon, may I speak to my brother for a moment." I said coldly, and he nodded politely and took a few steps away and leaned up against a tree. "Galen... even if they are Gifted, I can't risk any of them ever going to the other side and turning you in. And besides, I'm not..." my voice starts to break a little.

"Gifted?" he said softly as he squeezed my hand, "This is where we have been headed all this time, Kayd."

I felt my temper rise, "You were afraid of him just ten minutes ago!"

He nodded, "That's because I thought he was like the other men he was with. One of them slapped me, but I'll stay away from that man." He promised as if this would be the only fear of mine. He smiled so hopefully, the way he always did when he wanted something and knew I couldn't say no. I wanted to just run away right then, keep us safe a little longer, but I knew he was right.

For all I knew, maybe this was part of his vision? He knew we had to meet up with Leon at some point... I just wasn't ready to be around people again. People were mean. People were betrayers. People were cruel... but I understood that to Galen, he didn't think of it that way. He just thinks of Leon, the person who is kind, and sincere, and someone we can trust.

And then it hit me: all this time Galen has followed me blindly, trusting where I led him without a second thought. Now it was my turn to do the same for him. And so, I nodded as we walked over to Leon. He smiled graciously and ushered us forward. God, I hoped Galen was right.

Leon guided us back to his camp, and once we arrived, I realized there were far more people than I would've ever expected. Men, women, and an occasional child, usually under the age of 5—making me assume the children had probably been born within the camp. I felt my childish fears rising in my chest as I held onto Galen's hand tighter. I leaned my head down and whispered, "Galen... don't tell anyone your Gift." He nodded.

I began to feel the burning glare of at least a hundred eyes on my neck, and I pulled Galen closer to my side. It was in that moment I remembered, once again, that Galen was not the short little boy who only came to my breasts before... he was almost 5'5, roughly the same height as me. He had hit his first growth spurt early compared to most of the boys I had known before. I looked at his face and realized, under his baby fat, I could see the chiseling features trying to push to the surface.

I quickly looked away, unwilling to acknowledge my brother would be a man sooner than I was ready to admit. I took in a deep breath and looked around cautiously. So many families and couples were staring us down as if we were criminals walking down Death Row. I realized that, besides the children and Leon, no one was less than 20 years old.

A few men seemed to charge forward unhappily towards us, but Leon raised a hand to them, and instantly they stopped in their place and went back to what they were doing. Leon finally walked us through one of the largest tents in the camp and led us to a very kind looking woman, who looked as if she might be in her late forties. "Kaydence, Galen, I would like you to meet my mom, Anna Hensley." He said, ever the gentleman, and Anna came and shook both of our hands.

"Kaydence? What a pretty name." she said sweetly, her voice was like a delicate song drifting on the breeze. Her smile was bright and cheery, and though her clothes looked a little old and worn, she was still glamorous. Seeing Anna Hensley made me wonder even more: Where was Mr. Hensley?

Galen and Mrs. Hensley began talking and she instantly began telling him elaborate stories about knights and goblins and maidens locked in towers.

I wanted to listen too, but Leon gently grabbed my hand, and I felt something warm inside my chest as I dared to meet his eyes. He looked towards the tent door and then back to me—he wanted to go outside. I took one more glance at my happy brother before nodding and following Leon.

He guided me past all the angry onlookers, and towards a loud stream. Once I saw the water, I realized we were already at Westin Falls. I remembered what Galen had said earlier about us being closer to the Falls than I had thought.

Everything felt familiar, and I wondered if I somehow was recognizing the future my brother had warned me about. Then I remembered when I had been here before.

My dad had taken me there when I was about six years old as a special Father-Daughter adventure. We drove for two days straight from our home in East Fork, formerly known as Arizona, towards Westin, which was once Central Oregon. Once we got there, we stayed for three days, laying on our sleeping bags staring at the starry night sky. He used to tell me what all the constellations were and how they got their names. It was so long ago now that I had forgotten them all. He made everything seem so magical, like every tree was harboring mystical creatures that were hiding from us.

"But daddy, we won't hurt them, can't we see them?"

He smiled at me with a big grin, like he always did, "Because if we see them, then they lose their magical powers and transform into those beautiful flowers you saw earlier."

I gasped, staring at a handful of the colorful wildflowers I had picked from the ground earlier, tears rose in my eyes, "These flowers? They were fairies?" I stood up and tried to push the flowers back into the ground, tears tumbling down my cheeks. He hurried over to me,

"What are you doing Kaydy?" he asked with a concerned smile.

"I'm saving them... I don't want their new lives as flowers to be over..."

I pictured him pulling my hands up out of the dirt into his own. I smiled at the innocent memory. How could I have forgotten?

Looking around now, however, it seemed even more beautiful than I remembered, though less magical, because back then I didn't need something beautiful, and now I did. I let my hand glide into the falling water, and I heard a childlike giggle leave my lips. I tried to extinguish the sound, but it seemed to bounce off the walls of the cave hiding behind the waterfall.

I closed my eyes as I let the water splash down my face, taking away the dirt and sweat of travel. I quickly looked to Leon, hoping he had not heard me, but he was smiling softly, "Kaydence, how old were you when you realized your brother had a Gift?" he said boldly, and I felt sick.

How could he know? Was it that obvious? Of course it was... I wasn't special, and anyone could see it.

Then I remembered that Galen had told him earlier and my pulse calmed a little, "He was about 5 when he started telling us about his dreams, but it wasn't until 4 years ago... he had a vision that no one could play off as simple dreams anymore. The Authority found out, and when they came to take him, just like my parents had warned would happen eventually, I took him into the woods." I didn't mean to say it all so quickly, but it fell from my lips as swiftly as the water cascaded down the rocks behind me.

He nodded, "So he is a Prophet?" he said quietly, his hands forced into his pockets, "I'm a Speaker." He said with a laugh, "I didn't even think it was a Gift, until one day... I realized I could make things happen just by thinking about something. May I show you?" he asked carefully.

I looked at him skeptically, my hands folded over my slowly blossoming chest. "Ok..." I said skeptically. He smiled and looked at a small tree near us, it looked strong and sturdy, but suddenly there was a loud cracking sound, and the tree's roots had been pulled clean from the ground, making it fall into the river and was swept away by the current. I was surprised it fell so suddenly, but I was still waiting for whatever Leon was going to do. He looked back at me expectantly and I raised my eyebrows, "So what are you going to do?" I asked.

He tilted his head at me in slight surprise, "I made the tree fall."

I looked back with unbelief at the river where the tree had been stolen away, "Trees fall all the time, that doesn't prove anything. I've heard Speakers are few and far between. Sorry, it just feels wildly unlikely."

He sighed deeply, "Ok, I'll say it out loud first then." He looked up at the sky and it was filled with slightly dark clouds, "Rain." He commanded, and within seconds rain began pouring down on us, soaking my already damp clothes, "Stop." He said to the rain and it stopped without question.

I was stunned, my chest tight with the shock of the spectacle, but I didn't let my wonder show in my expression. I didn't want to believe it though... it could've been a coincidence. "That doesn't prove anything. You could just be good at telling when something is about to happen." I said directly, trying to sound sure even though I wasn't.

He looked at me incredulously. I think he realized he could do any number of things, but I would not believe him. "How can I prove it to you?" he said almost more to himself, frustration evident on his face and in his voice.

"Do something that can't be a coincidence." I replied with a stubborn smirk, convinced he could not prove it. He'd given me no reason not to believe him, but call it pride or perhaps stubbornness, I didn't want it to be true. Speakers were too powerful, too close to being Dangerous Ones. Perhaps I didn't want him to turn out to be one of them.

He seemed to be considering something inside his mind, "I'd have to have you do something… and I prefer not forcing people to do things." He murmured apprehensively.

I laughed, trying to allow my façade to continue, not sure why I was even keeping it going, "Go ahead. Prove it." I challenged, and I could see a fire light inside his eyes, and suddenly I was afraid.

I knew he didn't have to say it out loud this time, because the moment my legs took the few steps left towards him, moving against my own wishes, and when my lips were touching his… I knew it wasn't my choice. I felt the blood drain from my face, as I pulled away and stared at the ground.

I could tell he was ashamed of himself. He put a hand on my shoulder, "I'm so sorry… I should've done something else…" his cheeks were red, but his expression was filled with anguish and regret.

I shook my head, a fog in my mind from the contact, "I wouldn't have believed you if you had me do anything else… I should've just trusted you." I admitted quietly, feeling a tingle where his lips had touched. That was my first kiss, and I didn't even mean for it to happen. I was forced. Though, if I had to kiss someone, I was glad it was him.

"I will never make you do anything again... I'm so sorry." He said, walking back.

I ran up to him and took his hand, "Leon... you gave me exactly what I asked for. I won't make you prove it again." I said with a small smile, "Please don't feel bad. I trust you." I said without meaning to. I couldn't help it though as the words fell from my lips.

He watched me with curiosity, and then it was as if he saw something in me, and his gaze softened. "I'll make everyone realize you and your brother are safe, don't worry."

With that he began walking back towards the camp and I knew to follow. And though I would never admit it, I wished that kiss had been my choice... because I wouldn't have let it stop. That was the moment I realized without a doubt, I was no longer a little girl, and I was glad I wasn't.

∎∎

Though Leon talked to all the men in the camp, only a handful believed that my brother and I really were simply runaways from the Authority. I didn't like being there, I didn't feel safe around all those people, but everyone quickly fell in love with Galen. After only a few days he was accepted as part of the group, though everyone seemed to still believe I was a spy or something. It was fine with me that no one liked me, but I didn't like Galen being so friendly with those strangers... it scared me. I tried to keep Galen close, but he was too excited to have friends again, and I suddenly felt useless.

I often felt myself drifting back into my unconscious past, the place where I always get lost, but I didn't like getting that vulnerable around people, not even Galen. I found myself wandering into the woods back to the waterfall almost every day when I wasn't forced to do chores around camp to prove I wasn't just going to run out on them. I felt horrendously alone as I watched my brother join back into society. He was special beyond just his Gift, but me? I was just his protector... someone who was now considered obsolete. For four years all we had was each other, and now I had nothing, not even hope.

At first, I would just go back to the Falls to be alone, feeling more at home there than with the gaggles of people back at camp. Galen came with me the first few days to keep me company, but he was far past being alone with just his sister. I knew he loved me, and I tried not to be offended by his desire to meet other people, but it was hard not to take it a little personally. For me, he was my only friend.

Three weeks after we had arrived at our new home, I felt myself drifting back into my memories. So, when I felt the familiar ping of foggy thoughts, I went to the Falls so no one would see me just in case I began to cry.

Whenever I came back to camp, I would hear whispers, "Did you see her run off by herself again?" one girl said coldly, scoffing.

"Oh, I'm sure she's telling the Soldiers all about us!" said another with irritation.

"Usually they at least pick kids who are attractive... she is filthy and gangly and not at all pretty." One of the girls scoffed with a cool laugh as she gathered the laundry from the line, "I don't know why Leon keeps wasting his time with her." She ended with a cold-hearted laugh.

I had heard so many ridiculous rumors and unkind words since being here, but I always just shrugged them off— this one hurt me, though. This was the one that sent me running back to my special spot where I could be alone. It made me so furious to be told that I was ugly... I hadn't seen a mirror in almost two years partly because that was always a hidden fear of mine. My mother was so beautiful that I just always hoped I would be too, assumed it must be hereditary, but instead I don't even get to keep the memory of my mother within my looks—just another reason why I was nothing special.

I furiously wiped away my tears as I pulled my legs to my chest, trying to make myself as small as I possibly could. Finally, after days of hiding my thoughts even from myself, I let myself drift back into the Happy Days.

I envisioned my mother cleaning up toys and vacuuming in case we had company, even though we hardly ever did. I could smell the bacon and French toast cooking on the stove, and I could hear my dad's gentle humming floating from the kitchen. I felt the smile rise on my cheek, my world was suddenly warm and joyful again. Nothing was wrong here. No need to be an adult here where there is loving parents, and a delicious breakfast every morning. Safe.

But then, like always, my perfect picture is shattered by a mistake. One misplaced phrase to the wrong person, and suddenly that picture was burning in the distance as I was forced to walk away from it.

I didn't hide my sobs this time... for the first time in four years. I thought I felt hands wrap around my shoulders, and I pictured my dad's strong arms protecting me. I pulled them closer, but daddy didn't smell right.

My eyes shot open and I realized Leon was holding me. I pushed him angrily away and tried to scoot as far from him as I could. No one was allowed to see me like this. No one could see me be the child I so often felt like, because how could a child protect anyone?

Leon stood staring down at me with confusion, a tender expression on his face. I felt something in my chest swell at the sight of him, and suddenly my lips tingled as if our kiss had just happened instead of three weeks ago. I looked away from him.

"I didn't mean to startle you. You were crying." He offered tenderly.

"No I wasn't!" I urged as I wiped my nose.

He smiled very lightly, "Of course not. But... if you ever were to be crying, I'm always here if you need someone." I looked at him hesitantly, analyzing his motives—certain he must be lying to me for some reason. But, as I looked into his eyes, I only saw compassion. He had no reason to lie to me about such a simple kindness.

"Well I wasn't..." I urge, though more gently, "but, thank you." I replied as politely as I could. My cheeks were warm, and I could tell they were going red.

He nodded and hugged me quickly. I stared at him in surprise. How simple a hug is, yet it seemed like the most incredible gift anyone could have given me. I couldn't suppress my smile, "You know Kaydence, you don't have to be alone all the time." He offers gently.

I stared at my hands, feeling lost and embarrassed, "I'm not... good with people." I said with shame, wishing there was something more eloquent to say about it.

He seemed concerned, "And you never will be unless you give them a chance." He said honestly, and I knew he was probably right, but people weren't to be trusted, right? I had lived by that truth for four years, and suddenly, just because Leon said it, I was supposed to change?

"There is no point." I reply with a frustrated shrug, "Galen and I are never around people long enough..." I replied stubbornly, trying to push him away, but I felt something in me hanging on.

He nodded, something akin to pity and frustration in his compassionate gaze, "And how long do you intend to live that life, Kaydence?"

It was like a slap in my face... because I *don't* know. I stare back at him with wide eyes and he takes a step closer, his face sterner than I'd seen it so far. My heart pounds wildly in reply.

"You make it seem as though you are doing Galen a favor, but what do you think is better for him: making friends and learning about his Gift instead of hiding from it, or wandering through forests until he is someday caught, forced to watch his sister publicly killed, and then turned into an experiment, himself? Because Kaydence... those are the options." He finished solemnly.

I wished I could be as levelheaded as Leon, because he was right. If we were caught, I would be discarded like old trash, and my brother would be turned into a monster. At least here, even around these crowds of people who clearly despised me, we have a chance to be safe, to be protected.

I finally looked up at him, the defeat of four years of loneliness bubbling up in my chest, "I don't know where to begin... the last time I had friends, I was 10 years old. My parents stopped letting me hang out with other children when my dad started training me to protect Galen and myself." Leon's eyes filled with empathy, "So, for six years, I haven't interacted with anyone besides my brother."

Suddenly it was as if a light bulb turned on in his head, "You're only 16 years old?" I could feel his shock as if this was the first time he had considered it.

"Well yeah, barely though." I quickly offer self-consciously, "I guess I'm basically still 15—at least that's how I feel. I think my birthday was only just last month if we are in October." I said, convinced the reason he was surprised was because he thought I was younger.

He came over to me carefully, that familiar compassion in his eyes and his voice again, "You were only 12 when you left home with an 8-year-old brother to protect?" I nodded, confused as to why he was surprised—I thought he already knew all this. He laughed with slight embarrassment coloring his cheeks as he scratched his head, "I sort of thought you were like 18."

I stared at him in shock, my eyes widened in unbelief, "If that were the case why would you call us both kids when you first met Galen and I?"

He smirked, really looking me over now, and then looking away again with a blush, "When you were covered in dirt, you looked like his twin, but once you had cleaned up..." he allowed a brief cough to interrupt before continuing with a small, nervous smile, "I just assumed you were my age."

The way he spoke those simple words, and the way he looked in my eyes when he said them, made me suddenly feel beautiful.

I sat on the edge of the bank and stared into the calmer water, trying to catch my reflection, and I scowled at the large forehead and wide lips. I looked like an awkward version of my childhood self. I pulled my feet out of the water and let my back fall to the ground as I stared up into the trees looming above me. I didn't know what to say to Leon, or if I should say anything, but without my permission, my thoughts came spilling out,

"But if I were your age, I'd be stuck looking like this probably for the rest of my life, if I'm not already forced to look like a big kid forever already..." I put my hands over my face so he couldn't examine further to see just how funny I really looked. I was sure that a man so handsome must have known hundreds of beautiful girls, all enamored by his looks and gentlemanly attitude.

He sighed, "Those people earlier, they were wrong Kaydence." He said, kneeling beside me and pulling my hands away from my cheeks. He smiled so sweetly as his eyes sparkled looking down at me. I felt my cheeks go warm again with that grin I couldn't hide. Why did he have this effect on me? "Don't let anyone make you feel like you are less than you are."

I laughed darkly, feeling the endless insecurities. I wasn't anything. But staring into Leon's eyes made me realize something—I wanted him to be my friend. "Um... Leon? You can call me Kayd." I said in a small voice, and he gave me a big smile.

"Kayd." He repeated happily and reached out his hand to me. I stared at it for a moment before sitting up and giving him my hand to shake.

We laughed like little children for a moment before we both lay on our backs staring into the slowly darkening sky. I hadn't laughed like that in years, fearful that a single laugh would mean Galen's death. I took in a deep joyful breath as I let the truth sink in— I no longer had to be afraid.

Chapter 3: More than a Vision

When I got back to camp that day, I tried to hide the giddiness I felt inside as Leon and I walked there together. We were still laughing and talking once we arrived, and I no longer cared if people thought I was there for the wrong reasons, because I had a friend again.

We got back to the tent and Galen grabbed my hand immediately and took me right back outside. Leon and I exchanged confused smiles before Galen took me just outside of the camp. He was panting from the excursion.

"So why did you decide to take me for a run?" I said with a humored laugh.

Galen grinned at me, "Don't you remember?" he asked, still panting.

I stared at him with confusion, "Remember what?"

"Three weeks ago, right before we met Leon, I told you about my vision..." I could tell he was trying to pull the information from my mind, but I wasn't helping him. He sighed deeply and began pacing; "Remember? I said you were in the vision with the Green-eyed man?"

I felt my face fall. I did remember. Didn't he say he had seen the Green-eyed man and me sitting by a waterfall, my feet dangling in the water while we talked? It had seemed like such a silly dream for Galen to have... but it wasn't a dream, it was a vision. When Galen's visions happened, however simple they may appear at the time, they are important.

When we were younger, he had a vision about a dog being hit by a car on Tenth Street, three blocks from us. It seemed like an odd thing to dream about or have a vision of, but it turned out that the owner of that dog was Hawk Reece, President Reece's nephew. If it had been anyone else's dog, it would have meant nothing, but my father was in the car that had run over the animal. Our family was then watched closely, with Soldiers constantly patrolling around our home. It was the beginning of the end.

So, remembering what an impact that small moment had caused to the grand scheme of things, I couldn't help but fear what this moment would mean. I couldn't even comprehend what possibilities could occur. Was it a mistake to share so much with Leon? What if the visions Galen had of Leon were actually ushering in another dictator that was even worse than Reece? I felt as if someone had hit me in the stomach and I couldn't catch my breath.

Galen was still staring at me happily. With such a joyful smile—perhaps the vision was not ushering in a new evil? I tried to recompose and bring myself back to earth. "You remember now, huh?" he asked elatedly.

I nodded with a small, forced smirk, "Yup." But there was a lump in my throat.

"It happened, huh! That's why we came. Kayd you are the one who is going to help him become the next President!" I stared at him in shock. Even if he was right, how would *I* help Leon? But there was no use questioning Galen again, because last time I did, I was quickly proven wrong. That couldn't happen again—I'd never hear the end of it.

Galen began excitedly speculating what Leon and I had spoken about, what about our conversation could've led to Leon's desire to become the Leader of our world. But nothing we had talked about could've led to such a thing. As always, Galen was in his blissful world where only good things dwell. I wanted to cry with the new fears that plagued my heart. "Did you guys talk about how strong the Gifted would be if they stood against President Reece? Yeah I bet that's what you guys talked about! Huh, Kayd?"

When we got back to camp, Leon smiled at me kindly, but I couldn't meet his gaze. I was convinced he was already plotting how to turn in my brother and I. Convinced he would turn into the worst kind of person, and I didn't want to un-convince myself by looking into the sincere eyes of my friend. I wanted to hate him so he couldn't surprise me if he changed into the monster that I was trying to believe he would be.

I didn't talk to anyone else that night, or the next day, though a few girls close to Leon's age tried to spark a conversation with me. I tried to explain I felt sick and wasn't up to talking. Most people took this excuse at face value, allowing me to stay hidden in mine and

Galen's tent alone. Another day passed without leaving my tiny makeshift-home, and without eating or drinking anything. My stomach began screaming at me with loud gurgles, but I just pulled my body into a ball and tried to fall back to sleep.

Finally, Leon came into the tent without asking to come in, "What's wrong?" he questioned almost harshly as he put a hand to my head to check my temperature. I wouldn't look him in the eye still, though everything within me wanted to. I wanted the reassurance of his friendship again, but my stubbornness was too strong, so I stared at his feet instead. "Kayd?" I simply shook my head and buried my face in my pillow. He sighed deeply, "Come on, Kayd. I'm getting you out of this room." He always talked about the tents like they were houses rather than ropes and fabric.

"No." I said to my pillow.

Leon stood, and I hoped that meant he was leaving, but instead, I felt myself lifted by strong arms from the ground. I yelped in shock, but was too tired even to scream in protest. I stared down at his feet, and then up into his eyes with confused horror. "What are you doing, Leon?" I said angrily, weakly trying to break free from his hold, but my body was too tired from food and water deprivation. "Let me go!" He didn't listen though, instead, he just kept walking towards the Falls. His face was a mask of indifference, and it terrified me. I knew I was right! He was taking me to the Soldiers, but protecting my brother at least. I guess I could live with that.

But just as I had come to terms with him giving me up, he lifted me up and tossed me into a pool of cool water behind the Falls. I clawed my way back to the surface, gasping for air. "God, Leon, what was that for!?" I sputtered and coughed in frustration and shock. He stared down at me with a smile, his hands on his hips.

"Figured it was time for you to wake up," he replied indignantly.

I coughed, "I *was* awake!" I called back angrily, trying to paddle back to the bank. But I was surprised by a large splash beside me. I looked for the source of the splash and saw Leon beside me grinning softly.

"No, I don't think you were." He said, coming closer to me, an odd look in his eye. I liked the way he was looking at me, and though my stubbornness told me to keep retreating to the bank, something else kept me planted in my spot. I considered maybe he was *making* me stay, but I knew better. Because in that three days of sulking, I had deeply missed Leon. I had only known him for three weeks—only *really* known him for a few days—but I wanted to know him forever. Even with the fears of what Galen's visions meant, I realized that Leon would not ever become a monster. It wasn't in him.

I smiled as he floated only inches away from me, "Do you think you are finally awake, or do I need to try again?" he said in a quiet voice with a mischievous grin.

I tried to pretend to be mad, but my smile couldn't stay away, "And how would you do that?" he came even closer, and I saw him look at my lips. I wanted him to kiss me. I longed for him to touch my lips again, but instead he splashed me with water. I squealed in surprise and began splashing him back. We laughed and laughed until my face hurt from smiling for so long. When we finally got out of the water, Leon helped me out and I surprised both of us as I hugged him tightly. He held me without question.

"So where were you for the last few days?" he whispered against my soaked hair.

I stared at his shirt plastered to his chest, absent-mindedly pulling the fabric from his arms, "You know where I was... I was in my tent." I offered nervously.

I could feel him shaking his head, "You know what I mean. I came to see you multiple times each day and you were basically catatonic. Where did you go?" I hesitantly let go of him and walked towards the shallow cave behind the Falls. I didn't know what to say. He shook his head, "Why do you always do that?" he asked in a hurt voice.

"Do what?" I asked, looking at my hands.

"You always run away just as soon as we are starting to have a moment." A moment? My breath catches as I remember the way he'd looked at my lips. I shake off the thought though. He must just mean a moment when he is starting to get to know me. He was right though—I was afraid for him to know me, not because I believed he would turn evil like I foolishly thought before, but because I wasn't sure I was ready to have him know my secrets. Not even Galen knew my secrets.

"I've been running for four years, Leon. Can you really be surprised that I wouldn't stop after only three weeks?" I managed to say as I dared to meet his gaze. He came closer to me again, though not as close as I would've liked.

He nodded as he put his hands in his pockets, "I guess not. I just wish…" he began but seemed to decide better of it.

"Just wish, what?" my heart started to pound with hope.

He smiled, "I just wish I could understand you."

I laughed, "I'm really not that confusing."

He gave me that odd smile again, "You'd be surprised."

As he looked into my eyes, I saw something in them I didn't understand. The only way to explain was that it was sparkly and blue, like what I had imagined those magical creatures my dad used to talk about looked like. From that magic in his eyes I felt an overwhelming goodness emanating from them, and something seemed to jump out of me and encircle him. Everything went blurry for a moment, and then the fog cleared. He gave me a confused look, "Are you okay?"

I shook my head as I felt my body begin to wobble, "Just food deprived, I'm sure." I said with a weak laugh. He nodded as he led me back to camp. I thought I remembered that sort of thing happening before with my brother, and a friend of mine, but I wasn't deprived of anything then. I shook my head, reminding myself it was nothing, just like I had done when it happened before.

Leon and I began going to the Falls almost every day after our chores were done, and I started feeling important again. Leon made me feel so special, and he made me see that I was more than just my brother's bodyguard. I began socializing with the others in the camp, and after a few months I felt like I was actually making friends. I was starting to feel like a real teenager just hanging out, until Kent—the man who had slapped my brother when he first met us—came up to me one day. He said he wanted to talk to me about something. I looked at my new friends and they assured me I'd be fine, so I agreed, but I still felt wrong.

He took me about a quarter of a mile outside camp – I felt more unsafe with every step. When we finally stopped, he turned to me with an odd expression on his face. My heart pounded madly in my chest, so loud I could hear it in my ears. Everything was begging me to see that so much was wrong... Then I looked into his eyes and there was something I didn't like, and somehow, I knew what he was going to do. He jumped at me almost too quickly for me to realize what was happening.

Grabbing my arms roughly, he pinned me to the ground. I was about to scream but he froze me to my spot, and I suddenly realized why Freezers were considered one of the Dangerous Ones. He brought his face close to mine, "What did you think was going to happen, you little whore? That Leon would just protect you forever?" he laughed cruelly as he kissed my neck. I wanted to puke, but I couldn't move. His breath smelled like rotting fish and cigars.

He looked me in the eyes then, and as I stared into the dead gray orbs. There was something ugly in them that grated me from the inside out, and I felt my entire body go warm. In that moment, I wanted him to stop, for him to not see me, even though I knew that was impossible.. The blurry vision came back, but this time he was a red blur in front of me. Kent seemed suddenly confused, and my body began to unfreeze. I pulled my shirt back down, sobbing and shaking as I ran back to camp without looking back.

I could hear him stampeding behind me, but it seemed that he was running into almost every tree. "Get back here!" he shouted. I ran straight through the camp, people staring at me in confusion. I ran all the way to the Falls where I always felt safe. I pulled my knees to my chest and cried.

Leon came running to me a few minutes later, and he fell beside me, arms ready to intercept me with warmth and acceptance. I cuddled into him and he let me cry for awhile. Then he asked, "What happened, Kayd?" he whispered softly in my ear as he wiped my tears off my cheek.

I was shaking, and suddenly I was back in that moment... back under that evil monstrosity of a human, frozen to the ground as he touched me... and I felt hate like I'd never known. "Why would you guys allow such an atrocious person to be here, Leon?" I asked through my teeth, mortified and infuriated at the thought of Kent's hands and lips on me. I shake my head, trying to shake the memory, but I know deep down that this will haunt my nightmares.

He sighed with hesitation, "Kent is one of the Dangerous Ones, Kayd—sadly it is helpful if he is on our side rather than the Authority's."

I pulled away in shock, "He tried to rape me, Leon..." he flinched, and then tore his gaze from mine, "You have children here! Is that the sort of person you want around children? Who cares if he could help you... he is a pig that doesn't deserve to live?" I was almost yelling, my voice hoarse from my sobs earlier.

He stared at my back, and his voice was too quiet, too apologetic. "If we killed him, we would be just as bad as the Authority..."

I turned on him with fire in my eyes, and he stared back in surprise, "Some people deserve to die." I replied coolly but with certainty. He gazed at me in shock.

"How could you think like that, Kayd? All Gifted deserve to live..." he began, but I scoffed.

I shook my head, standing up now as I stared down at him with deep anger, and he looked back up at me, wounded and stunned, "Not all *un*-Gifted deserve to live. So why are Gifted any different? There are bad people, Leon, and death does not discriminate." I replied in fury.

He sighed, "I'll send him away today, ok?" he replied with defeat.

I knew this was all he could promise so I gritted my teeth and forced a nod, "Fine." He tried to talk to me, to calm me down, to erase the agony building inside my chest. He didn't realize that all I could see was the darkness in Kent's eyes, the complete lack of goodness... I wish that man would die. He didn't deserve to just be sent away... and though I felt guilty for just a moment for my judgment, part of me felt my judgment was correct.

But when we got back to camp a few moments later, there was a scream coming from outside Kent's tent. Suddenly people were rushing over there, "What happened?" Leon asked as he pushed forward and saw Kent lying lifeless on the ground. I stared at him in shock.

A woman with long curly blonde hair cried as she pulled a bag of oddly colored mushrooms out of Kent's tent, "I told him not to eat them, Leon. He got them earlier today, saying they were the same ones he and Martha used to use in their soups. They must be the deadly ones I heard about when I was a kid."

Leon looked at the mushrooms carefully, "How long has he been like this?" he asked someone darkly.

"He got back about fifteen minutes ago," A man that looked like the woman's twin spoke up, "But only a moment ago did we discover him. Right before you and Kaydence got back."

Leon nodded, put a hand on Kent's head, and said a little prayer. There was silence all over the camp as everyone prayed for Kent. It was odd that he would die so quickly after trying to ravage me, and I wondered how just a few bad mushrooms could take down such a large man.

Part of me wanted to believe he deserved it, but I realized it wasn't my business deciding if someone was worth living or not. He was just a lost man, and I suddenly felt a little sorry for him. But after Leon and a few other men took Kent's body to a tiny graveyard they had created, I watched at least fifteen girls go to his grave, "Good riddance." A few women said, "You deserved to die!" Said another, but it ended with the girl who had supposedly found him, she was bawling, "They should've caught you—you filthy bastard! I will thank God everyday..." but when she saw Leon coming, she threw down the bag of mushrooms that killed him before kicking dirt over it.

I stared at the woman and suddenly I realized my impression before was correct. Life is a gift, and not everyone deserves to live. But who am I to decide?

Chapter 4: Who Decides?

Two weeks passed after Kent's death, and Leon was constantly busy. Apparently when someone dies in the Gifted camp, it becomes a pretty big deal. Leon was questioning everyone, just to make sure no one tried to kill him, but no one really seemed to miss him. Everyone had gotten tired of his rudeness and the way he used his abilities to hurt so many. But Leon was the type of man that treated every life as if they were the most important person to have lived. Though I didn't think someone like Kent deserved such kindness, I admired Leon's convictions.

I was starting to miss Leon though, so when he asked if I wanted to take a walk with him, I happily said yes. He was quiet as we passed our usual spot, and then passed through a part of the forest I had never been, almost six miles from camp. I was so excited to be spending time with him, I hadn't even noticed the large duffle bag hanging on his left shoulder. He pulled out a pair of small women's jeans, a pair of high-heeled boots with a loose top, a light pink tank top with frilly lace overlapping the fabric, and a dark gray and pink blazer jacket. I stared at the odd garments in confusion as he handed them to me, and I took them in my hands carefully, as if fearful they would burst into flames.

He laughed, "You and I are going into town today, and I need you to look like you are in your twenties. This is what most twenty-year-old girls wear nowadays, in the city at least." He smiled at my wide eyes, "Kayd, just put them on, I will give you some privacy." And he walked away. I gave another unsure glance at the thin clothes in my hands and began to undress. Within a few minutes I had put on the pants that I now realized were skinny jeans, and the boots came up over the bottom of the pants.

I called Leon back, though I felt uncomfortable in the tight clothes. His eyes brightened as he stared at me like I was a new person. "You look amazing! Would you mind if we did something to your hair?" he said carefully. I nodded nervously, and I felt my eyes shining with eager curiosity. He came over with a hairbrush and gently pulled my hair into an odd, loose bun on the top of my head. "I don't have any makeup for you, but I think this already helps." He said with pleasure as he pulled me forward.

"Leon, why are we going into town?" I asked as I naturally reached my hand up towards my hair to feel the peculiarity.

"We are running out of supplies, and since Kent died, a lot of people are afraid to eat the things we just collect from the forest." He sighed, "This sort of thing happens every so often." He shrugged with a small smile, "Plus…" he gave me a soft look, "I sort of missed spending time with you, and just an hour or two at the waterfall just didn't feel like enough." His words made me blush as I nodded with an elated grin.

I could barely walk in the tall shoes, but after a while I found I liked the way they arched my feet and made me taller. Occasionally they would hurt my toes, but they were still more comfortable than my three-year-old sneakers.

We came to the end of the trees and I felt my fear overwhelm me as our feet hit the paved streets. Galen and I never walked through cities. We tried a few times in the first year, but two children unaccompanied by adults tended to draw unwanted attention. I expected it to be the same this time: people staring at us with unhappy whispers and ominous movements. The affect Leon and I gave, however, was entirely different.

He quickly surprised me as he put an arm around my shoulder and smiled at the many onlookers. Leon looked down at me as if to ask permission for his arm around my shoulder. I gave him a small nod and an ecstatic smile. No one looked at us like we didn't belong, but rather almost with admiration. I felt safe with Leon's arm wrapped around me, and I let everything else fade out of my thoughts.

When we weren't in the eye of the crowd any longer, he pulled me closer and turned his lips towards my ear, "When I go into this store, you should run to the bathroom and grab as many toilet paper rolls as you can and put them in this purse. He then handed me a large brown purse with little lace strands hanging from different sections. I nodded, "Now smile like I said something sweet." I smiled instantly, but it was just having his lips so close to mine again that helped me oblige.

We entered the store and I followed his instructions as I walked into the bathroom that had a little woman with a dress symbol on the door. As I entered, I saw the bathroom was completely empty, but as I passed the row of round mirrors, I suddenly became terrified when I saw a beautiful woman passing by them. I turned around quickly as I searched for the woman I had seen, and then I turned back to the mirror slowly, realizing the woman was me. I was shocked… hadn't I just looked into the water a couple of months ago and saw the gawky 16-year-old? Instead I was seeing a twenty-something young woman with delicate features, lips that finally fit my face, and electric blue eyes that sparkled in the light. My red hair had changed to fire over the years, and a few spit curls framed my face. I smiled at my reflection, and the beautiful girl smiled back with perfect teeth that were surprisingly still white.

I wanted to cry as I continued to stare in shock until I heard the TV blaring from inside the main area of the store. I quickly ran to each stall and took every roll of paper, forcing it into my bag. And then, just as I exited the restroom, I noticed a small candy machine. I remembered loving those little treats when I was a child. I suddenly wished I could have just one little piece, as if maybe it would take me back to my innocence. I started to turn back towards the main part of the store when I heard the machine clang behind me. I jumped, and then noticed five pieces of wrapped candy had fallen to the ground unclaimed. I stared in surprise, but picked them up and threw them in the bag, happy to have such luck.

I tried to take slow steady steps, so I didn't look conspicuous, but after years of being a runner, it's hard to tell yourself to just walk. I could see Leon standing at the counter passing the teller a small card-like object—it looked like a computer chip connected to a long piece of gum. "Thank you, Mr. Yursi! Have a wonderful day." The teller said in a loud happy voice as he ushered the next customer forward.

Leon pulled his large grocery bag off of the counter, greeting a few of the young women fawning over him at the door. I couldn't help but envy his ability to blend and flourish in a society that so many feared. As we came outside together, he smiled as he took my hand in his, our fingers so perfectly intertwined. I tried not to look at our interlocked fingers, though I wanted to just marvel at the simplicity of something that felt so wonderful.

We were headed back into the trees, to the place where I would go back to being the awkward 16 year-old. The trees were only feet away when a strong hand grabbed my arm, and it shook me to my core. Suddenly every fear from the last four years came back to haunt me. "Where do you think you are going?" said a low male voice.

I stared at the tightly gloved hand and instantly recognized it as that of a Soldier, and not just any Soldier either…. I felt my entire body go stiff, ready to run at the drop of a hat, but instead, Leon just kept his calm composure and welcoming grin, "I'm sorry officer, is there a problem?" he said, coming to face the man.

The man's voice calmed a little, but it was easy to see he was trying stay authoritative, "This girl is not licensed." He replied coldly.

Leon laughed, "What makes you say that?" tilting his head slightly.

The Soldier turned me towards him, and I could not hide the recognition of the man who burned my parents alive… and the recognition in his eyes of the girl who got away. His grip tightened on my arm, brief shock moving through his eyes, and he pulled his face close to mine, "Is the boy safe?" he said in a surprisingly relaxed tone, but there was a bite that I didn't like to it.

"Please let go of me…" I said quietly, my body shaking from fear and uncertainty. This man destroyed my former life, stole my joy… I owed him nothing.

Leon tried to put his hand above where the Solider had his grip on me, but the fierce look the man gave him sent chills through both of us, "This young woman is under arrest!" he said furiously, pulling me away from Leon, a few of my worst fears happening before my eyes.

Leon smiled too calmly, and I noticed a shift in his eyes, almost like a sparkle, "No she isn't." he replied with too much warmth.

The man almost scoffed out a laugh until he looked into Leon's gaze carefully, and his expression instantly changed, "My

God... you are one... of..." and then he looked at his hand on my arm and pulled it away. He stumbled back for a moment, blinking at us in total confusion. "I'm so sorry miss. I thought you were someone else." He slowly wandered back to a group of other Soldiers. I felt Leon's tension instantly. The other Soldiers looked our way, and Leon grabbed my arm.

His calm had faded, replaced by caution, "Kayd... we need to go right now. If we get separated, I need you to just keep running, alright?"

"I want to stay with you..." I said quietly, holding his arm tightly as we began walking into the forest, trying to look like we were just taking a stroll, but it was easy to see our feet were moving faster than most of the others to pass by.

He kept peeking over his shoulder to the Soldiers who were trying to reach us, though they didn't seem to be hurrying yet. "Kayd... I can protect myself, but I'm not sure I can protect you too as easily. You may be safer if you aren't around me." I understood completely, because I always did the same to Galen, but I wasn't used to being the vulnerable one in need of protection. I agreed, and when we hit the tree line we began to sprint together, but the Soldiers were faster.

They were almost to us when Leon gave me a panicked look and mouthed a single word: *Now.* I nodded and began sprinting in a different direction. Two of the Soldiers followed me while the other three continued after Leon. I ran faster than I had run in years, but the Soldiers were too quick. I suddenly felt my years of hiding fade into non-existence. None of it mattered anymore, except that Galen is safe... for now at least.

My lungs burned, my face was on fire, and my legs were turning into putty as my feet screamed in pain from the heels. I glanced back to the Soldiers, and they were too close. I wanted to cry, but what would that do? It would just prove to them I was a weak little girl, and they would torture me, trying to get information about my brother. I prepared myself for the worst as I stopped in my tracks and turned to them. One of the men chasing me was the Soldier who had grabbed my arm. Why was he still chasing me? Hadn't Leon fooled the man to think I was someone else? Maybe his influence was only temporary.

The men almost ran past me before they realized I had stopped, the Soldier from my past grabbed my arm again, "You shouldn't be out here, Kaydence." He remembered my name? Why would a Soldier remember my first name? It was protocol for Soldiers to address you by your last name, even when you weren't Public Enemy Number 1.

I twisted my arm in his too-strong hands, but they didn't budge. "Please just let me go. I'm not causing any trouble..." I pleaded.

The man shook his head, and looked at the other man who had a helmet on. The other man removed his helmet and I almost lost my balance: it was my dad.

"Daddy?" I whispered. I gaped at him, tears stinging my eyes. I pictured him back in the house, begging the Soldiers to let he and my mother go... he surely had died. But now, looking into those familiar eyes that used to offer peace and acceptance, all I could think was, *He's alive! He's here!* He smiled as he flung his arms around me.

"Kaydy... I missed you." He whispered back.

I didn't hold back the tears this time. "But... how are you alive? I watched you and mom burn in the fire."

He looked at the first Soldier, "This is Garrison Bold. He snuck into the house and brought your mother and I into the trees just behind the house. We have been looking for you and your brother ever since you left, but I guess I taught you better than I thought." It all seemed too perfect. I wanted it to be true... I wanted it so badly, but there was a nagging feeling inside me... the reminder that if something seemed too good to be true, it probably was.

Pain seared my heart as I realized this wasn't real. It couldn't be real... and then I looked at my dad more closely—the scar from when he fell on the diving board at Water Mountain was gone, as well as any familiar markings. Perhaps he had covered them with makeup, but I remember my dad's words clearly:

"Don't trust any Soldiers, Kaydy... not even if they look like me."

"Why Daddy?"

"I promise, I would never pretend to be one of them..."

I stared into the man's eyes, "Daddy... what's my favorite color." It was a code we came up with when I was young that only he and I knew.

He gave me a strange look and smiled as if this was the easiest question on a test, "Purple." He said kindly, but the other man seemed to be considering my words carefully and he gave a single shake of his head in understanding.

The answer to the code was Pinkie, not even a color exactly. It was our way of knowing no one would just blindly guess, "Why do you guys want me?" I said distantly, my strength returning along with my coldness, accepting my fate.

The imposter offered a forlorn, mock-loving gaze, "I want to protect you and your brother, Kaydy."

I scoffed angrily, "Stop calling me that." I said with closed eyes and my fists clenched, "I know you are not my dad. What do you want with me?" I demanded.

"But Kaydy..." he purred miserably, as if my words had cut him... but I could see the truth now— it was all just an act.

"Finn, stop playing with the girl. She knows." Garrison Bold said gruffly, shifting his grip on my arm. "Just tell her."

My pretend dad looked at Garrison with irritation and scoffed out a sigh, "This could have been so easy." He said as he changed his voice to a New Yorker accent, "Fine. You know what we want. We have been chasing you for four years—it wasn't for nothing."

I pulled forward my fake tears, "Well my brother isn't with me... he's dead."

Finn glared at me, "No he isn't. Just tell us. It's better if we have you both."

I closed my eyes—so they did plan on torturing me, or killing me, "My brother is dead! I've been hiding out for two years on my own. He is in the ground... he won't hurt anyone there."

The New Yorker slapped my face hard. He grabbed my jacket and pulled me off the ground. I just stared at him, and a fire seemed to grow inside my chest, just like when Kent was trying to hurt me. I was furious at this imposter... this man pretending to my dad, and my vision blurred with anger.

"Let me go." I said through my teeth. His arms began to shake as the red glow encircled him, and he looked at hands in confusion. "Let me go!" I screamed, and he fell to the ground, allowing me to escape his grasp.

I meant to run, but as I looked at the imposter, I felt frozen to my spot as he cried out in whimpering pain. The other man watched me, cautiously putting on a pair of strange glasses with an odd blue tint to the outside, "How long have you known?" the man asked carefully, stepping over his companion who was still crying out in agony.

I stared at the man on the ground with paralyzing fear... what had happened? Why was he scratching at his head like he was being attacked from the inside out? "Known what?" I whispered, locked in my spot from terror.

He knelt beside me, "That you were Gifted."

I turned my wide eyes to him, my entire body quaking from the shock of everything I was enduring, "I'm... I'm not." I urged, but something in my mind tingled with knowing.

He tilted his glasses slightly, "We were looking for you." He said in honest simplicity, "All this time, it was you."

I didn't understand as I looked back to the other man, bloody scrapes were covering his nearly bald scalp. I turned away in disgust, closing my eyes, "For my brother." I agreed. I knew the story.

He shook his head, a long sigh leaving his lips, "Prophets are of no real use to us, Kaydence... not until they are older. We assumed you were a Speaker, or perhaps an Emoty, but now I see what you are," I stared at him with obvious horror. What was he saying? "You are a Decider."

I cried, I knew what the first two were: a Speaker like Leon, or an Emoty, who could change the emotions of any person. They were a bit of a persuader, similar to the Speaker, but only towards emotions. The Decider, however, was not something I had heard of... well, except for the memory of a bedtime story my father had shared when I was maybe 5, and the memory— the mystery of it—terrified me. If he was right and I was Gifted, and what had happed to the New Yorker was because of me... what was I capable of? I was so distracted, I barely heard Leon's pounding footfalls as he came running towards us.

"Excuse me sir, but there are some men who are hurt about a mile that way." He said in that soft voice that I was beginning to recognize as his Gift.

The Soldier sighed deeply and raised his glasses again, "I know what you are. And there is no need to use your abilities." He turned back to me, "Kaydence, I'm just leaving you with a warning: they are only looking for you, but your brother is considered a bonus. I wouldn't go back into the public any time soon." And with that he picked up his partner as if he was a bag of potatoes, "If I see you again, Kaydence. I will be forced to take you to the Authority. So, I hope I don't see you again." He said sternly as he stalked away.

Leon stared back at me in surprise, "Kayd, what just happened?"

I was still on the ground, staring at the spot that the bleeding man had been screaming in pain caused by me. What had happened? What was a 'Decider'? And what was I capable of? I just shook my head, no words coming to my mind that would satisfy him.

He kneeled in front of me and took my hands in his, "Kayd... did they hurt you?" he whispered so softly.

I shook my head, "They were after me..." I whispered, still holding the man in my mind's eye. His pain would be forever imprinted in my brain.

He nodded his head carefully, "Yes, they were running after us both." He replied, trying to calm my obviously feverish mind.

I shook my head, my fear swelling inside my stomach as tears trickled over my cheeks, "No... when Galen and I were children... they weren't looking for him." I turned my gaze back to him, my eyes wide with shame, "They were after me."

He stared at me in confusion for a moment, "You are Gifted?" I hesitantly nodded. He sat beside me, giving almost a betrayed look, "Why didn't you tell me?"

I burst into tears, "I can't be... I can't." I shook my head and looked at him with wide eyes, "No, no, no... Galen is the special one." I urged, and I could see brief understanding cross his face, though no understanding crossed mine.

"You didn't know?" He asked. I sob, shaking my head, "Kayd... tell me what happened."

I looked into Leon's kind eyes and I explained how I recognized the man from when I ran away with Galen. I told him how I had always assumed it was because of Galen's Gift of Prophecy, how it turned out that I was believed to be Gifted as well, and how my Gift managed to nearly kill a man just by demanding that he 'let go'.

"You are a Decider?" he said very quietly as if he was still considering the thought. He knew what I was before I even said the name.

I stared back at him with widened eyes. "What is a Decider? I've never heard of it before today."

He inhaled deeply, almost anxious, "Not much is known about them, honestly… except one thing…" he muttered nervously with a secret.

"What?" I asked, hopeful.

He looked me in the eye with warning and fear, "They decide if someone is worthy to live or if it is their time to die."

Chapter 5: What is Love?

I couldn't look at him. I didn't want to look at anyone again… not only could I kill someone with a single thought, the Authority wanted to use that power to their own advantage. The look Leon was giving me was no longer one of compassion, but one of concern and fear.

"Kayd… I know this is a lot to take in… but…" he cleared his throat, "Um… did you kill Kent?"

I stared at him in shock, "Of course not!" I said in horror, but I thought back to that moment… I had wanted him to die. I had told Leon that when we were at our waterfall… which would've been the exact moment that man had said Kent may have died. My mouth dropped, and tears rose in my eyes, "Oh my God…" I pulled my knees tightly to my chest.

"It's fine Kayd, you didn't know that you were doing it." He urged with tenderness, but I shook my head, hearing the deep fear within him that had the decency to try and hide.

"I'm not sure I could've helped it even if I did know…" I mutter quietly, my tears distorting my speech.

He dared to sit beside me again, but I could tell he was afraid to look me in the eye, "What do you mean?"

I stared at the ground, "I never thought it was anything… but when I was younger, I used to have vision problems sometimes. Everything would just get really blurry, and the person I was looking at would usually turn blue, or like a peach color."

He nodded his head slowly, trying to fully digest what I was saying, "And what were you feeling when those colors appeared?"

I let out a breath, rewinding back to those moments, "Well… I think when the blue blur comes… I feel close to someone, or I want to protect them." I tilted my head at the memory, "When I know they are good." I said with a soft smile looking back to him.

"What do you mean, 'when I know they are good'?"

I lifted my shoulders, trying to figure out the exact way to say it, "I don't know how to explain it… I just look into someone's eyes, and there's just something that tells me…?"

He looked at me carefully, "And what color was the blur when…" he seemed to bite his tongue, "With Kent?" he looked so uncomfortable, and I don't blame him.

I inhaled, "I'd never seen that color before… it was like a harsh red, like fire. When I looked in his eyes, there was nothing good in them. There was only hate, and ugliness, and cruelty."

He just continued to nod as if that was all he could do, "And did you see a color around me?"

I smiled softly, "A deep blue, different than the one I saw around my brother. His was like a baby boy blue, or a mint green."

"What does that mean then?"

I looked at him uncertainly, "It means you are good. I wanted you to be safe." I felt embarrassed over it all, and as he looked into my eyes, I felt that familiar electricity between us, "I guess…" I added to soften it all.

"One more question…"

"Go for it." I said weakly.

"Are you still Kayd?" he said with a knowing gaze trying to look stern, but a smirk was tucked safely in the corner of his lips.

Despite his smile, I felt the intense tension beneath his surface. I wanted there to be no more fear or contention, but I knew better. "Even if I am, I know you think of me differently now."

He looked towards a large tree nearby, the smile gone. He hesitated, pulling in a sharp breath, "Hard not to, Kayd. I believe you when you say you didn't know… but you may have killed someone." He replied harshly. I nodded sadly, tears fighting to slide down my cheeks again, but I couldn't let them. It was time for Strong Kayd again—there was no room for the weak version of myself I'd been becoming over the last few months. "I just need some time." He said, trying to sound kind, but all I heard was disgust. And could I really be surprised? He saw the man I had just mutilated with my mind… I was disgusted too.

"No problem." I choked out with a forced smile.

We collected our supplies that were strewn across the forest floor from running, and we headed back to camp in silence. My hand longed to be holding his again. It was odd for me to think that that wonderful moment had happened only today, though it was a world away from now. I just wanted to be alone, but I knew we needed to deliver our supplies, so I pretended to be indifferent.

Right before we got to camp, Leon stopped me with a hand on my shoulder, "Don't tell anyone about what happened, okay? And don't tell anyone about your Gift... I'd like to say everyone here is honest and good, but sadly they aren't. So... it'll just be our secret." I nodded, not wanting to even think about my sad reality anyways.

I dropped off my supplies at Leon's tent, and without a word to anyone I ran to the waterfall and jumped into the cold water. I tried to drown myself, realizing I was too dangerous to live, but sadly I'm too good at floating. I looked at my reflection in the water, gazing into the eyes of the monster that was a Decider, and suddenly I saw something in those eyes... something beautiful. My vision blurred and there was a pleasant purple surrounding my reflection, and I understood what it meant: innocent... and I saw goodness imbedded in those eyes.

I swam to a corner of the water cave that was a bit shallower, and I pulled my legs to my chest and cried. I wasn't worthy of death... that's what my gift told me, or was it just trying to preserve itself? I shook my head, knowing that nothing I had ever done was on purpose. Yes, I wanted Kent to die, knowing that his cruelty knew no bounds, but I didn't mean for him to die. We say things in our anger and our fear that we don't mean, not really, and I hadn't really meant it. I mourned for him then, even if he didn't deserve it.

I thought back through my past, trying to remember any moment I had experienced the blurry vision. I remembered the first time: I was 8-years-old, and it was with my best friend, Tamara. The Soldiers had just taken her older sister because she was believed to be a threat to society—she was a Rebel. Tamara was so heartbroken, not understanding the cruelty that was happening in the world. I hugged her tightly, trying to be uplifting, and then when I looked into her pale blue eyes, I saw that mint-blue blur around her. I felt such a goodness and love emanating from her, and I prayed that she would always be safe from harm.

The only other time I saw the blue blur, besides around Leon, was around Galen. It was soon after I had seen the blur around Tamara, when Galen's gift first started appearing. I was thinking how special he was, with his great big dreams, and I wanted to protect him. I wanted all his dreams to come true, and then it happened.

Then I remembered when I had seen the peach colored blur—it had been around my mother. She was so upset at me one day, and as I looked into her eyes, I saw something dark... I didn't know what it was until now—it was guilt. None of us had ever known who told the Soldiers about Galen, or me I suppose, but thinking back to that moment, I realized it had been my mom. I was the reason she was dead... and she took my dad with her. I never wanted her to die, but I wasn't close to her after that day with the blur.

I thought about it more, and my hand went to my mouth, "She knew about me... she knew I was Gifted..." I said through my hand.

The realization was blinding. My mom had given her children up...
and for what? Had she hoped it would protect her and her husband,
whom she apparently loved more than anything else? Well that
didn't work very well in her favor. The betrayal I felt was beyond
belief. The woman I had so wished I could look like, that I could
emulate, I now wished I could strip from my mind forever.

I slept in the cave that night, and I was shocked when I woke
up that I had not been eaten alive by some ravenous animal. When
daylight poked its head into my cave, I glared and turned away in
hopes that no new days would come my way. I let myself float in the
water, my arms bracing me against the cold rock surface.

Galen came to visit me as it was nearing noon. At first when
he saw me, he shouted out to me in a panic, and when I didn't reply
he ran over to me and turned me over, surely expecting to see his
sister had drowned. But to his relief, and my chagrin, I had lived
through the night.

He hugged me tightly, "Kayd... I thought you had died! I saw
the most horrible vision..." he began, but I didn't want to hear
anymore visions with me in them,

"Not right now, Galen..."

"You were killing dad!" My eyes popped open and I looked on
at him in shock.

"Wh—what did you say?"

"In the vision, you were staring at Dad, and your eyes went
red and all of a sudden he was bleeding and shaking on the ground. I

hoped it wasn't true... maybe it hasn't happened yet, but I don't want it to ever happen."

I sighed, closing my eyes again to shut him out, "It wasn't dad... it was a Soldier masquerading as dad so he and his partner could take me in to help the Authority." I expected him to question this, since to him I was his un-Gifted sister, but he just watched me in anticipation, "Aren't you wondering how I could help them?"

He shook his head with a shrug, "You are a Decider. They've been looking for you all these years." He said as if it had been common knowledge. I titled my head at him in surprise.

"How long have you known that?" I ask in total shock.

He shrugged his shoulders, "Since I first had my visions." He continued to stare at me in anticipation, "Now tell me what happened." He said with curiosity, and I told him everything that had happened—there was obviously no point in hiding it from him since it appeared he basically already knew.

"And now Leon won't even talk to me..."

Galen waved his hand encouragingly, "He has secrets too. You just reminded him of himself." I stared in wonderment. When had Galen mastered his Gift so well that he was seeing into so much of our lives? "He will come around soon... maybe even today?" he said with a happy smile as he hugged me again, "I'm just glad you are okay! And Garrison and I had an agreement a long time ago. He promised me that if he found us, he would let you go at least once."

"Why would he make you such a promise?" I ask skeptically.

He smiled, "Because I told him about where his daughter would be so he could save her life. She was being held in a torture chamber on May 4th a year after we left." He said nonchalantly. I was so surprised by the way he spoke about the horrors of the world as if they were nothing. How long had he been aware of such things? Had I been fooling myself all these years when I thought he was still a naïve child? Everything I thought I had known just a month ago, I no longer knew to be true.

"How long have you been having such intense visions, Galen?"

He smiled mischievously, "Since they started. I used to tell you about them, but you were always convinced they were just dreams. You and mom and dad didn't start believing them until I was 7. By the time we left I was able to look into any person's future as long as I could touch them."

I sat back, trying to take in this news, "Galen... why didn't you ever tell me about all that?"

He shrugged again and looked at a fish swimming through the waterfall, "I didn't want to stress you out. I knew you already were taking it all so hard..."

"So... you know about mom and dad, then?"

He raised his head, "What do you mean?" my chest tightens, and I instantly felt horrible, "Like where they are? No. I've looked into tons of people's futures trying to find out their location, but we just haven't met the right people." I considered keeping him in the dark a little longer, but it was truth time.

"Galen... they died in the fire." I finally admitted the secret that had been destroying me from the inside out for four years, and sadly I saw instantly that it did the same to him.

He stared at me, his eyes filling with angry tears and he shook his head, "No... they couldn't have!" he said, standing up, "You're wrong."

I watched him with regret. I shouldn't have waited four years to tell him, "I watched it happen Galen. I'm sorry... but they are gone forever."

He screamed like he was in pain and continued to shake his head, "No, no, no!" he fell to the ground, "Why... why wouldn't you tell me...?" he howled. "You let me believe they were alive for *four years*! How could you, Kayd?" he screamed as he ran from the cave.

I watched after him and glared at my reflection in the water, "Great... now I've lost my brother too." I had no food with me, but I made sure to drink from the spring all day. No one else came to see me that day, and I didn't go back to camp. The next morning it was raining, and I was glad to have my cave to protect me. I watched the droplets hit the water, and tried to let it lull me into a pleasant sleep, but my trained ears suddenly heard an odd clomping sound outside the cave.

I prepared myself to dive under the freezing water, but then Leon's face appeared. I sighed and pulled myself back out of the water. He held a large blanket out to me, and I gratefully accepted. He sat beside me silently for a few minutes and watched the rain fall with me.

"I'm sorry for being a jerk, Kayd." He says after a moment of silence, his voice filled with sadness and regret.

"How could I expect anything else? I'm a monster." I said, though I still remembered looking at my reflection that told the truth.

He shook his head, looking regretful and miserable, "It just made me face some of my own demons Kayd... things I didn't want to admit."

"You couldn't know what it's like, Leon." I said, rolling my eyes sadly.

He lets out a long sigh, "I understand having a power that you can't stand." He paused and I found the shock overwhelming as I looked at his guilty gaze. He stared off into the water like he was watching his worst memories on live TV. "I've learned to control mine, but I did quite a few awful things before realizing I was the cause of it." He admits with agony.

"Like what?" I whisper.

He let out an uncomfortable sigh, closing his eyes tightly. He rubbed his hands nervously over his thighs, and finally continued, "I hoped I'd never have to tell you, or anyone really. I like to just be the good guy that everyone believes in, but instead, deep down, I'm cruel." He finishes as if he was admitting the worst sort of crimes already.

I took his hand in mine without question, "Leon, you are not cruel."

"Yes I am, Kayd." He argued with a pained expression, "When I was a boy, I hurt people. I used to have a horrible temper, and when I would get angry, my thoughts would race and I would just think how I wanted to hurt them, and when they would come back to scold me or apologize, I would think how I wished they would hurt themselves. When my father's assistant committed suicide—a perfectly happy and kind woman—my dad and I realized what was happening. He explained it all to me, and helped me to train my abilities."

That's when I remembered the interview I had seen when Leon was 12, "That's why you were ashamed to be Gifted." He looked at me in confusion, "I saw the interview when your dad brought you in and talked about how being Gifted was a blessing, and you seemed so unhappy about it." I quickly explained.

He nodded, "Someone had died because of my anger. I carry that shame every day... that's why when I made you kiss me I felt so awful. It's just when I get angry or emotional, I can't stop my mind from doing what it wants. That's why I always try to stay so calm—I don't want my Gift to decide what I do."

"I want to be able to control mine, but I never mean for it to happen." I reply quietly, throwing a pebble into the water.

"You said before it only happened when you were looking someone in the eyes, right?" I nodded, "Then don't look people in the eyes, unless you feel like you need to." As I looked into his eyes now, I knew he was right and that he had faith in me.

"So will you help me?" I asked with hope.

As he took my hands in his and looked at me carefully, "I will always help when you need me." He said softly, staring deeply into my eyes, and his hand brushed my hair away from my cheek. I felt the pull towards him, and I went to kiss him, but he turned away quickly, suddenly breathless. "I'm so sorry... I didn't mean to."

I watched him carefully... was that really him convincing my mind to kiss him? My mind so often desired this on its own that I wasn't convinced. "Then why did you?"

He looked back at me with pure guilt, "I told you before that when I get emotional or angry, my Gift takes control." He was still facing away from me, though he gave a gentle glance back towards me. I still longed to have his lips touching mine again, and the desire was so strong I closed my eyes as if I could feel it happening. Was I still under his control?

"You don't seem angry to me." I replied softly.

He smiled with an uneasy chuckle, "I'm not."

My body moved towards him, but I knew now it wasn't him pulling me—I wanted him on my own, "Emotional then?"

He laughed, watching every move that brought me closer to him, "I suppose so."

"If you didn't mean to make me kiss you, then why would you try?" he seemed to understand my meaning now. I wasn't accusing him before, I was trying to see if he really wanted me or if it was on accident.

I felt my cheeks blush as a small smile caressed my lips. He turned to me and I felt his gaze as it swept across my skin, "Because I wanted to." He admitted with a smile before turning away again, "I always want to kiss you..." he confessed quietly, totally breathless again.

"Why would you want to kiss me?" I asked in honest surprise though I wanted him too so badly. "You have gorgeous women fawning all over you every single day, and even more so when we went into town. You could have your pick, Leon. So why would you want the awkward 16-year-old with no experience." I had waited for so long to ask him these questions just in case he ever admitted his desire for me, the way I always wished.

He turned to me in surprise, "Kayd... do you not realize how beautiful you are?" he asked in shock. I stared at the ground as I picked at the dirt, allowing it to sift through my fingers. He tenderly took my face in his hands, "Kayd, you are one of the most beautiful women I've ever known." I shook my head with a weak smile as a tear waited in the corner of my eye. I remembered back to the gorgeous girl I had seen in the mirror—she had been me, hadn't she?

He lifted my eyes to meet his gaze, and his eyes were so honest and kind as he smiled with total sincerity, "But it's more than that. You are so strong, so loving, so..." he took in a deep breath, "Breathtaking." He whispered as he brought my face closer to his, "I would choose you every time." He continued and I blushed fiercely, trying to look away again with embarrassment, but my eyes always seemed to find his again.

When I was younger, I had always envied the love my parents shared. Every single morning, they greeted each other with a long, drawn out kiss—my mother's arms wrapped around my dad's neck affectionately—as if it was the first time they had seen each other in weeks. I never doubted their devotion to each other, and I always longed to have that same love someday. Of course, at 12-years-old, I had already basically given up on any such hope. I had made a covenant with my brother that made it clear we would never stop until we were safe. I just hadn't expected that safety to come in the arms of Leon, the Green-eyed Man. I smiled at the thought as he pulled me gently towards his lips.

He put his hand back on my face. My body began to shake in anticipation, "You are pretty easy to fall for," he whispered in my ear, and I could feel his smile against my cheek. Though it technically was not my first kiss with Leon, it felt like it. I think that's how it feels when it is the right person kissing you back—like magic. He was so gentle as he pulled me closer, and I fell into him and he fell into me.

Just like before, I never wanted that kiss to end. He pulled away only once, still breathless as he grinned, his gaze locked on mine, "Still Kayd." He said softly as he pulled me back into his embrace. I don't know how long we kissed, but it never seemed long enough. As soon as we would pull apart, one of us would pull the other back into another kiss. I never wanted the moment to end. It was the first perfect moment I'd had since the time my father and I lay under the stars camping when I was a child.

When Leon and I finally parted, we were both smiling like breathless fools. I almost felt guilty for the joy, but why shouldn't we be happy? So few people are allowed to find true happiness these days, especially those who are Gifted. We must take our happy moments any time we can get them.

We laid together on the blanket as I lay my head on his chest, my hand waiting on his stomach over his shirt as he entwined his fingers with mine. We fell asleep there, and that's when I knew... the little girl was gone, and I was a woman.

Chapter 6: Falling

After that day, Leon and I were practically inseparable. And though Galen was still mad at me for a few days, Leon finally talked to him for me and calmed him down. That first couple of weeks with Leon seemed perfect, and I felt as if everything in my life could continue going perfectly, until the day Galen came running to mine and Leon's hiding place. "Kayd! Kayd!" he shouted as he practically slid into the raging river. Leon and I pulled away quickly as we ran over to him to help, convinced he was hurt in some way. I tried examining him, but he pushed my hands away. I looked into his eyes, and recognized the frazzled look—he had a vision.

"Is everything okay?" Leon asked kindly. Galen looked at him as if he just realized Leon was there.

Galen looked back at me carefully, "You already kissed him... didn't you?" he asked in a whisper. I looked back at Leon and nodded with a blush. "It's too late..." he said as he shook his head and he fell to his knees.

"He kissed me the first day we were here, Galen..." I said as if I was trying to hide our other numerous kisses.

Galen wasn't buying it though. He shook his head again, "Not that one... I mean when it was raining." It still baffled me to have him know my moments so easily. I wasn't sure I appreciated his ability to peek into my future as if it were a picture book he could consult whenever he wished.

"Um... yeah. What does it matter? Are you saying you saw the past?" I asked carefully. He looked so defeated. I sat beside him and put my arm around him,

"I had it a while ago... but it seemed like it was further away. You looked so much older." He confessed sadly as he stared at his hands.

"Galen, why does it matter that I kissed your sister?" Leon asked with concern as he came to the other side of him.

Galen shook his head, "It's not that you kissed her... it's that *she* kissed you." I was confused, but Leon somehow seemed to understand some hidden meaning.

"How long until they get here?" Leon said with defeat like he knew the exact vision my brother spoke of... and the meaning that vision had carried.

Galen began to cry, "Hours." He said simply.

"I had hoped we could stay here longer." Leon said sadly as he stood up.

"Does someone want to explain to me what the Hell is going on here?"

Leon looked at Galen, "I have to warn the others so we can collect as many supplies as possible before we leave. Galen, can you explain it to her? I will see you guys back at camp in a half hour, no later." He said commandingly. He briefly brushed my lips with a kiss before running back to camp.

"Galen... what's happening?"

He looked at me with care, "You weren't supposed to kiss him yet..." he said darkly.

"Why? I don't understand!"

"You aren't strong enough yet." He explained as if that was all I would need to understand. But my baffled expression caused him to sigh as he turned to me, "I told Leon a long time ago that something would happen between you two, and that when it was your choice, that's when the Soldiers would come. I thought it was a year away at least," he repeated, "Or I would've cautioned everyone sooner. But I just had a vision of the Soldiers coming here now. The man who looks like dad is guiding them. He lived through your last meeting." I thought about it all carefully.

I understood that Galen's Gift often gave him hints of events that would happen, or what events would cause others to occur, but none seemed so crucially flawed as this one. I tried to think of some way to fix it all, and then I remembered the day Kent died—after the red blur had appeared, all I had to do was think he needed to die. I looked back at Galen, "Is the man leading them?" Galen scrunched his eyes shut as he thought to it and nodded, "Ok... I think I know a way to distract them. I need you to go back to camp to stay with Leon though, okay?" he nodded and ran back to meet Leon.

I inhaled a deep breath as I envisioned the man who had lied to me. The man who nearly convinced me he was my dead father. I allowed the anger to consume me as I spoke the simple words, "Finn, you deserve to die." I swear I could feel him as he instantly died, his life forever snuffed out. I heard my brother's scream come from camp and I ran back as quickly as I could. Galen stared at me with an almost betrayed look, but he quickly wiped it away.

"You killed him..." he whispered. I looked around at the people who were standing around him in concern. They stared at me in surprised panic.

"I had no choice, Galen." I whispered back, but I knew everyone heard us.

"Who did you kill, Kaydence." Said Layla, a girl who had become one of my closer friends at the Gifted camp.

I looked back at her, not knowing what to say, when Leon came to my aid, "The Soldiers are coming after us. I sent Kaydence to stall. Apparently one of them needed to be killed." He said darkly, "Now let's get going, everyone! Collect the things you can't live without and follow me. 10 minutes!" he shouted through the silent camp. Everyone seemed to nod in unison, as they got moving. Within the ten minutes we are all packed and ready to go. Leon pulls Galen and me to the front of the line as we begin our descent into the next unknown.

"Where are we going?" I ask him quietly.

He sighs, "Just somewhere to hide for now. But once they find our old camp, they won't leave it unguarded. This has happened before." He explained sadly, "We will never be able to go back there." He turned his attention to Galen with authority, "Galen... *never* reveal your sister's Gift again. Not any sort of mention of it. If she has to kill someone, or hurt them, ask her about it in private. No one can know." He said a little too harshly for my taste, but I understood... now was one of the worst times possible for my Gift to come to anyone's attention. No one wanted to leave their homes, and to know the whereabouts of a Decider is basically guaranteed safety from the Authority for life. Galen nodded quietly as he took my hand.

"I'm sorry." He whispered to me. I nodded back to him. We were about four miles from our old camp when I heard the gunshots in the distance. The group began to panic as women began grabbing their children and tried to run in a different direction. Leon whistled loudly and everyone stopped in their tracks and looked towards their leader. Though Leon was one of the youngest Gifted members of the camp, no one ever doubted his abilities, and he was a natural born leader. Maybe it was a gift from his father who was a naturally gifted orator.

"There is no time for panic! We have to keep moving together!" he shouted, and everyone listened. He began moving faster, and everyone followed without a second thought. I'm not sure if it was just him using his Gift on those fearful of death, or whether they truly just trusted him with their lives, but either way it was breathtaking to see the effect he had on such a large group. I was beginning to understand why he always made an appearance in Galen's visions about the Green-eyed Man who would overthrow the President.

Just as we were nearing the area that Leon guaranteed would keep us all safe, there seemed to be a shift in the earth below us. I stopped dead and turned around to see the first person drop to the ground. She didn't even scream as the Soldiers killed her with a silenced weapon. I don't think anyone would've noticed the Soldiers disguised as civilians blending into the back row of our group.

I don't know what possessed me—the girl who had to stare someone in the eyes to kill them— to attempt to fight a large group of men, but I couldn't stop my feet. I felt almost every pair of eyes watch me as I flew to the back of the group—that's when the screams began. A few of the others with stronger gifts, like the Shockies, began trying to fight off the men, but it was like they knew every move we were going to make. That's when I realized who these Soldiers were... they were President Reece's pets—the Dangerous Ones he had been collecting for the 12 years he had been president. They were Gifted.

"Run!" I heard Leon's voice shout over the crowd, and most of the people in the front listened, but those of us in the back already seemed to be trapped by the Colossals—massive men that could control the earth—who had slowly surrounded as many of us as possible. I felt it then, as those in my crowd began to drop like flies

88

on a summer day, the blur inside my gaze, but it was different this time. Everything around me seemed to be covered in a black haze, and my skin began to burn. I looked around and suddenly at least fifty of those in the group I was in began to glow red. I didn't need to question as the words left my lips, "Stop." I said in a voice that seemed to echo. Every one of them stopped instantly, staring at me, mesmerized by something I could not see. "Let the others go." I said to them in an even tone, and those from my camp were sent running back towards Leon.

"Who are you?" one of the Dangerous Ones asked, truly in awe as he gazed at me. He was a tall, handsome man with dark brown eyes and black hair.

They were all frozen in their spots, and I had the feeling I was somehow the reason behind it, "I'm Kaydence..." I said with less strength than I had moments before. Leon came running back towards me, but I turned towards him with a lifted hand, "Don't!" I urged and he stopped with a confused expression. I turned back to the others, "I'm a Decider."

They all stared on at me in shock, "*The* Decider? You're the one they've been looking for all these years!"

"Isn't that why you came after us? Weren't you looking for me?"

The man shook his head, "No, we were just sent to retrieve any other strong Gifted, and kill all others." He said almost too calmly.

I felt my fury rise, but I didn't want to kill them, "Well these people are not to be harmed... *Ever!*" I shouted with that echoing voice again. "Forget where you found us, and forget about finding me." They all nodded, hypnotized by my voice and my power. Without another thought, they went running in the other direction. Once they were far enough away, I fell to the ground, my body exerted from the unknown force that managed to save the rest of our group. Leon ran to me and pulled me into his arms and stroked my face.

"Kayd, how did you do that? I have a feeling they weren't just listening to you because they were in awe."

"I think my Gift can do more than just protect or kill people... I was able to spot which of them were bad, and focused all my power on them. They listened to me, and they froze to their spot. I don't know how I did it... I just did." I reply in utter shock. Even remembering the scene made me shiver with uncertainty.

He continued to push the hair from my face, "It was spectacular, Kayd." He whispered, "I've never seen anything like it."

I sigh distantly, "Well if it was really spectacular, it would've happened fast enough for me to save all of you..." I say, closing my eyes as I picture the horror-filled faces of those whose lives were stolen.

He turned me around, so I was looking into his eyes, "Do you realize you saved more people than any of the rest of us could've hoped to?" his voice was deep and honest and loving. "Those were the Dangerous Ones, weren't they?"

"Well yeah..."

He nods encouragingly, "Then either everyone would've been killed or they would've been taken to the Authority. I don't think you have heard of what those Dangerous Ones are capable of under President Reece's control. When he sends them to attack a Gifted camp, they all end up dead while the more powerful are taken to by the Soldiers. Without you, we would've lost everyone. Thank you." He said kissing my lips tenderly. It made me smile.

When we caught up to the others, they were already reaching the deep cave hidden by large trees. For an area that seemed so much safer, I didn't understand why they had ever been in such an open area. Leon and I got inside, but everyone was locked in whispers. Once I came into view, the room went silent. Leon watched their hungry stares, "She's Gifted!" shouted an older woman accusingly,

"She has already been lying to us, and the way she talked to those Dangerous Ones, she was probably in cahoots!" A few people in her circle agreed loudly.

"She was probably the reason they came for us!!" another man shouted.

I knew this day would come, but having everyone prepare to throw me out the door so quickly still hurt my heart. A mob seemed to be forming of all those who believed me to be just biding time before handing them all over to the Authority.

Leon tried to calm them, but my anger was rising too quickly, and I couldn't stop the words from pouring out, "They would've killed you all!" I shout, and the room went silent. I stare around, making sure to look in the faces of all those I had started to call friends, "The Authority only wants the Dangerous Ones! And I don't know this because I'm a spy, but because a Soldier told me this a few weeks ago when I first found out about my Gift."

Though I could see many of the people were beginning to believe me, a few skeptics still lingered in the crowd, "If that were true then why would a Soldier let you go?"

Galen stepped forward, "Because years ago I told him the whereabouts of his daughter in exchange for protection for Kayd at least once. He let her go because of me." Suddenly there were more believers.

"Besides, don't you realize that Kayd is the reason you are all safe? If it had not been for her instincts, we would all be dead!" Leon's voice echoed through the cavern, and any person who had doubted me a moment ago quickly pushed their skepticism aside. Not one person was used to seeing Leon angry, but somehow, I bring out that emotional nature within him.

By the end of the night everyone was settling into their new home. A few children were crying at the loss of their parents or another loved one who had been killed or injured by the Dangerous

Ones, and there were scattered couples holding each other close, thankful that they managed to live another day. I wished I was in one of these groups, but it didn't feel like home for me, who was still being ignored for lying to the others. I lost no one, thank goodness, but Leon was busy tending to the wounded and helping those affected by the change. I found myself sulking in a corner with Galen as he held my hand so I wouldn't be alone.

The next day I tried to help a few of the girls I had come to think of as friends as they set up their new homes, but even they pushed me away. I felt alienated, and somehow alienation was worse than being on my own with Galen, because at least then it was by my choice rather than someone else's. I thought about leaving, about going back out into the lonely world that now hunted me, and I even considered leaving Galen behind where he might be safer, but had I not been here, I wouldn't have kept these people safe. This Army was coming for our camp already whether I was a part of it or not.

I was bombarded by my thoughts, and I felt myself drifting back to that world I thought I had left behind. Without my permission, my memories overtook me, and I wandered back to when I was a child. I went back to a moment I forgot even existed— the last time I saw my parents before we were running off in fear.

My mom, Galen, and I were sitting on the back porch together staring into the thinly treed forest behind our home. I usually enjoyed watching the birds hopping from tree to tree, but today I wanted to help my dad work in the garden out front. My mom urged

Galen and I to stay out back as the light shifted from morning to afternoon. I could feel the earth vibrate beneath my feet and I didn't understand what could cause such commotion. I could hear people crying out on the streets—that's when my dad came running out to us screaming at my mother for being so careless about us being outside. She urged him that there was nothing to worry about. He pushed her inside.

"Tom, make sure they come inside. I don't want to be without them!" she said hysterically, but her eyes were shifting from side to side as she stared towards the door. She was biding her time as she fought with my dad to keep her children close as if we meant more to her than anything. I wished I could've told her I knew the truth. I wish I could've yelled and screamed, and asked her why she would turn us in.

My dad instantly became calm, almost as if he finally understood what was happening. He came over to her and whispered something through his teeth with anger before he brushed past her and took mine and my brother's arms and led us outside. My mom called after my father, telling him it was useless to run.

That was the first time I ever saw my dad afraid. He looked back towards my mom, and then to me. He knelt in front of me, kissed my forehead and whispered, "It's time to run, Kaydy. You and Galen have to run… and never look back. Don't get caught. I love you both."

"Ok Daddy." But when I started walking away with my brother, I turned back, "When will we see you again? Where will we meet?" I said dutifully, remembering that this is what we had planned when he prepared me for the day my brother and I would leave.

My father's face looked so sad as he stared at me with all the love and grief a father could give as he says goodbye for the last time. He simply shook his head as tears poured quietly from his eyes. I wanted to follow after him, to give him my last hug, but I couldn't. I ran to the tree line on the other side of the street and watched as the Soldiers beat my father, pushing him back into the house.

"We killed them." My father shouted with feigned disgust, "They were monsters! I thought that was what we were supposed to do when we found out our children were Gifted!" my father shouted at them, but the Soldiers kept pushing him back into the house. I saw the face of the man who threw the first bit of flame onto the wood frame of my home.

"He's lying!" My mom screamed at the top of her lungs as they locked them inside, "Please let us out! I'll tell you where they are!" I could barely hear her say as she pounded on the doors and tried to break the windows.

Galen kept trying to look towards our home, asking why we couldn't go back. I simply forced him into the forest in front of me in hopes that he would not see my tears.

I felt the tears still on my cheeks as if they were new. I wiped my eyes, and, with it, my memories faded back into the deep place I stored them in my mind. Everyone was asleep in our large cave, and I no longer cared how long I had been out. I didn't want to be around them. I quietly crept past the rows of people lying on the floor, and I walked out into the cool night. I wandered for a while, hoping that the pain inside my heart would heal from some fresh air, but it wasn't working. I tried running, but the tears still came, and nothing would stop them anymore. I fell to the ground finally, not knowing where I was or how far I had traveled from my new home, and I just cried.

I pulled my knees to my chest. How could we live in a world where parents are killed for trying to protect their children, and children are forced to run for their lives? It wasn't right! I was so angry at President Reece, suddenly pinning all my misery and misfortune on him. It was his fault I was running, after all. His fault my mother chose to give up her children...

Then an idea came to me—if we could find Leon's father, maybe a rebellion really could happen. If we could find him, then he could overthrow the President, and all of us could live peacefully. Peace had happened once, hadn't it? Maybe it could happen again.

When Leon found me some time later, I didn't doubt that my eyes were thoroughly puffy and red, so I wasn't surprised by the pity in his eyes as he pulled me into his arms. "Don't let what everyone said earlier get to you, Kayd. They would be dead without you." I nodded into his shoulder.

I was quiet for a long time as I let his warmth fill me, let it ebb away the frozen pain my memories had brought out in me. I pulled in a shaking breath and sighed through the agony, "My mom was the reason Galen and I had to run." I threw out randomly in a near whisper, and he looked down at me in surprise.

"What?" he asked in confusion.

I sighed, "I'm sorry... I shouldn't have said it. I just can't get these thoughts to leave me alone." I knew I wasn't making any sense, but I couldn't stop the stream of thoughts pouring out in conversation.

He pushed me away slightly so he could look into my eyes, "Kayd, what's wrong? Tell me." He urged compassionately.

I stared into those green eyes, and I knew that if anyone could help me, he could. "I just had this intense memory... and it made me face something I never thought I'd have to face. My mom... she was the one who gave us up to the Soldiers. She was the one who I saw surrounded by the peach blur... it meant guilt. I know now that she was the reason my brother and I have been running for four years." Fresh tears fell over my face, and I angrily brushed them away.

He shook his head in shock, "Why would she do that?" he gaped.

I gazed at him carefully, "She loved my dad more than she loved us. I heard her once..." I began as I picked at the grass under my knee, "She had told him that it was his fault that we were alive. She said that she had never wanted children in fear that they would be Gifted. I guess my dad had assured her that they would have non-Gifted kids, and in the end he was wrong. She was afraid of us." I glared at the blades of grass sticking to my palm, "And now I know... she was actually just afraid of *me*." I shook my head as I threw the grass out of my hands.

He hesitated, "But what if that was just a coincidence? Just because she felt that way doesn't mean she actually gave you guys up to the Soldiers."

I shook my head with a pained smile, "I've been thinking about my Gift more, Leon..." I dared to look at him, "That color gives me more than whether someone deserves to live or die—I know what their secrets are. I always just thought I was being ridiculous when thoughts like that came to my mind, but now I know that I was seeing everything!"

He gazed at me in cautious awe, "But... isn't that a different Gift? That sounds more like an Emoty."

I nodded, "There are a few of the other Gifts that I can use too, I think." I said quietly. "I'm pretty sure I have yours too." I whispered and he just stared at me with his mouth open,

"How... how do you know?"

I looked away from him, suddenly feeling embarrassed, "When I controlled that Army today... they were all highlighted in red, and I just told them what I wanted them to do. You saw it... they did whatever I told them—forgot what I wanted them to forget."

I felt his eyes trained on me, and though I could tell he was trying to hide it, his uncertainty looked pretty close to fear, "I'm confused... I thought you were a Decider? Deciders only judge life and death, right?" he suddenly sounded a little scared.

"Think about it Leon—no one really knows what a Decider does. I remember a story my dad read me when I was little, and it mentioned the Deciders. None have lived for over 200 years because people always killed them as soon as one was found. What if they could literally do anything?" I felt the fear creep into my voice as well, "What if Deciders actually 'decide' what they can do in the moment? Maybe there is the main Gift, but they can be trained to do the others also?"

He was silent for a while before he dared to speak again, and what he said next was enough to silence me for life, "Now I see why they weren't allowed to live... the Deciders were the real Dangerous Ones..."

Chapter 7: Dangers unseen

He was afraid of me now too, great... I glared at my hands, "Leon... please don't hate me. You can help me! You can train me..." I said desperately as I turned to him and grabbed his hands. He considered me carefully, "Please... don't be afraid of me like the others." I cried.

He pulled me into a tender hug, "I love you, Kayd." He whispered sweetly in my ear. I felt my cheeks go warm at those words.

"Even knowing all this?"

I felt him nod, "You aren't like the other Dangerous Ones, Kayd." He said as he pulled away and took my face in his hands, "It is still known that those who have the Dangerous Gifts usually have a desire to do evil. No one knows why they have it, but maybe it is a mutation in their genes? But you are kind, Kayd. Honestly, if anyone could have all those Gifts and still be good, it's you." He said with an affectionate smile, "I know that I couldn't handle it. Most people get a taste of that kind of power and it consumes them, but I think you could change the world with it."

I smiled back at him and hugged him tightly. "Thank you." I said quietly. I felt his arms tighten around me, "I love you too, by the way." I said looking up at him with a bashful grin.

He laughed happily, "I hoped so." He said as he kissed my lips softly. I hoped I'd never lose him. I knew there was no one else I could ever picture my life with. I didn't want to picture my life without him. He was mine and I was his. We might be young, me especially, but I know with certainty that this is a love that can last.

He held me close as I fell asleep in his arms over the blanket of leaves acting as our bed. When we woke up, he guided me back to our cave, which was actually pretty far away from where I had meandered to in the night. I looked back to Leon with a smile realizing he went far from camp to look for me .

When we got back, we heard a little chatter from the few people who were still awake, and then all at once, the cave seemed to go silent seeing Leon's hand around my waist. I almost pulled away in fear that we were upsetting people, but he put a little pressure on my waist to let me know I was safe in his arms. A few girls looked truly upset by this development as they glared viciously at me,

"Leon, don't be fooled by this monster!" An older man said coldly, and a few women nearby him shouted in agreement. Suddenly the little bit of support Leon had last night after his speech had gone with the night.

Leon's eyes seemed to turn to fire, "Monster? Who here couldn't be considered a monster in someone's eyes?" His voice bellowed, and everyone went silent, "We are all here, *together*, because we are all considered monsters to the non-Gifted! Yes, Kayd has a Gift that is difficult to understand, but after only knowing a few of you, and being shunned by almost all of you, she still *chose* to help you. I will not allow anyone to make her feel unwelcome!"

"She is an abomination!" the same man shouted out.

Leon glared at him, "But Kent was an angel?" He shouted. That silenced everyone instantly, and suddenly quite a few women seemed to be more attentive, "Kent was truly a monster, a cruel man that we allowed to be in our group. Does anyone remember why?" he questioned, but no one answered, and most of the elders in the group seemed to stare at the ground in shame, "We hoped that having a Dangerous One on our side would give us some sort of protection. Funny how few people mourned him when he died, this angel of a man." He called out coldly. I felt the emotional power rise in him, and I touched his hand. He looked at me, and the fire dwindled as he took in a deep breath and closed his eyes.

"I would never hurt any of you. I did not know I was Gifted until a few weeks ago, and I was therefore not hiding it from any of you. When I found out, I tried to keep my distance, fearful that somehow, I would hurt someone, but that's not how my Gift works. All I can say to you is that if anyone ever needs a helping hand, or you are afraid, I will do my best to help you, just as I did before I knew about my Gift. A few of you dared to be my friend when everyone else thought I was a spy... so why not allow me the same courtesy now that you know I am Gifted? This was meant to be a place of protection for the Gifted... please allow me this same kindness."

I spoke as authoritatively as I could. I think for many of those in the crowd, it was the first time they had heard me speak. Almost all the girls who had started warming up to me before, came up to me and embraced me, "I'm so sorry." They each repeated in their own ways. No matter how many times I accepted their apologies, they just continued. But as I stared out over the crowd, I knew I had convinced them, and, maybe most importantly, I convinced myself.

• •

I felt the world shake again as I watched my memories flash before my eyes again, forever haunting me with the moments that could have been so easily changed if my mom had only had as much devotion to us as her desire to preserve her own life.

One night, five months after we had come to the cave, Galen came to me, shaking me awake from the nightmares of my past, "Galen? What's wrong?" I said, wiping my sleepy eyes.

His eyes seemed to be glazed over with a white film as he gazed at me, "The tipping point is coming. You will have to decide what is more important... and no matter what you choose, there will be intense heartache. Someone is going to die." Galen said in an odd voice. His eyes changed back to their usual blue as he fell forward into my arms. I had never seen Galen act that way because of a vision, and it scared me as I held my little brother in my arms. Leon came running over as if sensing my fears. He picked up Galen and took him outside. I followed cautiously.

"What did he say to you?" he whispered as we walked out into the brightening world outside.

"He said something about a tipping point coming, and I'd have to decide? He said someone was going to die." I replied quickly, staring at my brother still lying peacefully in Leon's hands. Something was horribly wrong, but I couldn't place what it was.

"He just came to Annabeth a little while ago and told her to come to me to tell me what he had said to her." Leon met my gaze, "He said that if the three of us stay with the others, we will all die. We have to get going right now, Kayd."

"But... is that all he told her?" Leon shook his head as he looked back at Galen,

"No. He told her that we would all burn. He said the Soldiers were coming for the three of us. One of the Dangerous Ones in the president's Army remembered you, and now they are looking for you." I thought back to what Galen had said to me: Someone was going to die. What if Leon or Galen would die if they came with me? Maybe I should leave without them. This would cause the heartache, but at least this way they wouldn't be the ones to die.

Galen sat straight up, his eyes blue again, but his face was oddly relaxed as he turned to me, "We must travel together." He said in the ominous voice from before. He hopped out of Leon's arms and began walking to the East of the cave—back towards the town

Garrison had found me in. I looked at Leon and he grabbed my hand as we started following after my brother.

"Is he usually like this when he has visions?" Leon asked me quietly, leaning close to my ear.

I shook my head, "I've never ever seen him like this."

Leon nodded, and at first was kind of quiet, "He had a vision about me, didn't he?" he asked carefully after awhile.

I looked at him in confused surprise, "Now? Not that I know of."

He shook his head, pulling in a sharp breath, "No... I mean before."

"Why do you ask?" I asked, not wanting to make eye contact at the memory of every story I heard of the Green-Eyed Man that Galen had told me.

"Whenever he looks at me... it's like he knew me already. He has looked at me like that since the day I found the two of you." He took in a deep breath, "He gives you the same look."

I laughed, "But he has known me."

He shook his head seriously, "There's something different to it, Kayd. He looks at me like I'm special. He looks at you the same way." I looked at him for a moment, realizing I recognized the look he was talking about. Galen had not always given me this look... it hadn't started until he started getting his visions. And hadn't Galen told me that he had known about my Gifts since his first vision? Why would he know that about me unless he had a vision specifically involving my Gifts? My hand went to my mouth,

"Oh my God..." I stopped suddenly. This all seemed familiar, and I remembered back to what I had told Leon months ago about my different abilities, like that I could decide which Gift to use. I quickly ran over to Galen and touched his skin. He jolted suddenly, and my mind was instantly flooded by his memories and his visions, all mixed together in a nonsensical blur. I tried to decipher them, and I found the vision I was looking for (*how did I do that?*)—his very first one.

It was me, at least a few years older than I was right now, standing in front of the president, "I will never be part of your Army." I said to him coldly.

President Reece smiled as he stood and tried to approach me, but he froze where he was, and I could tell it shocked him. "What are you going to do, kill me?" but he didn't sound scared... he was cocky.

I shook my head, "Not yet. You deserve so much worse..." my teeth were clenched, my fists tight at my side.

"Then do it. You have already decided, haven't you, Decider?" he said tauntingly. And even though he seemed to be losing, he was too sure of himself. He smirked coldly as he looked just over my shoulder. I turned around and my chest tightened in shock as I stared at my father.

"Daddy?" My grip loosened on the President and he fell to the ground. "But you died..." He shook his head with a sad smile, but his

words were too quiet for me to hear, and suddenly the vision became distorted and blurry.

I tried to hang onto it, but it fell away. I lost my balance and almost fell to the ground as I looked at Galen in shock. Had that really been what he had seen? Not only was I up against the most horrendous man in our nation, I would see my dad again? But he couldn't be real. My dad died... I was sure of it. But as I looked back into my memory of the day I thought he had died, I realized I only heard my mother's screams. How had he gotten away? It couldn't be possible.

"Kayd?" Leon asked carefully as he held me up, "What did you see?"

"I—I'm not sure." I admitted, still staring at my brother.

Galen turned around and looked at me with his head tilted slightly, "Now you see why we must go. You have to face the president someday." He said in an even voice. I nodded once, my heart feeling as though it was stuck in my throat.

"But only me... I don't want the two of you to get caught in this..."

He shook his head, "No Kayd, we all have to go. It can't happen without all of us." He said like he was programmed to say it. He held his palm out to me, "Take my hand, Kaydence. I will show you." I stared at his hand in fear, and I felt Leon's eyes on me, "Now." I took his hand and saw what would happen if I left Galen and Leon: they would burn. They were the ones that would die. It wasn't the group that would suffer, though they surely would suffer if we were with them, but Galen and Leon would be the ones that would truly suffer.

Then I saw further ahead, or I guess closer to our current future. The Soldiers were already following after us but if we took a left instead of a right at Westin Falls, the Soldiers would lose our trail.

I pulled my hand away and looked into Galen's eyes, "You always knew dad was alive… didn't you?" I asked him instead of asking about the newer vision he showed me.

He shook his head, "You saw a part of the vision I couldn't see before. It was always blurred away, like I wasn't meant to see it. When you watched it just now was the first time I saw the whole thing."

Suddenly his words sunk in—you can watch more of the vision than what you first see. "Have you ever tried to look at the visions again to see more?" I asked hungrily.

He watched me with an odd look, "You aren't supposed to, Kayd." He warned.

"How do you know? If you don't try…" I continued hastily.

He shook his head and put a hand on my shoulder, "No Kayd, I mean… you are not supposed to see more. Just because you *can* doesn't mean you should."

I felt my anger rise, knowing that the truth I had waited to know for years was within my grasp, but within my brother's mind locked away. "Just let me look at it again. I'm sure I can see if it was really dad." Galen looked at Leon with worry.

Leon took my hand, "Kayd, calm down." Tears rose in my eyes and I looked between the two, feeling a betrayal from them that wasn't really there.

"Leon it was my dad! He might still be alive! If I could just look back at Galen's vision, I could know for sure when I'll see him." I continued, becoming hysterical.

Leon's eyes looked so pitying as he gazed into me, "Kayd, where are you?" he whispered.

At first those words made me so mad, but then I understood. I wasn't being me. If I looked at my reflection right now, would I see someone worthy of life, control, or death? I closed my eyes and took in a deep breath, and as I let it out, I let my anger out as well. When I opened my eyes again, he smiled with relief, "Still Kayd." He said as he kissed my lips.

But even though I had let the anger go, I could not rid myself of this new knowledge, and this new knowledge was possibly enough to put me over the edge. I would never be able to forget the fact that my father may be alive. My brother continued on, guiding us towards the direction his vision suggested we travel. Leon took my hand as we all walked together silently. I saw him look back a few times towards those he had led for so long, but he never turned to go back to them, and he never asked if he could tell them what was happening.

Though Leon was an incredible leader, he also knew how and when to follow. I envied his control and his strength. I looked back at my past every single day with regret, and now, knowing that my father may still be alive, all I wanted was to search for him day and night until I found him. I would risk everything to find out the 'what if' that called out to me so tauntingly. I often forgot my place or my duties when I got lost in my thoughts, and my thoughts were steadily taking more and more control.

We had been walking for hours before Galen stopped suddenly and stretched with a wide yawn, "We should rest now." He said tiredly, and he finally resembled my little brother again instead of the strange young man he seemed to be becoming more every day. Leon and I laid out blankets for each of us and we sat down on our parallel beds. He looked at me with dissecting eyes, "Kayd... are we going to talk about what happened earlier?"

I stared at my sleeping bag, "What?" I said, avoiding his gaze.

"The vision, Kayd. What happened with the vision you saw?" I felt my cheeks flush with anxiety.

"I saw a vision that my dad was still alive." I muttered simply, trying to hide my feelings, knowing deep down that I would never stop searching.

He nodded his head, "I figured that out by what you and Galen were saying. I meant... what happened to you after you saw it. You weren't yourself anymore, Kayd." He murmured gently with concern.

I didn't want to look at him, but my eyes always had a different plan when it came to Leon. As I met his gaze, I suddenly remembered the first time I had looked into those eyes, realizing who he was, but who was I? Galen always saw Leon in his visions as a hero, but the first vision he ever saw of me, I was a monster. How could he have ever looked on me with favor? And Leon had seen what I was capable of more than once... how could he look at me with love? I quickly looked away as I blinked away tears.

"I won't use the Prophetic Gift anymore..." I muttered quietly, "Though I used quite a few of the other Gifts to keep the President's Army from our group, the power didn't consume me. But there is something about looking into the future..." I shook my head with shame as I remembered the intoxicating power as I saw what was to come, "It was just too much. I don't know how Galen handles it was such grace. Because after only a single vision, I was lost in the power." I replied guiltily.

"What exactly did you see?"

I took in a deep breath, "I was talking to President Reece a few years from now... he wanted me to join his army. I told him I wouldn't, and then I used the Freezer Gift to freeze him to his spot. He seemed so cocky still, even though he obviously had no chance against me... and then when I turned around, I saw my dad." I sighed, "It may not sound like much, but there was something so wrong about it all. That's why I wanted to see more. I thought that if I could just figure out the truth, then I could know..."

"And even if you did know, what would it change?" he asked, and I realized he was right. What did knowing really help? Whether my father really was alive or not, it did not affect what would happen. But there was an advantage I now had: I knew my dad, or someone who looked like him, would be behind me when I was about to carry out my judgment on President Reece. I would not be distracted when it really happened, even if it was years away.

"You're right... that's why I won't look into the future again."

He nodded as he put a hand on mine, but I felt the distance between us. I lost him a little bit today. Leon was the next to fall asleep, and I was left with my thoughts keeping me awake. When I finally fell asleep, my dreams were tainted with the possibilities. In the first dream, Galen and Leon were burning in a fire that I could not put out. I tried to go in to save them, but my Gifts were gone, and I was useless. I fell to the ground screaming as I watched the last people I loved die, the same way my parents had died. Was the fire supposed to be a sick joke reminding me what I had already lost?

The next dream was a repeat of Galen's vision of me, and it kept repeating. Every time, even knowing that my dad was behind me, dream me always turned to him. It was almost as if my desire to see him was stronger than the knowledge of his existence. I screamed at myself to not turn, but the President always just smiled that smug grin as my attention went to my father.

When I finally woke up, I was drenched in sweat, and my lungs hurt as if I had actually been screaming. Leon and Galen sat staring at me with concerned looks on their faces. I wiped my eyes and sat up as I gazed back at them, "Why are you guys looking at me like that."

Leon seemed sad as he looked into my eyes, "You have been screaming for hours, but we couldn't wake you. We tried everything we could think of—I even tried using my Gift to wake you, but you were completely unresponsive. I'm sorry."

I waved him off as I rubbed my temples—my head was pounding with a fierce headache, "Don't be sorry. I'm sorry I was lost in nightmares." I said coldly, my voice hoarse. I didn't feel like myself, and I didn't like it. I felt like someone else was possessing me as I growled, "Stop looking at me!"

Leon huffed out a breath and sighed. He stood up and paced away.

"Stop it, Kayd." Galen said harshly, and he tried to reach out to me.

I pushed his hand away and stood, "Stop what? I already said I wouldn't look into the future anymore." I said bitterly, but I didn't understand why those are the words I chose. He obviously was not talking about me using a Gift, but whatever was controlling me had taken over my tongue.

He gazed deep into my eyes, "Kayd... stop it!" He screamed and I screamed back, and suddenly my brother was on the ground seizing uncontrollably. I wanted to hold him and make the pain stop, but I just stared helplessly. I screamed out to him, and suddenly I woke up for a second time.

Galen and Leon were still sleeping, and the sky was barely turning into an orange-blue to announce daytime. I cried fiercely as I held my knees. Leon woke up soon after I had.

"Kayd? Why are you crying?"

I shook my head at him, "I can't—I can't do this!" I said through my tears.

He pulled me into his arms. I tried to push him away, fearing somehow that I would hurt him like I hurt Galen in my dream, "Kayd, what can't you do?"

"Be with you guys… I'm just going to end up hurting you both." I wept.

He pulled me onto his lap, and I no longer protested as my arms naturally wrapped around his neck, "The only way you would hurt us is if you left us."

I nodded as my tears began to calm a little, "I know, Galen's vision showed me what would happen if I left you guys."

He shook his head as he took my face in his soft hand and turned me towards him, "No, I mean if you left us, we both would be shells of who we really are. You mean everything to your brother, Kayd, and…" he pulled my face closer to his and my body went warm as he caressed my shoulder with his free hand, "You are my love." He whispered in my ear. "I've waited my whole life for you, Kayd. When my father was captured and imprisoned by the Authority when I was

15, I decided there was no point loving someone. I knew that all the people you love disappear, but when I found you, I knew I could never be without you. I realized that I could protect you." He smiled as his hand went to the nape of my neck, and my eyes closed as my body filled with calm, "I never want to leave your side, Kayd. I will always be there to help you, to protect you... to be with you." I could hear him rifling through his bag,

"I asked my mother for this a few weeks ago..." he said, and I opened my eyes as I saw a small box in his hand. I stared at it in surprise as I pulled away from his face a little. He smiled sweetly as he opened the box and a brilliant diamond sparkled in the growing light of the new day. My hand went to my mouth, "I know you are still young, and I know we have only known each other for half a year, but I already know I always want to be with you, Kayd. I want to be with you forever." He said lovingly as he pulled the ring out of the box and began placing it on my left-hand ring finger, "But I will wait forever if that's what it takes to marry you." he whispered. I smiled as fresh tears sprung from my eyes.

"I love you more than words can express, Leon... but I'm so afraid..."

He shook his head as he kissed my lips softly, "So am I, about a thousand different things, but I will always be here for you. No matter what happens, I will always love you." Those words, in their simplicity, were what I needed to know. In my dream he seemed to hate me, but these words, his real words, showed me the truth: Leon was devoted to me. But the problem was my age.

"I'm only 16, Leon."

He nodded pulling me closer again, "I know, and that's why I know I may have to wait a few years, but you are worth the wait." He kissed me again, and I realized I didn't want to wait.

"I want to marry you. I want to be with you." I whispered back to him, my body shaking. "Our laws say that a girl can still marry at 17 if her parents are no longer in her life. Whether my father is alive or not, he has not been in my life for four years, with my brother and I believing he was dead. I have basically been an adult since we left. In five months when I turn 17, I want to marry you..." He smiled softly as he pushed the hair out of my face.

"Why are you in such a hurry?" he chuckled.

Something in my chest tightened, "Why wait? We know we want to be with each other, so I see no point in waiting." He nodded considerately.

"Then we can get married then, if you are still sure by then." He said with a knowing smirk. I nodded.

"I love you." I replied simply and he kissed me with a surprising heat behind it. But even now, in this moment that most young women wait their entire lives for, something felt wrong. I thought back to my dream in which I had hurt my brother—I was no longer controlling myself. And the way I had just answered Leon, those words did not feel like my own. I was patient... I had been willing to wait my entire life just to find a safe place. Kaydence was happy to wait if that was what was necessary. Kaydence would be happy to have simply found love, and would've been happy to wait as long as she needed... so why wasn't I willing to wait? What was the inner monster within me planning? Or was it simply that my fear to lose another person I loved was too great.

I pulled him away for a moment as the truth really sunk in, looking into Leon's green eyes—this thing guiding me might not be bad the way I had feared in my dream. I so often run from things that scare me, and I've never been as afraid as I was now looking at the man I knew I would love for my whole life. I was being guided to be with him before I could run away. I smiled delicately at the thought... maybe I was not so unreachable as I had made myself believe. I was not a monster—just a girl in love.

Chapter 8: End of the Road

The next morning, we reached Westin Falls again, and I smiled as Leon took my hand affectionately. He kissed the ring that encircled my finger so perfectly. We had not told Galen yet by my request, because I didn't know how he would take the news. Or, more likely, he already knew, and I didn't want him to tell me he knew years ago. Galen was being oddly quiet as we turned left and started walking into a part of the forest I had never been. The path began winding up a large hill towards the top of the Falls, and by the time we reached the top, we could actually see the Soldiers who had been following us.

"Which way did they go?" a younger man asked too quickly, and an older man—the leader, I thought—smacked the boy in the face,

"Don't speak!" He said loudly, "They must have gone right. The man told us they would go right." With that, they started traveling along the river in the opposite direction than us. I smiled at my brother who was grinning broadly.

"We are safe now." He said smugly as he sat down happily and began acting his age again. Leon and I smiled at each other as we sat across from Galen, and I saw him look at my hand carefully and then back at Leon, "Huh." He said with an odd, disappointed sort of look.

"What?" I asked him carefully, trying to hide my ring finger.

He looked at Leon with a small smile, "In my vision, you asked my permission to marry Kayd." He said with a shrug and he laughed. Leon and I laughed with him.

"So you knew this was going to happen?" Leon asked with a laugh, but it was warm, sweet.

Galen smiled, "Leon, I know lots of things." He said, and for one moment, I felt like I could see the expanses of visions inside his head.

I couldn't help but laugh, suddenly feeling free in a way I hadn't felt in a long time, "It's funny for the boy who could never keep a secret, he sure can keep his mouth shut about future events."

Galen smiled softly and nodded with care, "It's something you will learn also, Kayd." He said more seriously, suddenly feeling more like a sensei than my brother.

"Are you saying I can't keep a secret?" I said with a smirk and he shook his head,

His tone was far too somber, "No, you keep plenty of secrets, very well actually." I was surprised how little hurt accompanied those words, "You will use the Prophet Gift again... don't fight it, Kayd." He said simply as he lifted his hand, sensing my objection before I could even fully open my mouth, "You will, and the sooner you learn to control it, the better off you will be." He says almost harshly, and my eyes widen in surprise. "The longer you wait, the more bad things will happen. But, once you see the future, you cannot tell people what is happening exactly. You can give hints, but if you just give the ending, it could make people panic, or ruin the surprise." He said with a sudden wink towards Leon, who met the wink with a grin.

I bit my lip hard, tearing my gaze from his as guilt consumes me, "I don't like what it does to me, Galen. Your Gift is just not for me." It came out a near whisper.

An odd fury seemed to rise in him as he stood, his fists clenched tightly, "Don't you get it, Kayd? You have been given all these Gifts for a purpose. You can't just choose which ones you like and the ones you don't. You have to master all of them to reach your destiny. And if you wait too long, the powers will control you rather than the other way around." He warns darkly.

I just stared at him for a moment, hardly recognizing him anymore as he spoke like our father—a college professor, "When the heck did you become an adult?" I joked and he tilted his head at me slightly showing that he didn't really get the joke. I stopped chuckling, huffing out a breath, "Ok... I get it."

"I can help you if you wanted." he replied softly.

Leon squeezed my hand encouragingly, and I nodded, "I would like that."

Galen smiled happily. He scooted over to me and folded his hands in his lap as if he were meditating, "Now, obviously you won't be as good as I am, because let's face it—I'm a master." He said with an arrogant smile that made Leon laugh.

I nodded, holding back my retorting smile, "Of course." I pretend to be skeptical, but, honestly, at 12-years-old he seemed to have his Gift pretty well mastered.

"Now first thing's first: when a vision comes, don't force it. Allow it to enter you like someone is telling you a secret." He said calmly, pulling in a slow breath, "Now take a deep breath and focus." So, I did as he said and waited, but nothing happened. We sat there for at least five minutes before the summer air, mixed with the chattering birds, started getting to me.

I start tapping my fingers on my folded knees, my teeth gritted, "When is it going to happen." I urge with irritation.

He smiled with his eyes still closed, "I never said anything would happen." I felt my frustration swell, and Leon continued to laugh.

I focused on Leon, expecting to chastise him for laughing, but instead I fell into his mind, and suddenly I was sifting through his memories as if I were skimming through a photo album. "Whoa..." I said as I put a hand to my head when the memories faded. I realized as I looked up at them both, that I had fallen to the ground.

"Did you have a vision?" Leon asked, pulling me back up with concern edging his tone, and then Galen opened his eyes.

I shook my head, my eyes wide with uncertainty and Galen spoke for me, watching me with a furrowed brow, "I forgot the Emoty Gift came before you learned the Prophet Gift." He said snapping his fingers, "I get my visions mixed up sometimes." He explained delicately.

Leon looked at me in confusion, "Emoty Gift? But the Emoty's see your secrets. What does that have to do with what she is doing now?"

I felt my body shake, my cheeks heated, "I am so sorry... I sort of ended up in your thoughts." I said softly, tearing my gaze.

His cheeks flushed with embarrassment as he shifted his gaze quickly to Galen and then back to me, "You read my thoughts?" he whispered. I shook my head with a smile, seeing that something he was thinking was obviously meant to be very private.

"More like your memories. But it was like I fell through a hole in a photo album—only seeing fragments of moments." I tried to explain.

Leon chuckled, brushing his fingers through his hair nervously with a nod, "Well, I suppose maybe that's better."

I forced a smile, but when I looked at Galen, he looked almost frustrated, yet equally calm, "What's on your mind?"

Galen let out a long sigh, wiping his hand down his face. "Well, for all of your Gifts, you have to focus, right? Part of the reason Kent died was because..." his tone was a little harder, more authoritative.

I sat up straighter, scoffing with pained frustration, "Was because I didn't know, Galen." I said defensively. "I would not have let that happen had I known I was capable of that."

Galen watched me, "But would you have even said he deserved to die if you had not been emotional?" he said softly. "That is what I meant, Kayd... with all of your powers, I think you have to be careful of your emotions. You have so many Gifts, that any one of them could be sparked at any time if you are not careful."

I felt myself justifying what I had done in the past, my chest tight with regret, "But what about when we were ambushed by the President's Army? I acted immediately! It was like my Gifts already knew what to do."

He nodded, but he was hesitant for a moment, "They do, Kayd, but do *you*?"

I was standing now, my fists at my side, "What are you trying to say, Galen?"

"Do you know what to do with your Gifts? Do you know how to use them?" I thought about his words, and my glare softened,

"Well I must..."

He sighed, shaking his head with resolve, "Ok, freeze me to my spot." He said boldly as he stood, "I won't even move to make it nice and easy for you." He offered tauntingly, his arms out like an invitation.

I bit my lip with aggravation, and Leon put a hand on my shoulder, "Kayd, you don't have to prove yourself."

"Yes, I do." I said harshly as I stared into my brother's eyes and a flash of yellow blurred in front of them. I instantly let my guard down and let my fists relax. I felt the way he froze solidly to his spot.

I looked away from him. I wasn't even totally sure what had happened here, but the distance in my brother's eyes at that moment was enough to silence me. Somehow, my anger towards my brother had caused some power within me to lash out at him. Horror overwhelmed me, knowing I had done that... I had frozen him, but it wasn't me. It was my gift on its own... just like Galen had accused.

He blinked suddenly and stared at me in near repulsion, "Well I guess you proved me wrong." He said, barely holding back his hurt, and Leon watched us with confusion.

I think Leon desperately wanted to understand my Gifts so that he could somehow guide me, and I think the fact that Galen already seemed to know everything about my Gift, made him a little jealous. But if Leon really had understood it, I think I would see even more fear in his eyes than I already see. Because as I looked into Galen's eyes, the boy who sees everything, I saw deep terror. My brother had not foreseen whatever power had just struck him, and I could tell that it shook him to his core.

He didn't look at me again as he sat closer to Leon, creating distance between us, and breaking my heart with every move he made, "I'm going to take a nap. I'm not feeling so great." He said quietly as he pulled the sleeping bag over his head. Leon stared at the bag with concern.

"Kayd, can we take a quick walk?" I nodded as we walked far enough away to be out of earshot but close enough to still keep an eye on my brother, "Kayd... what just happened exactly?"

I gazed back at my brother's sleeping form, "I'm not totally sure. When he kept pushing me... it's like some power deep within me reached out when provoked. I guess it was the Freezer power... but I didn't like it." I clenched my teeth with pain and regret. "Galen had been right: I wasn't controlling it myself. My power controls me, Leon... and now my brother is scared of me." I said as tears burst from my eyes, and I bit my lip to hold back the flood.

He pulled me into his arms without question, pulling in a long breath, "We have to fix this."

I peeked up at him, clutching him like he was my lifeline, "What do you mean?"

He took in a deep breath, and everything went foggy for a moment as Leon said, "You have to stop using your other Gifts, Kayd..." he whispered so softly I almost would think he hadn't meant me to hear it. For just a moment, I wasn't even certain it was fully his voice.

I pulled away as I gave him an exasperated expression as the fogginess faded away, "Don't you think I would if I could? Ever since I met with the President's Army though... my Gifts just seem to happen even when I don't want to use them. I would never use them if it were up to me, Leon... so if you have an idea please let me know." I said with frustration.

He stared at me in baffled confusion, pulling away, "What are you talking about? All I said was that we needed to help you control your Gifts..." he replied with his brows furrowed in deep concern.

I shook my head, pushing away from him entirely, panic enveloping me, because I know what I heard, "No... no, you said that I had to stop using my Gifts."

The look he gave me scared me—part panic, part worry, part fear. "Kayd... I know you are doing the best you can with what you have to work with... and I would never have said that." He offers in a soothing way. But he did say it, I was sure. I felt confusion overwhelm me. Suddenly my head began to ache as the world spun around me.

The world became foggy once again, and I found my eyes moving to his, and he looked so nervous, "Every single day this gets worse... I don't know what to do anymore... her power is so terrifying." The problem is... his lips didn't move.

The world stopped spinning as I understood: I was reading his thoughts, "You are terrified of me?" I gasp out the words.

His face fell, eyes wide with an ache I couldn't help to fix, "You read my mind...?" he said with hurt,

"Is it true...?" I whispered, forcing myself to meet his eyes even though it cut my soul to see him afraid of me.

He quickly blanched, turning defensive, "Ok... yes, I am a little afraid of your power. But honestly, Kayd, aren't you too?" he questioned. I froze then... because he was right. I was horrified by my abilities, and could I really be upset that he felt the same. "I've never seen anything like the power you are capable of, but that doesn't change how I feel about you Kayd." He said, pulling my hands into his. "I have been afraid of myself many times, and the only way I overcame that was by learning to control my abilities." He urges, touching my cheek. I close my eyes to hold off the fresh wave of tears. "I just don't want you hurting yourself or someone else."

I nodded without meeting his gaze, "I'm so scared all the time." I whispered with intense guilt. "I had a dream last night that shook me... and when I saw that look on my brother's face today, I suddenly felt like the dream was about to happen."

"What was the dream about?" he questioned softly, rubbing comforting circles on my back.

I sighed, looking down at the crackling fire, "I was mad at my brother, and you were walking away like you were fed up with my Gifts... and as I gazed at him, all of a sudden his eyes looked so distant and he fell to the ground seizing. And then today, when he was making me so mad, I felt the power surge from me, and his gaze became so distant... and I felt the power still trying to attack him, but I let it go. I was not going to let my powers hurt my brother."

He pulled me closer again so my face lay against his warm chest, "You are so much stronger than you realize." He said so tenderly in my ear, and I felt so broken at those words,

"I know... I can't stand how much I still don't know." I reply with disgust, trying to push him away, but he held me tighter for a moment, keeping me still.

I felt him shake his head, lifting me so I met his eye, "No, Kayd, I mean *you*. You are stronger than your Gifts—they are *not* stronger than you. Just don't forget that." He said, and I smiled gratefully, wrapping my arms around his neck. I felt his smile against my cheek.

I felt that warmth in my chest again that only he seemed to give me. Something felt wrong around us though, and I couldn't deny the deep loss I felt in my heart. Leon whispered something in my ear, and it took me a minute before I realized he had said, "Do you want to go down to our old spot?"

But my eyes were glued to my brother as an odd light seemed to shower him as he slept. The world seemed to blur, going in slow motion as I walked over to Galen. Stepping past Leon, I touched my brother's forehead to make sure he was alright. As soon as my fingers graced his forehead, I realized what I had been seeing over him—he was having a vision. I was instantly pulled into a focused glimpse into the future—my future.

"Kayd you can't do this!" Leon warned, but I kept moving further into the thick foliage, "Kayd please! What about us?"

"What does anything else matter, Leon? If you can't support me, then maybe we aren't really meant to be after all." I was so cold as I spoke to him with venom on my lips.

"Kayd..." His voice was softer, "You can't save him... he is dead."

I turned on him quickly, "I have every Gift that ever existed, Leon, what makes you think I can't somehow bring him back? It could happen..."

He shook his head, as he pulled me into his arms, "No, Kayd... it couldn't. You just have to face it... your brother is dead."

I fell to the ground with a thud as I scooted away from my brother's shivering form. Tears welled up in my eyes as Leon came to my side, "Kayd, what's wrong?" I tried to think of how old I had looked in the vision, was this going to happen soon? In a few years? The panic overwhelmed me as my brother's eyes fluttered open and he stared at me carefully, perhaps pity was waiting there for me. "Kayd what did you see?" Leon urged.

My brother's eyes also filled lightly with tears, but he wiped them away before Leon could see them and he shook his head at me with a tired sigh, "She saw my vision." Galen said quietly, trying to hide the shaking in his voice. Leon looked between us, "Nothing to worry about." He urged. Leon hesitantly nodded, but I could tell he didn't believe him.

Leon stood, watching both of us apprehensively. He hummed out a slow breath, "Well I'll go get us more firewood. Kayd, did you want to join me?" I looked at my brother and shook my head,

"I realize I haven't talked with my brother for a long time." I pulled him into a mock noogie, and Galen forced a laugh, while pushing me my hands from his hair, "Us siblings have to catch up." I said with a forced grin.

Leon smiled softly, but I still felt how skeptical he was, and he should be. "Not a problem. I'll leave you guys be for a bit." He nodded at me before walking into the forest.

I looked back at Galen readily as I waited for his encouragement. I wanted him to explain that I hadn't seen what I thought I'd seen... that he wasn't going to die.

"You weren't supposed to see that." He whispered with frustration as he kicked a large pebble into the low fire, keeping his gaze as far from mine as possible. He looked so low, and my heart shattered slowly.

"What did I see, Galen?" I urged, grasping his hand as I knelt beside him.

He glared at me, "You don't have to know everything." He said grumpily as he stood and trumped off towards a nearby tree.

I watched him with deep sorrow, "Galen... what did I see?" I said as softly as I could. I needed to hear him say it wasn't what I thought. I could be patient for that... I could be calm. Of course, he wouldn't die... he's only 12, almost 13. That's too young. Too young...

He stared at the tree before turning silently back to me, agony hiding in those too-strong eyes, "I didn't want you to know." He said so miserably as he let out a deep breath.

I felt like everything in me was splintering as I looked at him. There was a painful ache deep inside my chest, and I felt as though I couldn't breathe. "How long?" I whispered in a barely audible voice.

He sighed deeply, lowering his head in defeat, "Not long, Kayd."

I wanted to cry, but I needed to be Strong Kayd again, because that's what Galen needed. "Why didn't you want me to know? Because you didn't want me to stop it?"

He shook his head as his entire body trembled, "I kept trying to see different scenarios... hoping I could somehow change it myself. I didn't want you to know because I hoped you'd never have to know." He whispered and huffed out a frustrated breath. When he turned back to me fully, large tears streaked his cheeks, "I didn't want it to be true... but there is nothing I can do Kayd." He said so hopelessly, "This new vision was the first that had someone talking about my death... which means that it is set now." Those words... those ones shook me even more than the vision. I felt like I was being stabbed from the inside out. "And Kayd... you can't do anything either. This vision... it shouldn't happen. Now that you know I will die, you can't fall apart." He spoke with such warning. He walked over to me carefully and took my hand, "When I die, don't try to save me."

I heard his words, but they seemed so wrong from this beautiful boy's mouth. I was hearing my brother's last wishes, and it wasn't right. He was too young. Had I wasted the last four and half years of my life protecting him when I was somehow leading him to his death now? I shook my head, "I can't promise that, Galen..." He lifted my face, and I suddenly noticed the patchy-thin layer of stubble growing unevenly on his chin.

"Kayd... I want you to always be you. If you lose yourself in your powers, the quicker you will fade away. I already see glimpses of what will happen if your Gifts take you over. I don't like it." He said so calmly, but I also see the fear waiting in his eyes, the warning. I wanted to cry, and shout, and stomp my feet, but acting like a child was not the answer. There was no answer... my brother was going to die.

My breathing is labored, painful. "Can you tell me how?" I said quietly.

He laughed darkly, "You want to hear how I die?" he said like it was some sort of big joke. I just stared at him with agony, and his smile faded, replaced by grim resolve, "I don't know." He admitted quietly, "I went through so many scenarios that, as of right now, I couldn't tell you which way it will be. Sadly, I've watched myself die in so many different ways..."

I can't hold back the gasp, "When?"

He huffs out one more tired breath, "Not long after you marry Leon." My hand flew to my mouth at the thought... if Leon and I got married on my 17th birthday like we planned, then my brother only had about 8 months or so before he was a goner.

"What if we don't get married... then maybe you won't die..." I hurried out the words, desperate to find an answer.

He smiled compassionately, "I already looked at that scenario... it didn't change things. It's always the same day.... I'm not meant to live, Kayd. I just sort of wish I'd realized it sooner..."

I shook my head, not willing to accept the inevitable, and became completely hysterical, tears pouring down my cheeks as I pace beside him, my hands in my hair, "Maybe there *is* something I can do though... I could save you. I could..."

He looked towards the woods where Leon had walked off, and he cut me off, putting his hands on my shoulders firmly, "Kayd... No. I watched myself die hundreds of ways... watched hundreds of ways I thought could save me, and none of them work. I am meant to die that day, Kayd." He speaks with too much finality, and my spirit feels broken.

"But..." I feel as though an elephant is sitting on my chest.

He forces a very sad smile, "The sooner you come to terms with it, the better off you will be." He said almost unfeelingly, but I sort of understood. He obviously had been trying to see every possibility for a long time because he wanted to live. In the last 9 months, Galen had proven to me more than once that he was growing into a man that makes his own decisions, whether I liked it or not. And whether I liked it or not, my brother was going to die, though I had obviously wished it was later in both our lives, it was happening at some point in our near future. If there were any way to stop it, I know he would tell me.

I stared at the ground, realizing how lost I felt, and then realized how important it was that my brother have a normal life the rest of his days. We were silent for a while before I laughed and he smiled at me, "Coming to terms with it a little easier than I expected?" he offered with a raised brow.

I shook my head, forcing all my pain away, "I just realized I forgot your birthday…" He smiled a large grin,

"Good segway, sis." He said with a laugh as we both wiped away our tears as if they were simply an eyelash we were pushing off our cheeks. When Leon got back, I told him how it was Galen's birthday, and we began to celebrate with our limited supplies. I watched the two men in my life enjoy the sweet rolls and sparkling cider that had somehow been magically snuck into our bags. They were both smiling and laughing, nothing else in the world mattering except this brief moment of bliss. I wished I could join with them, but deep inside, I knew there would be few happy moments left for Galen, and that was enough to suck the happiness right out of me.

Chapter 9: New Steps

The nightmares were getting worse. I was being swarmed with memories that I had long since forgotten—images of my brother playing with the girl next door right before the Soldiers yanked her away from her parents... and of my mom kissing me goodnight when I was seven, right before she realized I was a monster. Every single day my head would pound as I fell back into my past. I tried so hard to stay in the present with my beautiful brother, and amazing Leon... but it was getting so hard. The memories beckoned to me like an old friend... begging me to fall into them and never come out.

"Kayd?" I heard Leon's voice reach to me through the fog, but I was too tired to fight the memories anymore. I knew he had called to me more than once, but I wasn't sure how long I'd been out. That's when I heard him sigh, "Come back to me Kayd." He whispered in my ear in that special way I had begun to recognize as his Speaker voice. I instantly fell out of the dreams and into his arms. I stared up at him—his face was red and swollen, but not as if he'd been in a fight....

I wiped my eyes as I sat up, "How long was I asleep?"

He shook his head as he sighed miserably, "Kayd... you know you weren't asleep." His tone was tired, resigned.

I considered him more closely—he had been crying. I looked around in a panic, suddenly harshly aware of my brother's absence. I stood quickly and Leon grabbed my arm, "Galen is just at the stream." He wiped off his pants and went to the tent. We had not kissed in over a month and a half, not since I found out my brother was going to die in the near future. I just didn't know how to be normal anymore, but I wanted to be. I was sure that Leon was rethinking his proposal, with good reason. I was too broken to be fixed...

"You can't let him just go out by himself, Leon. He could get hurt..." I urged harshly.

Leon slammed his fist on his knee, "Kayd what's going on?"

I looked at him in alarm, still wanting to scan the forest for my brother, "I just don't want to lose sight of him. I have to protect him."

He nodded, forcing his face into his hands like a sanctuary, "Kayd... we have to talk."

I stared at him with sharp pain in my heart. Though I left home so young, I still knew that those dreaded words were not something to be taken lightly. I sat beside him, trying to calm my series of nerves that were jittering inside. I stared at the fire, suddenly aware of how hot it was today. "What about?"

He scoffed, "God..." his fists grabbed at his hair before he let go and relaxed, "I wish I even knew, Kayd." He looked at me, and I began to recognize the man I had fallen in love with. The desire to kiss him, to hold him, overwhelmed me, and I turned away. He groaned as he came in front of me on his knees and pointed at me accusingly, "Like that!"

I pulled back in shock at his severe tone, "Like 'what', Leon?"

He shook his head, "Whenever you and I start to have a moment, or we get close to being intimate, you turn away and drift into your little world. Or you randomly start freaking out about Galen." He sat down in front of me and put his hands on his knees, "You don't talk to me anymore... or look at me, Kayd." As I look at him, I'm stunned by the anguish staring back at me from those green eyes.

"Well I can't just forget about the fact that we are always going to be chased and..." and in an instant Leon pulled himself to his feet and pulled me into a kiss. Whether it was from our time apart or my deep need for him, it was the most passionate kiss we had ever shared. I didn't want to pull away, but my brain reminded me that I couldn't be selfish. I couldn't be happy if Galen was going to die. It wasn't fair to live life joyfully or passionately if Galen wasn't going to get to.

I pulled from his lips and turned away, but Leon wouldn't let me drift away as he came in front of me again, no matter where I turned, he wasn't going to let me forget him this time. I pushed him away, but he just came closer, "Talk to me." He finally whispered with affection as he pulled my forehead to his.

I could hear Galen walking back to camp, "Kayd." I heard his voice call out. I lifted my head instantly towards his voice. Leon still looked into my eyes then, brief understanding passing over him,

"Is something going to happen to him, Kayd?" he whispered so gently.

I could almost picture Galen's face staring at me, "Tell him." He whispered. He was so far away still, but it was like he was right beside me.

"Where is Galen?" I hurriedly say.

"Here I am!" Galen called out as he came to sit beside us. I'm not sure if I had been seeing a vision or reading his thoughts, but even sitting next to me, I could see the telling look on his face that he had truly spoken to me from far away. "I found a cave that we should go to. It's safe for now. No one will come for at least a few months." I nodded with a small, forced smile, always enjoying the way he knew things.

I looked at Leon and he nodded as he began picking up camp and guiding us towards the directions Galen had given us. He was distant, and the distant part of me was thankful for it. It was easy to ignore the ache he caused in me when we weren't face-to-face.

We had never been so quiet, and I felt the pull towards the past, but as if sensing it, Leon grabbed my hand tightly. When we got to the cave, I almost laughed because Galen had obviously tried to set it up earlier to look like a real home. He pulled leaves and vines around certain holes to look like windows, and had tied together thick vines to cover the main opening like a door.

"I set up rooms, so that we can have more privacy." He said with a wink towards Leon. "And... speaking of privacy... I'm going to go to my room. Your rooms are to the right." And with that he wandered towards a small corridor to the left, his footsteps echoing distantly.

He waited until we no longer heard the *tap, tap, tap* of Galen's feet. "Are you ready to tell me yet?" I sat on a makeshift chair made of rock as Leon gazed at me.

"I'm just having a hard time." I admitted, averting my gaze as I rubbed my hand over my arm nervously.

He nodded, huffing out a breath, "I can understand that. But you don't have to hide from me, Kayd. Why would you push me away?"

I looked at my hands on my lap, "I'm not pushing you away." I lied.

He grabbed my hands and sat right in front of me. "Yes, you are. Every day you are further and further away from me, and having you right next to me makes it even harder." His tone is sharp, honest, and it cuts me.

I began to stand, tears trying to fall from my tired eyes, "Well I can go somewhere else then... I can leave you alone." I choked out weakly, feeling my barriers starting to shatter.

He shook his head and stood too, putting a gentle hand on my waist, and I realized how much I wanted him to hold me. I wanted him to kiss me. I wanted him to love me. I closed my eyes. "Kayd... tell me." He said, near exasperation.

My eyes opened slowly, watched as he looked into me. I looked back at him and the protective walls started to shatter entirely, "It's not right for me to get to love you... and have you... and be happy..." I admitted with defeated tears.

"Why?" he asked in confusion, cupping my face in his hand.

My tears fell desperately down my cheeks, "Because he will never get that." I choked out. He smiled softly, wiping my tears away, clearly not understanding.

"Of course, he will, Kayd. Eventually he will be older and will find a nice girl, just like I found you." I shook my head... my entire body was shaking. "I don't understand. Why wouldn't he?"

"Because he's going to die!" I said louder than I expected, the sobs quickly choking out all my echoing words.

Leon's eyes widened as he looked towards my brother's direction. He pulled me into his arms, not even questioning my words. "I'm so sorry, Kayd. Why didn't you just tell me?" he whispered against my cheek.

"Because I don't want you to know." I said harshly, trying once again to be distant.

He considered me, "Kayd you were out of it for two days, and before that you were in and out of it for two weeks." He warned me, and those words seemed to wake me up a little, "We could hardly do anything because of how catatonic you were. I've noticed that's what happens when you are sad." He pulled me close again, "Do you really think that's how your brother would prefer you to be? Because, I can't imagine that happy little boy could ever be ok with you forever drifting further into a little pity abyss?"

I couldn't help but chuckle, "'Pity Abyss' huh?" he smiled back.

"Now that's the Kayd I remember." He kissed my lips gently. God, I wanted him! Every time he kissed me, I fell more and more into him. I looked at him carefully.

"What is today?"

He laughed, "You are the queen of randomness. It's the 10th of July."

I nodded, "That's what I thought. Only 3 months till my birthday." I said with a simple smirk.

He chuckled again, "Is that so?" I nodded, "And what does that mean?"

He raised his eyebrow at me, and I ran a hand down his face, pushing away my agony so I could have a moment with him that didn't include sorrow, "It means... that, if you'll still have me, that we can get married."

He smiled tenderly, "I would marry you now if I could, or in 10 years if that was what you wanted."

I looked deeply into his eyes and embedded my fingers in his hair lovingly as I pulled him close, "That's not what I want."

"To marry me now?" he tried to hide the pain that caused.

I shook my head, "No, that I would like. I don't want to wait another day." I whispered. "I'm so sorry I've been so distant. But being close to you now… I don't think I could handle being like that again. I needed you so much, but I was afraid to show it." I admit, pulling him closer.

Leon held me so close then, whispering sweet things, reminding me of all the reasons he loved me, but there was something far off that distracted me. There was something off about all of this… or maybe it was just something new I was sensing in the future. Everything was just a little hazy, almost like it was distorted like a funhouse mirror.

Leon kissed my lips, pulling me closer and closer to him. What was this odd feeling inside my chest? I was afraid one of my powers was trying to lash out at him because of the untamed feeling it gave, but it was something more unexpected—my desire for him.

He picked me up and carried me to one of the makeshift rooms. Galen had been kind enough to put a thick layer of moss and vines in front of the opening to the cave room. My body began to shake as Leon laid me gently on the surprisingly comfy leaf-and-sleeping-bag bed. He pulled off his shirt and lay beside me on his side. His chest was so warm, and I cuddled in closely, suddenly harshly aware of what was about to happen.

My eyes widened as I stared at him and down at my own loose clothing—buttons already broken. How had that happened without me realizing? I sat up straight and pulled the ripped clothing around my bra and my bare stomach. I put my feet back on the floor and pulled my body tightly together. This wasn't right. This wasn't right... and then the world seemed to stop tilting, it flattened back out like normal.

Leon took my hand gently and I dared to look into his eyes, "Kayd, what's wrong?" As I looked at him, I realized his shirt was still on... and we were still in the entry area of the cave. I looked down at myself again and all my clothes were still intact. I shook my head and cried. He pulled me into his arms, "Kayd... what just happened?"

I gazed back at him, "I'm not ready..." I whispered in shock.

His eyebrows rose in confusion, "Ready for what?"

"To..." I gazed at my feet, not wanting to even say the word my parents had not yet explained to me before I left, "You know..."

He watched me carefully, "Marry me?" he said uncertainly.

I shook my head, "No... I mean maybe... I want to be with you forever, but I'm not ready for..." I bit my lip hard.

His touch on me seemed to retract slightly, "I understand. Marriage is a big commitment, and I told you before that if you needed time, I would wait." He said with a resigned smile.

He pulled his hands away from me and I sobbed. What was happening? Why was I so haunted by visions of things that had yet to happen? I was used to visions of the past, but this was something I couldn't handle. I wanted to marry him, I did... I wasn't afraid to make that commitment, but I was afraid of the dreaded 'S' word. The one thing reserved for mommies and daddies... that's all my parents had shared with me before I went venturing off into the unknown.

I grabbed Leon's arm before he could go away from me, "No... I want to get married to you... but I'm not ready for something that you will expect." I said, shaking.

He tilted his head at me, "What do you—" He stopped, his eyes wide as his lips mouthed a simple 'O'. I could feel how uncomfortable he was now too, his cheeks slightly pink, "Well..." He let out an uncomfortable sigh, "We don't have to until you are ready, Kayd." I glared at the ground. Of course, we would have to... that was part of marriage. Even as a child I understood that. I didn't know what to say or do, but I was thankful that Galen had given us privacy.

"I'm just... terrified." I admitted, still shaking from the vision.

He looked back at me with a tender gaze, "Kayd it is natural to feel that way. And that is why I would never force it on you. Let's just wait a few years to get married. I never want you to feel pressured." He assured me.

I thought back to those times I had seen briefly into his mind, into his desires, and almost laughed, "But you want to... I've felt your feelings about it, Leon. It is a constant desire of yours."

His cheeks flushed bright red, and now he looked away in embarrassment, "I wish you wouldn't do that..." his tone was gruffer.

I sighed, suddenly feeling regretful for even saying it, "I never mean to... but whenever you think it, it seems to overpower everything else around me. I just..." He put a hand to my lips, looking me in the eyes once more.

"Yes... I want you. I always want you." He spoke with such devotion, such honesty.

"Leon, you don't have to—" My cheeks heated, my heart pounding wildly in my ears.

"I want you to hear this out loud, Kayd. You may overhear my thoughts, or my feelings, but you don't hear them all. Yes, I would love to make love to you, but that is what I want, Kayd—to *make love*, not just have sex." I blushed at the word. "There is a difference. And honestly Kayd, if you have a question about it, just ask me. It doesn't have to be something awkward." His tone was so sweet, understanding, and it comforted me.

I shouldn't have to have my boyfriend be the one to explain such an intimate affair... or maybe it made more sense? This was one of those moments I missed my mother more than ever. She always explained things in such a calm and loving way. Why did she have to end up being the villain in my story?

"I shouldn't have to ask anyone!" I replied miserably, suddenly defensive. At my yell, I could hear Galen rustling through the corridor. I realized I was standing, with my fists clenched at my side. I sat down quickly, feeling overwhelmed, "I just wish I had been normal, with parents to guide me through all this. But instead I have to learn about all this from the man I'm about to marry?" He smiled softly, "Why are you smiling?" I asked as I wiped away a few more tears.

"Why would you be embarrassed to ask me?" he asked, his head tilted in an annoyingly adorable way.

My cheeks were burning, "Because I don't want to talk to a boy about this..."

He nodded, a soft smile brushing his lips, "That is understandable... my mom was the one who had the 'talk' with me. My dad was so busy trying to help everyone else that I never saw him. He only seemed interested in being around me when he found out I was a Speaker. So, my mom was the one that had to help me through everything, and yeah it was terrifying to have to ask my mom those awkward questions, but she was just trying help me." He pulled me onto his lap affectionately, "My point is, I do understand how awkward it might be to have to ask someone of the opposite sex about what you are feeling or going through, and though I might not be able to answer every question, I am at least here to answer them for you the best I can and to listen." He said, hugging me.

I thought back to my vision of Leon and I—so passionate and consumed by love—and then back to what was happening. Could that really have been a potential future? Together we were now so mellow and reasonable that I couldn't picture that other vision as a possibility. I appreciated Leon's kind offer to answer any of my questions, but deep down I still knew it wasn't likely that I would ever come to him about my fears in this regard. Which, in its own way, probably spoke volumes of how unready I was to pursue such a relationship anyways.

Galen came through the corridor into the main living area that Leon and I were still sitting in. I quickly tried to stand so Galen didn't see me sitting on Leon's lap, but Leon was still holding me. Galen looked concerned, "I heard you yell." He said to me.

I looked back at Leon, "Nothing serious, Galen. Sorry if I scared you."

He smiled softly, "Is it ok for me to be out here with you both now?" he asked, though I felt as though he was implying something.

"Yeah, of course." I said, and Galen smiled happily and sat next to us. Leon loosened his hold on me long enough for me to jump up and sit on the other side of my brother. I put my arms around Galen lovingly and we both just swayed back and forth for a moment as Leon spoke to Galen. Leon watched us with an odd look, almost envious.

He looked away, "I wish I had a brother or sister." He admitted softly. I sat up straighter and considered him.

"Why? I'm sure you got more of your parent's attention as an only child." Galen said, taking the words out of my mouth.

He laughed, "My world was nannies, scheduled visits with my father, and dinners with my mom. I always felt horribly alone."

I looked down at Galen, "Most brothers and sisters are not as close as Galen and I." I chuckled at my thought, "Honestly we wouldn't even be this close if it weren't for having to run away from the Soldiers for so many years."

Galen laughed, "Yeah, Kayd used to think I was really annoying!" he said with a broad smile.

We all laughed together, and Leon smirked, "I doubt she thought you were annoying." Leon's eyes were affectionate as he watched me act so freely around my little brother.

I nodded strongly, "Of course I did. Still do most days." I said with a wink at Galen as I gave him a light noogie. He pretended to push me away. "I mean, yeah, I definitely got annoyed because I'm the older sister. As an older sibling you almost feel obligated to be annoyed by your little brother." I put my arm around Galen and pulled him closer, more affectionately now, "But I have to admit, there is something very special about the love a brother or sister has for you and you have for them. Unconditional." Galen nodded.

"Kayd took care of me when our mom stopped caring about us." Leon's eyes widened at my brother's words, and I looked at the floor.

"Your mom didn't stop caring about you, Galen. I'm sure she just got confused."

Galen shook his head, so solemn, "I knew for a long time, Leon. I still loved her, but she just didn't love us anymore. When she found out about me when I was 6, she stopped hugging me or tucking me in, always telling our dad to do it instead. Then when she found out about Kayd…"

"Galen stop…" I urged, my hands now in my lap.

Leon watched me, but Galen continued, "When she found out about Kayd, she…"

"GALEN!" I said with my voice raised. He didn't stop though, oblivious as always.

"She stopped talking…"

I ran away then, not wanting to hear the truth that I always pushed away. Having Galen talk about the past was pushing me into that world I didn't want to drift to now. But it was too late—I was stuck. I fell into that moment when I had seen the orange blur around my mom.

"So, what are you going to do today, my little angel?" she asked kindly.

"Present shopping of course."

Mom laughed as she continued to clean another dish, "Your dad told you again, didn't he?"

I tilted my head at her in slight confusion, "No… you just said so a while ago."

She stopped moving, "When did I say that?"

"You said that you were going shopping for birthday presents today. I'm sorry, was it a surprise?" Mom's eyes were so wide with fear, and I didn't understand why. I had not realized that I had been using other Gifts so early. That must have been why no one knew what I was. My mom just let the moment fade, changing the subject.

Though I hadn't heard her next thoughts, my Decider Gift knew that she would be guilty—she was thinking of turning me in.

I was pulled out of the memory as I heard Leon and Galen's voices, "You shouldn't have kept talking about your mom when Kayd didn't want you to." Leon said gently.

"Kayd doesn't like to admit that our family wasn't as perfect as she thought." Galen replied simply.

"To Kayd, she never had anything to look forward to though, Galen. You had your Gift, and you could see the future. For Kayd, she felt nearly useless except to protect you, and she felt broken knowing that she had watched her parents die. She had nothing to look forward to, or anything to make her feel special."

"But I always tried to tell her about you, Leon!" Galen said happily, "I always told her how she would meet you, and that she would help you become…" Galen stopped short.

"Help me become what?"

"Nothing… nothing."

"Galen, what am I going to become?" Leon said almost fearfully.

"Kayd has to tell you. I'm not supposed to be the one who tells you. It will make everything wrong."

Leon was silent for a few before replying, "Galen… what did your mom do when she found out about Kayd?"

"I thought you didn't want to know?"

Leon sighed, "Please tell me?"

Though I didn't see them, I was sure Galen was nodding, "She would lock us in our rooms, or in the basement, when our dad was at work. By the time I was 8, mom basically stopped talking to us. Kayd would always get lost though... and she never realized what was happening."

I sat against the wall with my legs against my chest, listening to a part of my past that was not accessible to me, "What do you mean 'lost'?" Leon asked quietly.

"It is one of the Gifts... I'm not sure which one. She gets stuck in her mind, blocking out a lot of her memories. About the same time my mom started being so distant to Kayd and I, was when my dad started training her for the day her and I would have to leave. It was because I think he was afraid that my mom would tell someone, though he never thought she really would."

"I just don't understand how your mom could do that, no matter how afraid she may have been. You both are her children..."

Galen was quiet for a moment, "I thought Kayd told you... our mom never wanted us, Leon." I put my hands over my ears, because even though most of this was old news, it made me feel sick to hear all of these sad things at once. "Our dad wanted us, and she was afraid that if she had children they would be Gifted."

"Your mom didn't want children just because she was afraid you'd be Gifted? Besides, nowadays it is so unlikely a child will be Gifted, the only way a child would have gifts is if one of their parents was Gifted."

I uncovered my ears slightly, suddenly aware that my brother had the secrets to my constant confusions, to the reason behind my blackouts, and possibly to all my questions about why I am the way I am. I peeked my head out of the corridor just enough to see Leon staring distantly, looking as though something had just hit him, "Galen... if your parents weren't gifted, how did they end up with not one, but two children with Gifts. And besides just having Gifts, you and your sister have some of the stronger ones I've seen. That doesn't happen if neither of your parents are gifted."

Galen nodded darkly, "Dad was Gifted. When I found out, he had me swear not to tell Kayd." I sat up straight, my ears poised like a cat. "Dad helped me train my Gift..." he almost looked ashamed, "But I don't think he was a Prophet. Honestly I'm not sure what he was."

"Well how did you catch him? What was he doing?"

Galen shifted uncomfortably in his seat, as I sat perfectly still, fearing that they would realize I was close by and stop talking, "I'm not sure how to explain it..."

"If you don't want to tell me, Galen, you don't have to." Leon said as he put a firm hand on his shoulder.

"I caught him in the past... he was the first person I'd ever seen the past of. It was a vision... and in it, he told a Soldier to leave, that he wouldn't find what he was looking for there."

Leon waited patiently for Galen to say more, "Okay? How does that show he was Gifted?"

Galen sighed, "Because the Soldier was coming for *him*—he even had a picture. Dad just smiled at the man and said, 'I'm not Tom, and there are no Gifted people here.' And then the Soldier apologized and walked away."

Leon sat back and nodded, not needing to be told twice considering this was his own Gift, and he knew how easy it was to control another person's mind, "So did you confront him?"

Galen suddenly looked like a very young boy as he continued to make himself look smaller and smaller the more they talked, "No... he knew. He knew I had seen it somehow. He didn't get mad though, he just told me that no one could know the truth. But I'm not even sure what the truth is, Leon. I know you might think he is a Speaker, but I didn't get that vibe."

"Why didn't he want Kayd to know?"

Galen sighed, "Because he said she wasn't supposed to know. He said it was supposed to be a surprise for her."

"A surprise? But now he is gone for good..."

Galen shook his head, "He is alive, Leon. Kayd saw him in the vision."

Leon waved it off, "But she saw a man who looked exactly like your dad before, and it wasn't him."

Galen looked terrified, and I couldn't understand why, "Leon... my dad is the one who has been testing her all this time. Soldiers wouldn't still be looking for us... He has them all controlled, doing his bidding. I recently saw it in a few visions in the farther off future."

"But they are always trying to take her to the President... he wouldn't have them take her to the President—it would be like murder."

Galen nodded hesitantly, "Dad wants her to be with him so they can help the President together."

I hit my head on a rock as I pulled my head back towards the wall. The thud stopped my brother and Leon instantly, but those words still rang through the hall for me. My dad was working for the President, and he wanted *me* to help the evilest man in the world? I shook my head—it couldn't be true. Galen seemed to hyperventilate, "No! She wasn't supposed to hear!" He said, running off to his room in fear as if my dad would swat him right now.

Leon came around the corner, and I sat there quietly, not knowing where to move. I felt so lost. Leon knelt in front of me and took my hand, "You heard all of that, didn't you?"

I stared into his eyes carefully, "Yeah..."

"Kayd, it is ok to be afraid or shocked..."

I scoffed, shaking my head as I looked back at him as the fire inside of me surely was lighting my eyes. "I'm furious. I thought my dad was the good one, Leon... but instead he is just as bad as my mom!"

Leon shook his head as he put a kind hand on my cheek, "Kayd, the President brainwashes people... and yes, he may now be controlling the President's army, but it doesn't mean that he always meant for this to happen."

I pushed his hand away, the anger fueling me now, "Leon... my dad is the reason I have fought so hard for my brother and I. My dad believed in me so much, helping me and training me, and I really believed he was the greatest guy in the entire world..."

"He still might be, Kayd. You haven't seen him in 4 years, aren't you at least happy that he is alive?" He urged, and I realized he was right, but the new betrayal I felt wanted to override my happy thoughts.

"I'm glad he lived... but in my eyes, whether he is alive or not, I am an orphan."

Leon looked at me with wide eyes, laying a gentle hand on mine, "Kayd."

"It's done, Leon. He made his choice, and so have I." I said standing, letting his hand drop sorrowfully to the cold rock chair. I tried so hard to hold back the tears as I stalked back to my new room. I lay on the bed and burrowed myself in the sleeping bag and drifted into unconsciousness.

Chapter 10: Awakened

Leon was incredibly reserved for the last month, though he would still come kiss me every morning, he would wander off during the day and not come back until well into the night. Galen and I started playing cards with a deck we had not picked up basically since meeting Leon. Whenever Leon would come back to our cave, he seemed as though the life had been sucked right out of him. He would kiss me on the forehead and go right to bed. Galen kept assuring me that Leon was fine, that he just had to prepare. But I didn't understand what he was preparing for. Eventually he started leaving before the sun had even risen.

One morning, I pulled him aside, "Leon don't go." I pleaded.

He looked at me in surprise, obviously not prepared for me being awake as early as him, "I need to get some things done, Kayd." He murmured gently. I grabbed his arm with both my hands longingly and he looked down at me, his eyes softening at my tears. He sighed and sat beside me, taking my hands in his, "Ok, what's up?"

He still felt so distant, even being so close to me, like his mind was on other things. I didn't know what to do to keep him there, "I just don't want you to leave today. I don't want you to get caught or anything."

He laughed darkly, "The great thing about my Gift is how easily it lets me blend in. You don't have to worry about it."

I shook my head, feeling how much he wanted to leave, "Please. Don't go, Leon."

He sighed again and kissed my hands, beginning to stand back up. "Kayd, I have to get things ready…"

"Ready for what?" I asked, feeling my fear and temper rise. I felt like Leon was getting annoyed with me.

He bit his lip like he had said too much, "There is just stuff I have to do…."

"Every day you have to do this?" He looked towards the door fleetingly. He started walking towards it, but my hands were still holding his.

"Kayd, please, I've gotta go." He urged.

I did the only thing that made sense at that moment—I kissed him passionately. He seemed incredibly shocked by the abrupt change, and he put his hand in my hair, he pulled away with a smile as he chuckled, "Is this what you are going to do whenever you aren't getting your way?"

I smiled, my fingers embedded in his soft hair, "Probably. Is it working?"

He laughed and nodded as he kissed me again. He caressed my cheek, "But I really do have to go, Kayd. I'm getting some things ready for the future."

I pull back in surprise, "You mean for when we get married?" I asked curiously.

Leon seemed to stiffen, tearing his gaze from mine, "Um… ya. Well I gotta get going."

He was almost at the door when I spoke up, "You don't want to marry me anymore… do you?" My heart felt frozen, my body stiff with the shock of it.

Leon stopped in his steps and turned back to me with an ache in his eyes, "It's not like that, Kayd…"

I shook my head, sitting back on my bed, tears raised and ready in my eyes, because I could tell I had figured it out, "Leon I know I sounded harsh about my dad the other day, but did it really make you not want to marry me?"

He came back over to me, kneeling in front of my knees, affection and devotion in his eyes, "Kayd, I want to marry you." He assured me, and I almost smiled, but then he sighed, and I felt my body tense again, "But I don't think you are ready. There is more to marriage than just being together, and I don't think you are ready for that part. I will still stay by your side, just as I've promised to. I just don't want you to feel obligated to do anything that you are not ready for."

Oh God… I thought, realizing exactly what he was meaning, "I'm ready… I am. I promise."

He considered me with doubting, but comforting eyes, "Kayd, it's okay not to be ready to 'be together' like that."

I took in a deep breath, and mirrored his humble stance, taking his face in my hands, "I want to be with you in every way." I began, my body shaking as I thought carefully about what I was telling him.

He shook his head and touched my hands as he pushed them gently to my lap, "Kayd, what's the rush? I told you when I asked you to marry me that I would wait an eternity if that were what it took. I will never leave your side, and we can get married when everything is right. It doesn't have to be right when you turn 17 next week."

What *was* my hurry? I couldn't think about what it was except that I was afraid he would disappear, or change his mind. But in all honesty, I did want him in that way too, but I just was terrified of what that meant. "And I appreciate that... but I am ready now." I said firmly and he raised his eyebrows, "I'm serious."

He smiled softly and gently kissed my lips. "Ok. Well we can talk about this later."

He went to stand but I quickly leaned in and kissed him, and I whispered, "Stay with me..." I don't know what was behind that kiss, or those simple words that finally stopped him, but as he looked back into my eyes, a sweet smile brushing his lips, he didn't try to leave again. He kissed me deeply then, and as he kissed me, he pulled me closer and closer, and before I knew it, we were on my bed. His hands explored my waist and my back under my shirt and my body felt hot. I wanted to have him close like this forever.

His lips caressed my neck, and I began to ache for him in a way I'd never experienced before. Suddenly my vision from before came back to my mind, and I realized the vision was of this moment, not of that day a month ago. I pulled away as I looked down at my unbuttoned top, and the deja vu was undeniable as Leon placed his soft, gentle hands on my shoulders. I turned my cheek towards him as his hands pushed my shirt off my shoulders and he kissed my arms, and then my hands as he turned me towards him again. Our fingers became intertwined as he put his free hand under my head, cradling my neck.

He lingered over me slightly, and then came so close, our naked skin touching for the first time. I felt him reach for my bra, and I wanted to stop him, but I didn't. Suddenly I felt as if I was watching it happen rather than experiencing it myself. How was this happening? Just a few weeks ago I was so afraid of this moment that I was ready to postpone our marriage, and now I was jumping in headfirst without a second thought? This shouldn't happen yet. We can wait, at least until the wedding... at least that is what I tried telling myself, but those words just couldn't leave my lips because my entire body was consumed by how good it felt to be so close to Leon.

I felt him touch my still-clothed-legs, as I helped him with his own complicated belt and buttons. But as I touched his hipbone, I stopped, my entire body going stiff. I wanted to pull away, but my body was still refusing to listen to me. I turned my face to take a breath as I looked around the room, vastly aware of the sounds and smells around me—Leon's heart was thumping loud enough to be a drum. "Are you okay?" he asked breathlessly.

I looked into his eyes, sifting my fingers through his messed-up hair and I smiled, "We can wait, Leon. I want you... but we only have to wait a week... I don't think we should do this now."

Leon nodded kindly, but I could see how hard it was for him to pull himself away from me. An odd look came to his face as he looked at my nearly naked body with confusion. He looked away instantly, almost embarrassed, and handed me my shirt without meeting my gaze, "You don't have to stop looking at me just because..."

He continued to look away from me, guilt and uncertainty plainly painting his cheeks, but he shook his head, "That's not it, Kayd... I didn't know this was happening... I—I thought this was a dream." He explained with a shaky voice.

I felt my body freeze as I stared at him in shock, "What do you mean?"

"I mean... I swore I was asleep, Kayd. I would never do this to you, especially knowing how much you didn't want to." He sat down with his hands in his hair, "I don't understand how this happened... I was just telling you I was about to leave, and then everything went blurry." He stood, pulling his shirt back over his bare chest, "I am so sorry. I am so sorry..." he said with shame as he walked out of the room.

I stared at my hands in confusion... what had just happened? Then I realized how it all began—with me telling him to stay, and, in my heart, I knew what I had wanted. I had pictured that vision from before, of our bodies connected and filled with lust, and somehow I must have imprinted that vision into his mind like a command. It was not *his* dream but *mine*? Nothing made sense at that moment. My powers were like untrained stallions, running wild. Every time I thought I was finally getting a hold on my Gifts, I was made instantly aware of my lack of control.

Leon did not come back that night. When he finally came home it was nearly 5 am the next morning. I heard his familiar footsteps approaching our hallway, but he didn't enter, he just sat down outside the door. I quickly pulled back my vine-door and looked at his red face—it was covered in blood, and then I saw the his entire body was completely covered in it. I stared in fear, reaching for him to check for wounds, "My God... what happened? Are you ok?"

He looked up at me, realizing I was there for the first time as tears wiped away streaks of blood from his cheeks. "They are all dead, Kayd..." his voice was a whisper.

I watched him in horrified wonder, afraid to ask my next question, "Who?"

He put his face in his soiled hands, "The group. They were massacred, Kayd... Thomas, James, Hannah... and I couldn't find my mom...." He shook his head.

I gasped. "I—I don't understand… why would this happen?" His eyes were so wide as he looked at his red hands more closely and he wiped them harshly on his jeans. I knelt beside him and lifted his chin with my hand, his eyes were wild, "Leon, why did this happen?"

His anger swelled, "Because of me!" he growled, jumping to his feet.

My eyes widened as I watched him, "Why would it possibly be your fault, Leon?"

He sighed deeply, obvious pain in his voice, "I have been taking them supplies for the last month. They moved closer to where we are… I found them one day when I was collecting wood, and the Soldiers must have followed me when I started visiting them." He seemed to pull his hair out as he thought about it all carefully, "They made it personal, Kayd…" he growled out the words.

Fear and shock radiated through me, but I tried to hide it from him, to stay strong for him. "I'm sure they had just been looking for them for awhile, Leon." I offered quietly as I patted his hand.

He shook his head, yanking his hand from mine, "They didn't spare anyone… *anyone*, Kayd!" he shouted, pounding his fist on the unleveled rock, his hand beginning to bleed. "They didn't even take the Dangerous Ones! They did this to *me*!" In the time I'd known Leon, I'd never seen such fire or fury in his eyes.

I stayed quiet for a moment, trying to think of any reason, any understanding, but there was none, "But why would they do that?"

fear crept over me along with the guilt… I knew what he was going to say before the words left his lips.

"Because I am with you, Kayd!" he said coldly, though his expression began to calm a little when he saw the horror on my face. He wiped his face with instant apology apparent in his eyes, "Gah… I'm sorry Kayd… it's not quite like that, it's just…" his tone was still hard, but it was gentler.

Tears pooled in my eyes and I stared out the window. "You really think they would punish you by killing all those people?"

He nodded without hesitation, "They must have found out I had been leading them, and they already hate my father. They wanted to send me a clear message."

My fear was consuming me as I watched my fiancé, dreading his next words, "What message is that, exactly?" I whisper.

Leon gazed into my eyes and then tore his gaze away… but I already saw the devastation waiting for me in his gaze, "That if I'm with you, no one I love is safe." He said bluntly. His nearly detached gaze seemed unsure.

My breath caught in my chest, "Leon… what if they had been waiting for you? I kept you from going for at least an extra half hour… maybe they just lost it when you weren't there?"

He fell back to the floor, the horror of that realization hitting him too. Finally, he just sighed with agony, throwing his arm over his face, "I guess it doesn't matter why they did it in the end, since they have officially started a war with me. I will avenge them, Kayd." He says with dark promise.

Galen came around the corner and stared at me, "I told you." He whispered, and my heart broke… Galen knew that everyone would die. It wasn't about Leon—it was about me. This was going to happen no matter what, and it was because it was meant to be an attack on me, taking away something I loved. Since they couldn't take my brother, they were taking Leon. Though Leon was not dead, a piece of him was stolen, and I did not yet know if it was a piece that would change him completely or not.

"Leon… I am sorry. I wish…" He raised his hand to silence me.

The ache in his voice broke my heart, "I just can't talk about this right now. I don't need apologies." He took in a deep breath, "I just need to clean up. I'll be at the river." He said tiredly as Galen and I watched him walk out the door.

Galen came over to me and sat down, "I'm ready."

"Ready for what?" I asked in surprise, exhausted from the emotional trauma of the last 24 hours. My body felt exhausted, as if I had run for a mile instead of enduring an emotional battle no 16-year-old should have to endure.

He sighed, "For my lecture."

I looked back at him and almost laughed, but the pain was too present in my heart to even force out a laugh. I scoffed, "Oh, you mean how you should've told me when this was supposed to happen? How you should've told me that if he went back to the old camp every day that the Soldiers would follow him and eventually kill all of his friends and his mother?" I said darkly and shrugged my shoulders, and he nodded once. I closed my eyes tightly and offered a miserable sigh, "Though I could get mad, scream a bit, I have a feeling you had your reasons for not telling us." I peeked back at him and he nodded calmly, "Are you going to tell me what that is?"

He smiled sadly, "If I had told you, you would've been there and would have been taken, and Leon and I would be dead." I sit up then with horror, my heart beating like mad as if it felt that devastation, "If I told Leon not to go help the group, he would've went anyways, protecting them instead of being with us, and he would be dead too, or they would've taken him so that they could torture him." I tear my gaze again, the pain of that possibility pulling on everything inside of me, "You and him are important, and this was the only way I could be sure the two of you would not be harmed." He said in that mature voice I was still not ready to hear from him.

I nodded hesitantly, letting the silence fill up the room for a little while. When I finally responded, my voice was solemn, sad, "Leon isn't going to be happy about you keeping this from him, just so you know."

Galen shrugged, "You have more things to worry about than him being mad at me." He said quietly, staring at his feet as he leaned against the wall next to me.

"What do you mean?"

"There's just some things that are possibly changing... the air around you two—the future—it's shifting."

My heart aches at that, and I close my eyes. There's so much I want to say, to ask, but something inside me says nothing I could possibly ask would help. For one moment, I even consider looking into his mind, but I don't need to fall further in the rabbit hole of discontent.

When I finally look back at him, Galen seemed so distant, stuck in a different place that I didn't think I would ever understand. He sighed deeply, "Kayd, I'm so tired." He said in the saddest voice I had ever heard from my optimistic brother.

"Then go rest, Galen. I'll talk with Leon, and everything will be fine."

He shook his head as a few tears trickled down his face, and the shock of those tears filled me with grief, "I'm tired of seeing everything. I know you won't like this, but I'm kind of happy that I won't have to worry about it soon. You'll be okay without me though, I'm sure of it." He said with a small smile, hugging me tightly, buy I felt his agony, even if he tried to hide it.

"Galen, I could still save you." I whisper hopefully, but he shook his head with a long sigh,

"No, Kayd. Just go about your life, it is the safest way for everyone else." He replies too tiredly.

"Galen..." My voice breaks.

He hugged me again, "Knowing everything is more of a burden than I would've thought." He whispered with a sarcastic smirk. He looked at me with love and friendship. "You should leave Leon alone today... but you do need to talk to him, Kayd. There is something that has to happen tomorrow. If it doesn't, it won't happen for at least four years if at all."

I raised my eyebrow at him, "Why are you suddenly being so chatty about your visions with me?"

He shrugged, "I need you to know as much as I can tell you before I'm gone."

I nodded, ignoring the ache, ignoring the devastating pain that accompanies thoughts of my brother dying, and I kissed his forehead before leaving him. The day was tiring and long. I kept expecting Leon to come back, but he never did. Worry and fear raked through me, but Galen was as calm as ever, which at least told me I should be too. I tried to clean up the cave, but everything felt like busy work, and it did nothing to ease the ache in my soul.

"Kayd..." Galen says after I'd been keeping myself busy for several hours. I looked up at him in surprise, and he watched me with concern, "Kayd, maybe you should go down to the river and relax a bit?" he suggested politely, his brows furrowed in concern.

I chuckled miserably, wiping my hands down my face. I looked down my body and realized I was covered in dirt. "Is that a hint that I need a bath?"

He smirked, but it wasn't filled with as much humor as normal, "It means you need to go relax, Kayd."

I sigh deeply before nodding, "Ok..."

The sky is turning from afternoon to evening, with stars spotting the sky. As I wandered down to the river access, hearing the splashing of someone in the water, I was shocked to see Leon completely naked. I gasped, and I felt his eyes on me as I turned away with blushing cheeks, wanting to just go back to the cave.

"Oh, hey." He replied simply, suddenly not embarrassed or ashamed for his nakedness. I tried not to blush, but there was no way to look at him like this without my cheeks going red. "I'm covered, Kayd. What's up?" he seemed so far away even though he was only a yard away at most.

I dared to look at him again, and sure enough, he had managed to pull on some shorts, "I didn't actually know you'd be down here... where've you been?"

He lets out a tired sigh, wiping water from his face, "Honestly, I just have been walking or sitting by the water. I can leave you here if you want to be alone..." he says, his tone tinged with misery and regret.

"No... please..." I murmur, "I sort of figured maybe we should talk about what happened..." I whispered, again pulling my gaze so I didn't have to see him shirtless, because even now, the ache for him was so present.

"I don't want to talk about the group." He said bluntly, and I could hear splashing behind me, "I told you, I'm covered, Kayd. You can look at me again." His voice sounded so coarse and rough as he spoke to me now.

"Well how about we talk about the other thing that almost happened, " I said, finally turning back to him. I now could tell he had put on his briefs, not shorts, and the idea had me blushing even more as I looked at his perfect body.

Leon sighed as he splashed over to me. "I'm sorry I almost took advantage of you, Kayd. I seriously don't know what came over me. I usually have pretty good self-control around you..."

"It was me!" I said without thinking and he watched me in confusion.

"What do you mean? I'm pretty sure it was me that was basically ripping off your clothes." He said carefully, eyeing the opening to the cave, probably making sure my brother couldn't hear him.

I dared to take a step closer to him, the guilt and shame cutting at me, "I didn't mean to, but I wanted you to stay so badly, that when I asked you to stay, I think I accidentally put my own thoughts into your head."

His eyes widened with an un-suppressible smile on his face, "You're telling me you accidentally told me to make love to you?" he laughed as he dived under the water in a deeper section and came up right in front of the shore before me. "Well that's not something I ever expected to happen." The sadness touched his face again, but it didn't seem to overwhelm him as much for now.

I giggled, sitting down and dipping my feet in the water, "Me either. I think I wanted you to know that I wanted you too, so much so that it actually transferred into a command?" I said with a laugh.

He pulled himself out of the water and sat next to me, "So... you really think you are ready?"

"I think I am." I said, grasping his hand in mine, entwining our fingers.

He smiled softly, his gaze on our hands, and he sighed with hesitation "I don't mean just for that, Kayd. Yes, that is a part of marriage which, I'm not going to lie, I look forward to, but there is so much more. Marrying me means that you know you won't want to be with anyone else, because I don't ever want to be without you."

I nodded with a loving smile, "I know. I want to be with you forever, Leon." He pulled me into his arms, soaking me in the process, "We can wait however long you need though, I mean it, since I know you have had a really traumatic thing happen."

He held me closer and I could feel him nod, "Really... though I could wait forever, I would marry you tomorrow if we could. "

I looked up at him in surprise, "What?"

He smirked, "Kayd, we are a team, and I have a feeling a lot is going to change soon, and I would rather know that you and I are married as we go through it together." I smiled at the realization of what my brother had said: 'There is something that has to happen tomorrow. If it doesn't, it won't happen for at least four years.' If we didn't decide to get married now, we might have to wait more than four years, if ever. So, I gave my happiest grin and nodded.

"So, what if we *did* get married tomorrow."

His eyes widened a little but then they glowed with devotion and love, "Are you serious? I thought with the law you wanted to wait until you were 17?"

I smiled, "Leon, I'm practically 17 anyways. Besides… as far as anyone knows, my parents have been dead for years, so who would question me choosing to get married sooner? Besides, we live in a world where we've been on the run. The real question, though, is are you ok with all this, especially after what happened today."

He nodded, kissing my lips affectionately, "If anything, I think it made me realize I don't want to ever let you out of my sight. I know this is what my mom wanted, Kayd, for you and me to be together."

I nodded "Alright! Then… I'd love to." I said with a smile and I leaped into his arms. He kissed me happily, and I think for one moment at least, we were able to push off all the darkness in our world.

We rushed into the cave, and Galen had already packed all of our bags, ready for us to move on. Galen smiled, "I had a feeling you guys would want to get moving." He said knowingly.

Leon smiled back, "Of course you did." He laughs, feeling lighter. "I know someone that lives not too far from here that is an ordained minister. He's actually a prophet." He looks at Galen who seems to be bouncing with joy, "He told me a long time ago that he would marry us when I'd found the one I was meant for, and he said I could stay there as long as needed in the house connected to his. If we leave first thing in the morning, we should get there before 12."

"Why wait?" I ask, squeezing his hand. He looks back at me with affection, "Why not go now? I don't know about you, but I doubt I'll sleep anyway."

He grins back at me, eyes glowing with affection, "If you're sure."

I nod, lifting up on my tiptoes and kissing him. "I'm positive." I said with a smile, about to throw my bag over my shoulder when Leon took it out of my hand and slung it over his own shoulder.

"Okay, let's go." He said with a content grin, intertwining his fingers with mine in his free hand.

It was a quiet walk since we were taking the journey at night. Leon was used to being in a single spot for long periods of time, but this is where my skills take center stage. I know what it's like to not make a sound, to act as if we are invisible... sadly Leon isn't, and it sets me on edge.

We had been walking almost two hours when I heard rustling from the trees up ahead. Galen and Leon started quietly chatting, not realizing the potential dangers waiting at every corner. "Be quiet!" I growl to them, but it was too late. A man came jogging towards us from the thicker trees to the north, it seemed as if he came out of nowhere. I quickly pushed my brother out of the way behind a large tree, but when I went to do the same to Leon, he continued walking towards the man with a large grin. The man gave him a boisterous hug, "How did you find us?" Leon said with a chuckle.

The man was worn-out looking, between 40 and 50, with receding blonde curly hair and dark hazel-green eyes. "I have a Prophet, and he told me he saw you and two kids coming towards our town."

I came to Leon's side defensively, holding onto his arm, trying to pull him away, "Is this your friend we were going to see?" I whispered with a small, forced smile as I looked towards the man with as friendly of a nod as I could muster towards a stranger. As I looked at the man more closely, though, I realized he looked oddly familiar.

Leon grinned, "No, Kayd… this is my dad!" he said, hugging his father once more.

"Kayd?" His father asked, suddenly impressed as he offered his hand to me, "The Decider! And my son is friends with her."

Leon stepped back with anguished surprise, looking sick as he stared at the ground, and Galen rushed over to us, wiping off leaves and dirt, "And his fiancée!" Galen said, saying things he shouldn't like always. Jonathan Hensley smiled and shook Leon's hand with obvious pride.

"Good job, my boy!"

"Dad…"

"Ya know, I haven't seen my son in over 2 years! And I meet up with him again, and he is marrying the most famous girl in the Gifted world!" I stared at him with apprehensive shock before looking back at Leon.

"What is he talking about?" I whispered, pulling on his arm again. I felt out of place, and even though I'd always wanted to meet this man, I now felt as though I should be anywhere but here.

Leon sighed with a glare towards his father, "Dad sort of spreads word like wildfire… if even one of the other Gifted people that know you told someone he knows, everyone will know about you. By the way, thanks for that, dad." An angry fire seemed to light in Leon's eyes, "So since you already know about Kayd, do you know what happened to mom?" he asked bitterly, his fury growing.

Jonathan's face changed as he considered Leon more seriously, "What happened?"

Leon shook his head, "A lot of Gifted people were murdered either yesterday morning… hard to know when for sure. And mom…" he clenched his eyes closed, fighting with his pain, "I didn't see her… so they either took her or discarded her somewhere I couldn't find." I squeezed Leon's hand, hoping that I was offering comfort.

Jonathan put his hand over his eyes, suddenly near sobbing, but something felt off to me about it. He was obviously distraught that his wife had possibly died, but there was something wrong about his reaction… it almost felt staged. "I don't know how this could have happened…"

Leon shrugged with surprising coldness, "Like you didn't know..." he whispered bitterly. I watched him with care, finding myself mystified by the level of distance between them. I think the picture I'd created in my head had been of a happy family, of a father that was devoted to his child and wife.

"What was that?" I asked him under my breath.

He shook his head, and he grasped my hand in his again. I can see the way my presence seems to calm him a little.

"My God, Leon... I'm so sorry I haven't been there." Jonathan says, oblivious to his son's animosity.

"I assumed you had been captured by the Authority." I said, my words coming out without my permission. Leon looked down at me in slight surprise.

Jonathan replied with a small smile, though tears still wet his cheek, "That's what the Authority wanted everyone to think. But I have been rallying troops together since I left office!" he said too excitedly for a man who had just found out about the loss of his wife.

"Well as great as it is to see you dad, Kayd and I have something we have to do, so maybe we can see you in a few days or something?" Leon said hurriedly, so eager to leave the man he'd been so excited to see moments ago.

Jonathan slapped Leon's shoulder affectionately as he hugged him, "What's the hurry?" He looked to me warmly, beseeching, "Come on Kaydence, stay and chat with your father-in-law to-be!" he chuckled.

My emotions seemed to swell, and I felt the overwhelming urge to look in this 'visionary's eyes. I didn't understand where the urge came from, or why I would feel such a thing, but as he put his hand on mine and his other on Leon as if to stop us, I peeked back at him sternly, "Mr. Hensley, I don't mean to be rude but..." my eyes met his for only a moment, but I felt that odd sensation that accompanied the colored blur, and I closed my eyes with an involuntary gasp, turning away, "We need to go now." I warned Leon, trying not to meet his father's prying gaze again. Because even in that split second, I had seen something I never would've thought from the once-great Jonathan Hensley—reason for shame, though no shame could be seen. I didn't know what he had done, but he should be ashamed. I immediately knew that Mr. Hensley was not someone to be trusted.

He continued pressuring us, and the impulse to look into him became almost debilitating. I clenched my eyes closed tightly, gritting my teeth, but he wouldn't leave. He was determined, but he didn't realize his determination could lead to his downfall. I wished I could make him leave us, and then it was as if I felt my power imprint his mind to let us go.

Mr. Hensley smiled, "Alright, my future daughter-in-law! Well Leon, I am in Greensville staying with our old friends there." He patted Leon on the shoulders once more before heading back towards the direction he came.

Leon exhaled with frustration, "Well I'm glad he listened to you."

I felt a little guilty. "I made him... sorry."

Leon laughed darkly, looking back in slight surprise, "Eh, he will probably pat you on the back later, proud to know that he was forced to do something by the Great Decider!" he said in an annoyed voice, picking up all our bags again.

I followed after him, but I still felt his distance, "Are you mad at me or something?"

He sighed, shaking his head as he offered me an apologetic glance, "No. It's not you at all. I love my dad, but he is just so obsessed with the Gifted, that I feel like he doesn't really believe in the person, just their Gifts." He said with a shrug, though he clearly seemed frustrated about it, "And then the fact he just seemed to get over all those deaths so easily." He gritted his teeth and closed his eyes.

I grasped his hand in mine, "I'm so sorry..."

He offered a soft, sad smile, putting his other hand over mine, "It's ok, Kayd... I'm ok." We were quiet for a bit, allowing the silence to fill the space. After awhile, he looked back at me with sudden curiosity. "So why would you make him leave like that, though? I saw you look away from him all quickly, was something wrong?" he asked with a furrowed brow, pulling Galen from his hiding spot.

I didn't feel right sharing my presumptions since I really didn't know what I had felt or seen, "I just felt my Decider Gift trying to read him when I looked into his eye, and I fought the urge."

Leon chuckled, "Eh, go ahead next time you see him. At least when you look into him, he will be protected, right?"

I smiled weakly, not meeting his eye as we continue walking, "Well... if that's what the Gift decides. I told you before, I see someone's essence, and if its good then they could be safe, but if they are red or orange, then they aren't." I warn, hoping I don't have to say more.

Leon considered me as we continued forward, Galen watching us carefully in silence, "Kayd, are you afraid that my dad won't be considered 'good'?"

I sighed and forced a smile, "I'm sure he will, I'm just saying, what if he wasn't? I wouldn't want to be the reason something happened to him just because my Gift decided whether he was worth living or not."

He nodded hesitantly, "Fair enough." He took my hand, "I'm sorry about my dad, by the way. Obviously, I have missed him over the years, but whenever I see him again, whether it was from a long trip, or now, I quickly remember how irritating he is."

I smirk at him, "I could kinda tell." I chuckle and he smiles back at me, offering a brief kiss on my lips. "So how much longer until we get to your friend's house?"

Leon let out a breath, "Kayd, maybe we were being impulsive…"

Galen came running in front of us, making us stop in our tracks, "No! Leon… is this about your dad?" Leon flinches, then nods once hesitantly, "You can't let his mistakes guide you too! Just because he left you and your mom doesn't mean you will leave too…" Leon stared at Galen in shock. I watched them both in surprise… was that something Leon feared? Should I be afraid now too?

Leon sighed, wiping his eyes before he nodded, "You're right… you're right." He said tiredly.

Galen nodded, grabbing his arm. Leon looked at him uncertainly, "You aren't him…" Galen whispers, but I hear him. I look over at Leon and there's something in his eye that shares alarm transforming to relief.

We were quiet for a while before Leon quietly looked back to Galen, "Thank you…"

It took nearly three more hours, but we finally spotted a large home with a smaller cottage about a hundred yards away, slightly hidden by large wisteria bushes and trees. An elderly man with wavy white hair that lingered at his chin opened the door to the main house, a large grin on his face and open arms held out for us. Leon smiled back and met the embrace of the old man. Leon looked to me and grinned, "Kayd, Galen, I would like you to meet my grandfather, Paul Jackson—my mother's dad."

"I'm so sorry about your mom, Leon..." Paul said with tears in his glass-blue eyes, holding Leon's shoulder tenderly.

Leon peered back at him with a clear ache in his gaze, "Grandpa... how did you even know about that?"

Paul smiled weakly, "You know us Prophets can't decide what we see, Leon. I tried to send your dad, but God knows that man never seems to care about anyone but himself..."

"Grandpa..." Leon warned.

Paul waved his hand, "But that's not why you are here tonight. You are here for happier things." He said with a kind grin, "You must be Kaydence?" I nodded politely, looking between Leon and him with a soft smile. He smiled graciously back as he approached me and kissed my hand, "How beautiful you are in person! My visions never gave you enough credit." He said as I blushed. Galen seemed to be jumping out of his skin as he tried to shake Paul's hand.

"I had seen a few visions where I never got to meet you! I'm so glad I did!" Galen said as he excitedly shook the old man's hand.

Paul smiled softly at him, "I knew I would meet you Galen, if not now, later." Galen gave a sad expression.

"Well sir, I won't be around much longer." Galen whispered even though we all knew the truth.

The man nodded with a tender grin as he messed up Galen's hair like an affectionate father, "We were always going to see each other Galen. Make sure you enjoy your Gift though, while you still can." He said with a knowing wink before coming to Leon and me, taking Leon's right hand and placing it on my left hand. "Now as for you two, are you sure you are ready for this step?"

I smiled, "I have no doubts." Leon nodded, beaming, but Paul lingered on Leon.

"Leon, your mother died yesterday, why are you rushing suddenly to marry Kayd? I didn't expect to you for at least another month at least."

Leon sighed, "I can't be without her…" he said, his voice catching on hidden tears, "Mom may not get to see Kayd and I get married, but to honor her memory and her wishes, I want to marry Kayd now to show mom that my life will go on." He briskly wiped away a tear, "It was something her and I always agreed on if one of us ever died before the other."

Paul nodded, "But are you doing this for her, or for you?" he said carefully, a wise glint to his eye, and I watched with interest, understanding the weight of the question Paul was asking, and that they were for my benefit.

Leon kicked a rock at his feet, "I have wanted to marry Kayd practically since I met her… but the sooner reason is for my mom, yeah." He quickly looked at me with brief apology, "I just am so afraid to lose you next."

Paul smiled tenderly, "Leon, there are no wrong answers. I just wanted to make sure that you were really ready to do this for yourself too. I am of course happy that you want to honor my lovely daughter by marrying such a sweet young lady, but it had to be for you first, and her second."

Leon smirked, "Oh Gramps, always too wise." They laughed as Paul embraced Leon happily.

"I'm proud of you, Leon. Now go get some sleep, and then tomorrow, we'll get you two married."

Leon wrapped his arm around my shoulder, "I'll show you one of the guest rooms. Grandpa always had a few, and I have a feeling he may have one set up just for you." He peeked over at Paul who nodded back with a laugh.

"You of course are correct. Top room to the left, Leon. And yours is on the main floor... just like when you were a boy." He explained softly.

Leon nods, guiding me up the stairs to a room with soft pinks and whites. "I hope this room is ok... I think grandpa will probably put Galen close to you, if that helps."

I look around, running my hand over the soft ruffled fabric of the comforter. I know it's foolish, but I feel tears fill my eyes... because everything in this room is so lovely and light and pure. It reminds me of my room when I was young... actually almost to a T.

"Kayd? Are you alright?" Leon asks gently.

I turn back to him and he looks surprised by my tears. He reaches out and I sit on the bed, embracing the softness, "I just..." I bite my lip, "I didn't realize how much I missed all of this." My voice comes out a whisper. Leon sits beside me, taking my hand in his with a concerned look on his face. I look at our hands, and warmth fills my chest, "I don't think I ever expected to have a bed again, or be in a room like this…"

He wraps his arm around me and I lay my head on his shoulder, "He said we can stay as long as we are able to, Kayd…" He offers reassuringly, "Grandad just told me that he wouldn't mind if we stayed forever." He chuckles.

I can't help the small smile, but something still feels like it's missing inside of me, or maybe just that I feel as though I don't deserve this. "Even though my mom tried to destroy us—Galen and me—I… I still feel like it's wrong that I should have this, and she never will." I whisper, the tears beginning to spill.

"Kayd…" he murmurs, brushing his hand over my spine.

I shake my head, "And I know it's dumb," I sigh with irritation as the tears continue to flow without my consent, "But I sort of wish she could be there tomorrow… that my dad could be." I scoff at my own foolish wish. "I know it's ridiculous!"

He pulls me to his chest in a tight embrace, "Kayd, it's not ridiculous…" he murmurs against my cheek, "She was your mother… you loved her, and your dad. It's ok to mourn them, even though you know the dark parts of them now." I pull back to meet his eye, my heart longing to grab at the hope he offers.

"It just feels so wrong to be happy… to feel comfortable and safe." I push my face into the fabric of his shirt, soaking up his warmth, his smell... and just enjoying the feel of him. Leon is always so steady, so firm... always my protector, always my love.

He gently cups my cheek and I move into the touch, peering up at his waiting gaze, "Kayd, you have to stop living in the past." He says so earnestly that it rankles something inside of me, almost like he's using his gift, but I think it's more his words just have power in my heart. "I wish you could see the way it destroys you a little more every day that you focus more on the pain you think you should have because of your ghosts."

I go to turn but his gaze follows me, wiping my tears and holding my face now with both hands. The agony in my heart begs me to get out of his affectionate embrace, to go somewhere cold and bleak to sit and simmer in the ashy remains of my former life. As I meet Leon's eye, though, I stop fighting. Looking into his tender gaze, I actually see something good, something bright... something I want. I can almost see a future with Leon—us old, laughing, holding each other's hands as we sit in a couple of recliner chairs on his grandfather's deck. That life looks peaceful... and I want it with everything inside of me.

I run my fingers down his jaw, brushing my hand into his hair until his tender gaze turns heated, almost hungry, though he also waits for my decision, waits for my voice to say no. I smile as I pull him closer so our lips touch. Tomorrow we will become one, but for now I need him too... maybe just holding him, his lips against mine, will be enough to calm the ache in my belly, the ache that is mirrored in my soul. I don't think I ever realized that there was a gaping hole in my heart and my spirit until Leon starting filling it in with hope and love. I smile against his lips, and he meets that smile, filling me with even more warmth as he holds me tighter.

No, I have no doubts... I want to be with Leon forever. For tonight we will kiss, hold each other until dawn, and then tomorrow we will become one...

• •

I woke up to Leon still holding me against his chest. We both still wore the clothes we'd had on the night before, neither of us waking to even take off our shoes, and somehow that brings me the greatest joy. I snuggle in closer to him and he murmurs out a contented sigh.

"Come on kids, it's time to start the day!" Paul calls.

Leon stretches out beside me and I find I'm grinning at him. "I guess he's right." He leans in and kisses me, but it's not enough... I want more, "I have to go..." he urges, "I'm supposed to marry my best friend today."

A shiver runs down my spine and I look back at him. "Oh... right." I say, forcing a smile. He held me all night, but suddenly now I'm nervous about the next step.

He tilts his head at me in brief concern, "Kayd... are you with me?"

I bite my lip, holding back all my fear and my reservations, "Of course I am." I nod.

He smiles back and nods before hopping out of the bed, "Good. I'll see you downstairs."

I shouldn't be so afraid suddenly, but I find that I am. I pull my knees to my chest, and I look around this grand room again, and I feel a little sorry for myself, or maybe not sorry for myself, but rather sorry that I get any of this when others won't. My mind flashes to Galen and I ache more than ever before at the thought that sometime soon, I won't have his open optimism, his comforting laugh.... It's not fair to think that someone who is so full of life, will not be allowed to live fully the way he should! He told me he'd die soon after I marry Leon... so why in the Hell am I choosing to do this so early? God... why am I jumping into this so blindly? What if this is what signs the final death sentence of Galen!

Knock! Knock! I turn to my door, unsteady tears trickling over my cheeks. I realize I'm near breathless from the anxious thoughts, "Who's there?"

Galen opens the door, peering in with a sad smile, "I had a new vision this morning... it included you freaking out and trying to run from this."

My eyes widen and I hide my face, hating that my fears could've led to a new future. Wasn't my future so clear to me just last night? Would I really run from it...? I peek back at Galen, "Would it help to keep you longer...?" I dare to ask, biting my lip to hide the pained emotions spiking through me.

His brows furrow in concern and he sighs, shaking his head. He shuts the door and sits beside me, staring out the window instead of at me, "Nothing will change it, Kayd. I told you that already. If you leave him though, you'll get taken too. Just keep that in mind, ok, Kayd?" He murmurs almost protectively, "At any point, leaving Leon won't lead to you saving me, it will just lead to you being captured. Ok?" he warns.

My heart pounds wildly in aggravated fear, and I manage a tired sigh, "Ok... as long as you are sure..."

He pats my shoulder and then leans on it the way he used to when he was smaller. I lay my head on his, "I need you to know something important, Kayd..."

"What's that?"

He huffs out a long breath, "You need to live your life like normal. I'm begging you... please don't come looking for me when I go. I've seen some things recently, and all of them include you trying to come for me." He dares to meet my eye, and I can see his are misty with unshed tears. "It's pointless Kayd. Ok? Nothing you could do would save me... not a thing. Please don't come after me when the time comes."

I feel like someone is pressing down on my chest, stealing all my breath, but based on the earnest look in his eye, I can't help but agree, "Ok Galen..."

He nods with a forced smile, "Good..." he whispers.

"Galen?"

"Hmm?"

I pull in a sharp breath, "Am I making a mistake marrying him so young...?" I whisper back.

He hesitates, "I think you and Leon are meant to be together Kayd. You and him... you make things change together. Things might happen soon that, if you weren't married, could sway you, take you in the wrong direction. So, if you are really asking me, I say it would be a mistake not to marry him now..."

I peek back at him in surprise, "Wow, a solid answer from you for once." I tease, but I notice the look of pain brushing his face. "That's not your usual attitude towards the future lately." I say, my brows furrowed in concern. He clenches his eyes closed tightly, "What's the deal?"

He huffs out an unsteady breath, "When I told you that you can't just tamper with the future..." he begins hesitantly, his grimace confusing me.

"Yeah... that it could make people do things they aren't ready for, or something... right?"

He groans, nodding, "The more I test the future, it's starting to get muddy, Kayd." He admits darkly, "I'm getting things confused, getting lost in futures that may or may not exist anymore." He grumbles out a sigh, "But the worst part is watching as an entire new series of visions keep showing up in my head constantly..." he meets my eye and I'm surprised by the ache waiting for me there, "So much is changing Kayd... and I'm getting scared."

A wave of sorrow rakes through me, "What could possibly be making *you* scared, Galen?"

"I'm afraid that if I tell you, it'll make it worse... but if I don't say it, maybe you'll fall right into it?" He says nervously.

"Come on Galen, at this point could it really make it worse by telling me?"

He stares at his feet, "Kayd... I saw things about you, about what you could become..." he clenches his eyes closed tightly, and the shock of his obvious fear breaks my heart, "I can't see the reason it happens... but it's clear that at some point, you could completely lose yourself." I flinch away from him, my world seeming to shatter at the seams, but he doesn't stop, and though I want to understand, I'm afraid to hear more, "What I know for sure, is... it's if you get separated from Leon. You stop being you... and you... you end up helping the Authority."

I can't help the horrified gasp, "There's no way, Galen. I would *never* do that! Never. Even if they captured me..."

He grasps my hand, forcing me to meet his eye. I realize my eyes are filled with misty tears, "That's the point Kayd... you don't seem like you in those visions. It's almost like who you really are doesn't exist anymore... they used you like a weapon." He whispered.

"How could something like that happen?" I murmur as quiet as possible, hoping Leon never hears this. He already sees the hints of darkness in me... what would he do if he heard this potential level of darkness I hold inside of me...?

Galen hesitates, "I don't know Kayd. I don't... that's why all I can say to you is what I hope will help. Ok?" He murmurs almost pleadingly, "Stay with Leon. Don't come for me. Live your life without me..."

It feels as if he's taken a knife to my heart and is turning it with every word he speaks. "You already told me all that, Galen..." I force out, "Of course I'll continue on..." I say, but it even sounds like a lie to *my* ears. I can try to pretend my entire world won't fall apart at his death, but I know it will. I can't hide the deep hope in me that somehow I could save him. Maybe there is part of me that fully could picture who I am slipping away at his death... I already slip away from myself daily, and that's with him standing right beside me.

He looks back at me skeptically, but he lets out a soft sigh, "Kayd... I know I don't say it much... but I love you." My heart swells and my eyes close tight to hide the tears waiting there, "And... I really just want you to be happy. I know this isn't the life you probably expected, but... I'm glad you are the one I've gotten to be with all this time." I bite my lip before it can quiver with emotion, "You... Kayd..." his voice breaks and I look back at them to see he's crying too. I wrap him in my arms and we say nothing else. He doesn't have to tell me… I know.

"Hello in there?" Leon's grandfather calls. "I hear someone in here is supposed to be getting married?" He chuckles good naturedly, but when he pushes the door open all the way and sees Galen and me crying, his expression softens instantly. I expect pity, but instead he just looks loving, considerate. "Oh come on kids, you'll see each other again!" He offers brightly, and it twists that blade in my heart again. "You're just getting married." He laughs, "It's not the end of you two."

It's funny how those words felt like an omen. *It's not the end of you two*… but on some level it was. I look back at Galen, and he's forcing a smile, but I recognize that knowing look he gives me—he's thinking the same thing as me. My marriage is the first guidepost leading to Galen's death. I wish they weren't connected…

Galen stands, shaking off his sorrow so much easier than I can. "He's right, Kayd… it's time for you to get married." He says with a suddenly light smile.

I look between them, trying to borrow some of their joy, to even remind myself that I should be happy, but all I feel right now is fear. "Galen, how about you get downstairs and help Leon get ready."

Galen glances back at me with an almost apologetic smile, and he nods, "Ok. See you guys down there." He says, and then he's gone.

I follow him with my gaze, my heart pulling towards the boy whose time was almost up. For just a moment, I picture that little boy again from my memory... the one with the blue bowtie and the flash of blonde hair that was always messy... and a tear falls down my cheek. He's too young to have to experience the things he's had to experience... and too young to have to see himself die. I promised him I wouldn't follow... so I wouldn't become what he fears I might, but can he really expect me not to go after him when he goes? Even if it kills me, I will follow Galen to the ends of the earth. I don't care. No one else and nothing else can matter in comparison to him... maybe he can't see every possibility?

I sit up, the realization that maybe Galen is wrong. He mentioned that he looked in several possibilities, but hadn't I seen part of one of his visions—that he couldn't see. Maybe he didn't see the whole vision? Maybe there's still hope...

Chapter 11: Hope

When I came out of the room, Paul smirked, "Though you are beautiful, honey, I think it's customary for the bride to walk down the aisle in a dress."

I looked down at my grubby jeans and loose-fitting buttoned blouse, "This is all I have though... I mean, I have a jean skirt that comes above my knee?"

"Follow me, Kayd. I have something you could wear." Paul pulled me up another flight of stairs and guided me through a beautiful wooden hallway, the walls covered in engraved butterflies and flowers. Paul smiled as he watched my gaze, "My wife carved the flowers and my daughter, Leon's mom, helped engrave the butterflies." He chuckled as he wandered in and out of his memories, "She used to say that every blossom should have a butterfly to remind us how beautiful and precious each flower is." He wiped his eye, though I couldn't see if he actually had tears.

Paul led me to a room hidden behind a deceptively short ceilinged entryway. The room was in pristine condition as if it had not been touched in years except by a feather duster. There was a large fluffy bed at the center of the room with a floral comforter. At the end of the bed stood a sizable emerald-green chest that Paul opened with a small silver key. As the chest opened, I saw a beautiful pile of white lace layered over white satin fabric. Paul pulled it out to show a beautiful wedding dress with a lace bateau neckline working down a swooping back with light pink pearls touching the top and the waist.

It was breathtaking to see the beautiful dress that I would be wearing when I married the man I love. My hand went to my mouth involuntarily as I stared happily, "This was my wife's dress. We were married 45 years before she was taken from me."

"Did you know..." I began and stopped myself quickly, feeling beyond rude for the question.

He nodded sadly as he caressed the soft fabric, "I did. But even when you know exactly how a tragedy will happen, you are never prepared enough." He sighed, "You are lucky to have the Gift you do, Kayd."

I scoffed, "Well I'm sure over time I might agree with that more, but I don't now..."

He sighed with a soft laugh that was filled with hidden sorrow, "The ability to protect those you love is something I would've liked to have." If anything, his words punctured a hole straight through my chest... because my powers will likely not be able to save my brother. Maybe I was able to save all those people that day months ago, but it didn't save them forever.

We're silent for a few minutes as I dare to approach the dress. "You never thought you would be wearing a wedding dress, did you?"

I smiled softly, running my fingers over the soft lace, "My family home burned to the ground almost 5 years ago now, and my mom's dress with it." I said simply and he nodded with a knowing smirk.

There's an odd twinkle in his eye, the same kind I'd seen with Galen after a vision, "You still didn't think this would ever happen though, did you?"

I laughed in surprise, holding back the ache, "No... I guess not. I thought my brother and I would be running forever. When I met Leon though... I just wasn't prepared."

"To fall in love?" he said with a kind grin.

I smiled back, "I never dreamed I would be lucky enough to fall in love, let alone with someone as wonderful and sweet as Leon."

He nodded solemnly, "Why are you wanting to get married now, though? You are only just 17, why would you marry him now?"

"Why wait when you know you've found the right person?" I say like it was obvious, but I felt something ping inside of me.

He smiled, "I'm glad he found you." He said, kissing my forehead like my father used to do. "Well I will let you get dressed, and if you need help, let me know." He said with a reassuring grin.

I held the dress closely for a moment, knowing that this would be the gown I would remember my entire life and, perhaps, my own daughter could wear someday. That thought suddenly made me more nervous—I could have children someday with Leon. Would I even be a good mother? Would they be forced to watch their parents die because of their crimes against the Authority? Or even worse... would they be taken by the President and made into mindless soldiers for a horrid man?

I set the dress on the bed and walked away for a moment, staring at it like it held the Black Plague. I tried to keep the nerves down, tried to kick the fears away, tried to convince myself I was being silly, but this was the world I lived in now. Children were not safe anymore, not as long as the President was in power, but that's when I remembered something important: Leon would overthrow the President, and Galen told me that I would help him in some way. Perhaps someday our future children would be safe?

So, I took a deep breath, picked the dress back up and pulled it over my head and it fell perfectly over my body. It was the first time I had ever seen this dress, but it seemed to be made for me, accentuating the curves I hadn't realized I possessed. I smiled at my reflection, as the beautiful woman smiled back at me again. I dabbed some pink-rose lipstick onto my lips and walked back into the hallway. Paul beamed as he gazed at me, "You look beautiful my dear. Would you like me or your brother to walk you down the aisle?"

I grinned at the thought, "My brother." He nodded and asked me to stay at the door while he retrieved Galen. Galen came in, his eyes wide as he smiled happily at me, no words spoken as a tear came to his eye. He took my arm in his and began walking me outside into the beautiful garden. The path from the backdoor led to a rose-strewn gazebo with flowers of every kind surrounding us on each side of the walkway. The smell of lilacs and gardenias filled my senses, and my heart swelled with love and excitement.

Leon stood inside the gazebo with a smile from ear-to-ear as he watched me approach. My cheeks were hurting from my own large grin as Galen offered my hand to Leon's outstretched palm. Leon guided me towards Paul who held a large, worn, leather bible in his hands. "Now, do you want the long version or the short version?" Paul said with a smirk.

Leon laughed, "How about the medium version, Grandpa?"

Paul nodded and began. My heart was pounding as he spoke about our covenant with God and each other, mentioning the promise we were making to each other and to our families. In that moment though, I pictured my father's smiling face, and his eyes that matched my own... and even though he may not be what I expected, and he may be betraying us either now or in the future, I find that I miss him... and I still love him.

"I do." I heard Leon say, and I was pulled back to the moment, suddenly aware of the tears that were streaking my cheeks, as he placed a ring on my finger.

"And do you, Kaydence, take Leon to be your lawfully wedded husband, through sickness and health, through darkness and light, the good times and bad, as long as you both shall live?"

I took a deep breath and shakily said, "I do..." Leon caressed my hand gently with his freehand. I felt my whole body shaking, but I dared to meet his eye, and the light waiting there for me in his filled my heart with warmth.

Paul nodded, "Kaydence, please place your ring on Leon's left hand and repeat after me: 'I give you this ring, wear it with love and joy. I choose you to be my husband: to have and to hold, from this day forward.'"

"Leon... I give you this ring, wear it with love and joy. I choose you to be my husband: to have and to hold, from this day forward..."

"'I pledge you my faithfulness to show to you the same kind of love as Christ has shown, and to love you as a part of myself because in His sight we shall be one.'"

I put the ring on Leon's finger and looked into his eyes, "I pledge to you my faithfulness to show to you the same kind of love as Christ has shown, and to love you as a part of myself because in His sight, we shall be one."

"I now pronounce you husband and wife! Leon, you may now kiss your bride." Leon beamed as he swept me into his arms and kissed me so sweetly and so passionately. I giggled as he carried me back up the aisle, flowers brushing through my hair and making me giggle. He grinned at me with such love as he continued towards the cottage only a few yards away. He opened the door and carried me across the threshold, kissing me more while we went up the stairs, and surprising me how graceful he was with his eyes closed. He stopped when we were inside the room, and he set me down on the bed, watching me with affection. I glanced around the room only enough to see how the floor is covered in rose petals, and the room is lit by candles. It's so romantic... and even the bed is so comfortable, but that's when fear briefly strikes me.

"I love you Kayd, my wife." He said tenderly as he kissed my hand, and with his confidence, his certainty of calling me his wife, that tiny hint of fear fell away.

Everything was a dream, and I was no longer afraid of what I knew was about to happen, what was about to make our love consummated forever. "I love you too, Leon." My body was shaking nervously, but I tried to keep it from my voice.

I could tell he was about to say something else, most likely about to ask me something, but I didn't want him to change my mind. I quickly pulled him to me, kissing him passionately, allowing us both to forget all our doubt, all our pain, and all our fear.

Everything went by so quickly—a kiss on the neck, clothes being pushed away, exploring hands, and two remarkably close bodies—a thousand little moments pieced together to make something so beautiful and so perfect. He held my naked body close to his when we'd finished making love, and I felt so complete. I looked around the room, suddenly seeing where he had thrown my dress on the floor, and where my last bit of innocence lays. I felt wild inside like something secret had finally been let out, and I smiled like a fool as I nuzzled into his shoulder.

I was his, and he was mine... nothing could ever change that. Not ever...

Chapter 12: Freeze

Leon and I woke up the next morning elated, and I felt utterly free. We walked together into the main house to meet Paul and Galen for breakfast, when we got there, however, an unexpected guest surprised us— Leon's father. For a man that had always seemed so admirable, and so kind, the sight of him suddenly made my skin crawl. When I met his gaze, I wanted to run back the way I had come, but Leon was holding me close. I felt something sharp in my stomach, trying to yield some warning, but I still could not tell what it was. I kept my eyes from his.

"Well hello my new daughter! I hear you two went ahead and eloped last night without inviting me!" Jonathan said with humor. I forced a smile.

"Daughter-in-law..." I said under my breath and Leon gave me an odd look, his brow raised in question.

"What was that dear?" Jonathan asked, still trying to meet my gaze.

"Nothing sir..." I forced a smile, keeping my gaze away from his demanding stare.

"Just call me Jon, or dad." He smiled affectionately. I wanted to puke at his sweetness. He wasn't even necessarily fake, but there was definitely something that left an unhappy taste in my mouth even speaking to him.

"Alright Jon." I say, but it feels bitter on my tongue... wrong. His expression dimmed a little, but no one else seemed to notice. Galen and Paul seemed tense, but I couldn't read why, I assumed that they knew something that Leon and I didn't.

"So, what brings you here, dad? I told you that we would come to see you." Leon said only slightly annoyed.

"Well, son, I'm afraid that the Authority is pushing back again, and the troops I've been rallying could really use some stronger players." Jonathan said, pacing across the kitchen as if he were concerned, but everything he did felt staged, like an actor who had planned out every movement and every line.

Leon sighed harshly, slamming his fist on the table. Everyone turned their gaze to him in surprise, "Dad, I told you when you first left that I would not fight for you... and besides, I'm married now, and I need to be here for Kayd."

Jonathan feigned shock, hiding the small smirk at the corner of his lips. "Actually son, I came to ask you *and* Kayd. If we had the two of you, we would be set!" I stared at him in shock, disgust and frustration quaking through my entire body, "So, Kayd, what do you think?" he asked, speaking before Leon had a moment to object.

"Dad!" Leon blurted with intense irritation and near horror.

"Let her speak, Leon." Jonathan said harshly. Leon went silent, not as if forced by a Gift, but from years of trained obedience. "Actually Kayd, how about we go outside to talk." Jonathan said, back to his sugary sweet tone. I held onto Leon's hand tighter.

"Um... I'd rather not..." I force out.

Leon kissed my cheek and whispered in my ear, "Kayd, it's ok. Just be you. I'm sure he just wants to talk to you for a minute." I shook my head at him with warning in my eyes, but Leon just smiled and kissed my lips tenderly. "You'll be fine." He promised, but it did nothing to calm my nerves.

I force a nod, pulling in a sharp breath, and forcing myself to my feet. I started walking outside stiffly and Jonathan followed after me. I went right outside the door into the back garden, but he continued walking to the gazebo where I had been married only a day ago.

"You don't like me, do you Kayd?" he said, turning back towards me with hooded eyes and his always charming grin.

I stared at him for a moment, "I don't really know you, sir—I mean Jon."

He laughed darkly, nodding once, "Listen, I don't know much about the Deciders, but there is a rumor that you have the ability to keep someone from death by a single look in the eyes." He begins, and something inside of me tingles with warning and fear. "I want you to do that to me." He says, finally sharing the motive behind his sticky sweetness.

I stared at the ground adamantly, the urge stronger than ever to meet his eye, "I'm not really sure that is true, but even so, it doesn't work like that." I growl back with caution. "My Gift decides if you are worthy of life." I warn more softly.

He smiled mischievously, "So what's the problem? I'm your father-in-law, I'm sure your Gift would recognize that sort of kinship." He says with far too much confidence.

I shook my head with a scoff, "It doesn't." I replied simply, trying hard not to look at him though he wanted me to so desperately, and so did my Gift... it felt as if it was desperate to judge this man.

He grabbed my shoulders and forced my chin upward so I would have to look at him. I closed my eyes tightly, panic striking my entire being, "Just give me your protection!" he demanded so suddenly, "I want to be able to go against the President and not die!" He said impatiently. All his pretenses had fallen away, and I saw the same man my Gift had glimpsed.

I push him away, "Even not having looked at you with my Gift, I know that you will not pass the test, sir." I spoke quietly but to the point, a tinge of anger filtering into my voice. My fingernails were puncturing my skin through my pants as I tried desperately to stay relaxed and calm so my Gift couldn't jump out on its own will.

He stepped back in slight surprise, letting go of me, "Why would you say that?"

I opened my eyes and looked at him closely, still making sure not to meet his gaze fully, though, "My own mother gave my brother and I up to the Soldiers, and my Gift sensed it before I understood what the feelings and colors meant. I have worked hard not to look in your eye because my Gift may decide that you are worthy of death, and one simple word from my lips would finish you off." I peek up at him then guardedly, "Do you really think that you have a guilt-free conscience, *Dad*?" I started approaching him more closely, and now it was his turn to back away in fear, "Because if you really think you will pass the test of the most accurate lie-detector there is, then I will happily help you out." I allowed a gentle but cold smirk to rise, and my devastating gaze must've done the trick.

He stopped moving and watched me, "How do you know?" he whispered, eyes wide in distress. For the first time since meeting him, I think I actually see a true peek of who he truly is.

"I'm not sure what I know yet, but I know it's not good. But if you ask me again to use my Gift on you, I will." I had never seen such true fear in someone's eyes before, and it guaranteed my original suspicions that Jonathan was not as good of a man as he tried to pretend to be. "And as to your question earlier to Leon and I—no, we will not fight with you." With that I walked back inside, and Leon considered me.

"What did he want?" Leon asked, looking up at me in waiting, his brow raised in concern.

"He just hoped maybe taking me aside, that he would be able to convince me to fight with him." I lied, biting my lip as I forced a smile and quickly grabbed a piece of toast.

Leon shook his head and slammed his fist on the kitchen table. Paul put a stern hand over Leon's hand, "You remember your grandmother's rules, Leon. You can get angry, but if you damage the table or the china you're in trouble." Paul said with wink. Leon nodded and relaxed his hand as he took mine, expelling a slow breath.

"All he cares about is fighting..." he forces out in a hard tone.

Something stirred in me at those words and I drifted somewhere distant. Everything was foggy as I stared at a man with a dark face, "Who are you?" I asked him harshly, trying to approach him, but he moved further into the shadows.

"You must fight... there is no choice, Kayd." He spoke in a low, breathy voice.

"There is no point to fight! I have to keep my brother and my husband safe. I can't do that if we are fighting for ours, and others, lives."

"Listen to me, girl! If you don't fight, if *you* don't lead, then everyone's a goner. You think the President is bad now? Just wait... you ain't seen nothin yet!" the man said with an odd voice, almost as if he was trying to hide what he really sounded like.

"Nothing could make me fight..."

In the darkness I could see the man grimace tensely, "There are two things..." the vision began to become cloudier. I ran towards the man, my body aching as I screamed at him. I felt strong hands holding my arms and legs, and I thrashed harder. "What two things!!"

"Kayd! Kayd!! Wake up!" Leon said to me fearfully. I couldn't come out of the vision yet... I couldn't! I needed to know what this mystery man was planning. I was finally woken when a large pan of water was dumped over my head. I woke up instantly in shock, coughing and sputtering from the surprise.

I looked around, angry and terrified as I realized yet another mystery in my future that I did not want to face. I couldn't handle only seeing glimpses. I wanted more. I needed more... I turned away from Leon who was happily hugging me, obviously glad I had not died in some bizarre sleep. But looking into those visions, feeling the hatred, the pain, the anguish, was like feeling a thousand people's emotions at the same time. I felt useless as I watched the unknown as it became another possibility in a line that I would never understand.

"Kayd? Seriously, are you alright?" Leon asked, holding me tenderly in his arms. I look over to Galen, and he has that knowing look in his eye again, the one that shows he knows exactly what I'm going through... and possibly knows what my vision was about.

I close my eyes tightly, forcing out the tears, "Sure. Yeah... I'm fine. It's fine." I force out.

Leon pulls me closer for just a moment, his concern clearly having escalated having me act so frustrated. He guides me up to our room, tentatively holding me, eager to help in any way he can as if I were an invalid. I knew in my gut it was wrong to feel that way towards him, to hold any kind of bitterness when he was simply helping me, loving me... but something was growing inside of me after that vision, and it was dark... angry.

Once I was on the bed, Leon sat beside me for a moment, quiet as he looked off towards the door. That strange irritation was bubbling up again having him just sit there, but I forced it down. "Leon... you don't have to stay with me. I'm fine. It was just a stupid vision. I'll be alright... I promise." I say with a feigned smile.

He sighs and then glances back at me with a muted smile, "Kayd... you didn't see what happened to you when that vision hit you, ok? I watched you change for just a moment." Fear ebbs inside of me, picturing the darkness I feel bubbling still. I gulp, "You weren't you... and then when you woke up from it, you still weren't. Even now, I see it in your eyes. You think I don't?" he says with affectionate sorrow, and it tugs at my heart.

I hang my head guiltily, "I guess I hoped you wouldn't see it..." I whisper.

He nods with a resigned smile, his eyes holding his agony, "I know you might resent me for wanting to stay close to you, but I will always be here to remind you who you are. Ok? As long as you let me... and as long as you are willing to stay true to yourself. Ok?" he takes my hand, squeezing it encouragingly, "I will stay by you."

My chest tightens with affection, but there's also brief fear. Because what if one day I can't stay true to myself? Will he leave then...? We made a vow, but it's new, fragile. What happens if everything shifts? "Thank you, Leon." I say, moving forward and laying my head on his shoulder. I let him hold me like that... let him wash away the darkness with his light.

∎∎∎

I wake up the next morning and everything feels off. I'm alone in the room, but the air feels filled with something… and it makes my head hazy. I almost think perhaps I'm about to have a vision, but this doesn't feel familiar. As I move through the back door, trying to hurry my feet, I'm painfully aware of how slow it seems like I'm moving. Panic starts to hit me the moment I look in at the kitchen, and my eyes widen at the scene.

Something felt odd as the room filled with silence and everything seemed to move in slow motion. I look around, seeing Leon's lips moving as hidden words left his mouth, his grandfather smiling as he offered his hand to Leon. Finally, my gaze fell on Galen who was staring at me sadly. Something was very wrong. He shook his head slowly as I felt the icy grasp on my reality take hold.

I closed my eyes to focus on the feeling and somehow, I envisioned a person I had never seen before—white-blonde hair, bright blue eyes, and a thin angled chin. The man was beautiful, though he reminded me of what I had once pictured Jack Frost to look like. He was hiding behind the door, with his hand touching the thick wood frame. While everyone else became entirely frozen, I walked by them like a slowly moving picture. I felt a surge of prickly, invisible frost puncture my limbs. I gasped at the odd sensation and a new anger cascaded through me as I saw the door open and the man came through easily and smoothly.

As he reached my brother, I felt a frenzy burst inside of me. A scream left my lips and I broke free of the frozen frame, my feet pounding towards him. He didn't expect me when the breath left his chest as he hit the floor with a powerful thud. My family remained frozen, most likely for at least fifteen minutes—the usual time a moderately strong Freezy could keep multiple people frozen—while I held the man to the floor.

He stared up at me in shock before looking back towards the picture he had created and back to me, "Ah, so you are the Decider I heard about?" he said in awed respect. He smiled devilishly as he dared to grab my waist, "I've been waiting to meet you for a long time, Decider." He pulled me closer to him and I slapped him hard in the face as I jumped away from his body.

"I want you to get out of here, *now*!" I hissed. He laughed, and it fueled the fire building inside me.

"We still have about an hour until your family wakes up anyways." My eyes widened at the thought, "If I promise not to touch your family again during that time, perhaps we can talk civilly?" he said with a devilish grin, pointing regally towards the table in the den for us to sit.

I considered him, "You can't touch me either." I warned with glaring eyes.

He smirked suavely, "I'll do my best to keep my hands off you." He said with a wink. Though I wanted to hate him knowing he was on the wrong side, there was something I found I liked about this stranger. I should keep up the anger, the frustration, the distrust, but something inside me didn't want to. I hesitantly nodded, trying not to meet his gaze yet. We went to the table and he sat across from me.

We sat silently for a few minutes before I broke the silence, "How can you keep so many people frozen for so long? I've only heard of Freezy's keeping that many people like that for like 20 minutes tops, and that's for the more experienced Freezer."

He laughed heartily, his brilliant eyes glowing with mischief and pride, "Starting at the big stuff, huh? Not even my name first?"

I sighed, "What's your name, Freezy?" I said with a scowl.

He grinned, "Jeremiah Thomas. And your name is?" but I saw something under the devilish likability that he was hiding.

"Kayd." I mutter with feigned irritation.

He seemed to be waiting for the rest of my name, but finally nodded simply before taking a deep breath and speaking, "I have been part of the President's Army since I was 5 years old." My chest tightens at the implication, and my heart aches for the 5-year-old boy with white hair and big blue eyes. Compassion fills my heart, but I try to stifle it. Jeremiah went on, clearly none the wiser about my internal dilemma, "He doesn't let our powers go to waste, so he makes sure we are trained as early as possible, and as strong as possible. My guide was an 80-year-old Freezer bent on keeping the Freezy's the strongest of the Dangerous Ones. So even though I'm only 18, I have the strength of at least a 60 or 70-year-old power."

I tried not to show my awe, but it was hard to hide, knowing that I desired to have that kind of control. Maybe this mystery man was the answer to my many dilemmas in the area of guiding my powers, "And why are you here?"

He watched me carefully, obviously trying to look me in the eye, "For you." He said with captivating ease.

I glowered playfully, "I'm being serious."

He smiled softly as he leaned back in his chair, "Me too. There are a few of the others who have quite the power-crush on you, and I decided to break away for now to see if I could find you." He replied conversationally, flicking a piece of grass off of his tightly fitted shirt. I couldn't help but notice the taught muscles beneath.

I scoffed, "You would really risk going out on your own just to find a little 17-year-old runaway?"

"I heard you were 16." He said with an interested smile.

"It's called a birthday. Even runaways have them..." He seemed to catch me off guard at every turn. I couldn't help but smile as I looked up at him bashfully.

He chuckled back with a friendly nod. I made a decision in that moment, knowing that of course there was the risk of Jeremiah failing the test, but something in my heart told me I already knew what would happen.

I dared to meet his gaze, and he seemed surprised as he fell into my eyes. The entire room filled with sparkling blue-green light like I had never seen before. It was so beautiful, and it sent shivers all through my body—he was not evil, not even a little bit. I looked away as tears filled my eyes for a moment. I felt a hand on my cheek as I looked up and saw Jeremiah kneeling in front of me cradling my face so gently. Leon was not in my mind in that moment as I looked at a man with a purer heart than I would ever see, and allowed his face to inch closer to mine.

"Kayd? Are you ok?" his voice whispered across the table. I let my eyes lift to realize he had not left his spot. Had that been another vision? Or had it been something I simply wanted after seeing such goodness?

I could not shake what I had seen, could not comprehend a backup plan for what to say as the words fell out, "You are so good..." I whispered in awe.

He stared at me curiously, and I could see how vulnerable he was under his mask, "What are you talking about?" he scoffed.

I shook my head, wanting desperately to say anything that felt strong, but those were not the words that formed on my lips, "You are not dangerous." I murmured.

He laughed bitterly, staring out a window, "Of course I am. You already saw my power." He said with that same mask of strength, but I saw something beneath it that ran deep.

I came over to him without question and knelt in front of him, and he looked down at me with surprised uncertainty, "Tell me how you are still good, Jeremiah." I pleaded, "Please... how do you stay good with these powers?" I couldn't help the unwelcome tears that filled my eyes as I begged for the answer

He considered me with soft affection and complete uncertainty, "You saw into me?" I nodded almost desperately, but he shook his head, looking completely crestfallen, letting my hand fall from his, "Whatever you saw, it must be wrong. I have not done a single good thing in my entire life. I guess the Decider gift isn't as great as everyone thought." He said distantly, but I could sense that he wanted my words to be true. After seeing that purity in him, everything about him seemed to be incredibly easy to read. All my Gifts seemed to work at once with him. I wished I could always have that kind of clarity.

"Jeremiah, my Gift is never wrong. That's why I won't look Leon's father in the eye—I have a feeling it won't be a good consensus." He gazed back at me in sudden surprise, "I don't look unless I am already pretty sure what I will see. I just expected to see you were not rotten. I have never seen anything like you, Jeremiah." The awe was too bold in my tender tone.

His eyes flashed with desire, and then he wiped it away, trying so hard to look cold and hard, "I came to take you with me, maybe even kill your boyfriend to get you." He replied cruelly, "Does that really sound like someone good?" he challenged with an unfriendly smile, trying to make it cold, but his eyes gave him away.

The air went foggy for a moment, and everything felt familiar as I watched our lips touch, but I knew it wasn't happening. I couldn't understand what kept making me think of it. I shook my head and he watched me. "I know you are with Leon Hensley, yet I would make you mine now."

I can't help the soft smile that brushes my lips. I didn't hesitate as I said with certainty, "No you wouldn't." it shocked him... I could see how deeply my words caught him.

He suddenly seemed furious as he stood, looking down at me, "How are you so sure?" He said, pulling me to my feet effortlessly, and pulling me close to him. I felt breathless as I looked into his pained eyes. He wanted to kiss me, but I could see his moral dilemma. Before he leaned in, I said quietly,

"Leon is my husband." Jeremiah stopped inches from my lips, completely floored by the thought, just like I knew he would be. He still tried to move forward, but right as his lips were about to grace mine, he quickly pulled away angrily.

"Why are you upset?" I asked, my head tilted as I watched him.

He shook his head, tears seemed to peek out on the corner of his deeply unhappy eyes, "I'm not good, Kayd..." he forced out, pained.

I sigh, nodding in understanding, "Just because you do bad things does not make you a bad person. You can stop doing bad things, but it is much harder to take evil out once it sets into your soul."

His face lightened, but I could tell he was afraid to believe it, "Hensley is lucky..." he replied simply, "Damn..." he says suddenly as he looks around, "I guess that emotional overload is messing with my power." He chuckles miserably. I follow his gaze to the kitchen and I see everyone's bodies seeming to move a little again. "I feel my effects wearing off on your family, so I should be on my way," he began as he headed for the door, but as his hand touched the handle he turned back, "I wish I'd met you sooner, Kayd... maybe we could've helped each other to fight that evil within us." The softness in his eyes was exactly the gentleness I had seen in the brief vision I'd seen after looking into his eyes.

I dared to come closer to him, and I felt that sparkling green-blue light again as I went to touch his shoulder, "We still could."

He smiled gently, taking my hand in both of his, patting it softly and setting my hand back into the empty air, "Not quite the same way I meant, Kayd." He said regretfully. As soon as the door shut, everyone began moving at the same time, running towards me in worry, but my heart still saw everything in slow motion.

Who was Jeremiah, and why did I feel like this towards him? A feeling so deep that I'd only thought my new husband could make me feel this way. Is this the reason 17-year-olds shouldn't get married?

Leon nearly flew past me as he went for the door, prepared to fight whoever he needed to get me back. I touched his arm gently and he turned back in surprise, "Kayd? Thank God!" He said, pulling me briskly into a bear hug. "Twice in two days I almost lost you... I can't lose you Kayd. I love you." He whispered in my ear.

"I love you too."

I wanted to say, *"You won't lose me."* But I had a bad feeling that he had already just lost a little bit of me in the half hour that he had been unaware, and I had been more awake than I had ever been.

Chapter 13: Reminder

Nothing was right anymore as I counted down the time till the next disaster, and I tried so hard not to let myself become distant from Leon, but Jeremiah was stuck in my mind. Leon was oblivious to what had happened, happy to snuggle in bed with his wife, while my mind wandered to another 'what-if' I had not seen coming. I was lost in an entirely new world of confusion and pain. I loved Leon, there was no doubt in my mind for a second on that account, but Jeremiah captured me. I had never even worried about being torn between two men considering I had never believed I would find a single man that would be captured by me the same way I was for him.

Leon had asked about what had happened, and my only explanation for him was that I had accidentally used my Freezy Gift. I felt guilty for not telling the truth, but part of me wanted to keep Jeremiah to myself, even if it was only the memory of him from a 20-minute talk. I had barely spoken to anyone in the five days since meeting him, but Galen hadn't spoken to anyone either. Though I still was feeling like being silent a little longer, I felt the need to speak to Galen.

I found him sitting outside in the garden, "Galen, why are you sitting out here all by yourself."

He sighed, "You met Jeremiah..." he whispered. I stared at him in shock, even though I should never be surprised by Galen's knowledge anymore.

I cleared my throat, not meeting his eye, "Well yes, but why does that have you so depressed?"

He shook his head and took in a very deep breath, his eyes closed, and said, "I'm afraid, Kayd."

My brows knitted together in instant concern, "Of what?"

"Of everything!" he said, almost shouting.

I sat beside him carefully, wanting to put my arm around him, "Is this about your vision about dying?" I said as calmly as I could, trying to dehumanize the thought, because that was the only way to push away the pain so I could be his tough big sister.

He shook with rage, "It's not just about dying, Kayd! It is about all my damn visions!" he screamed, pushing my arms away from him, pulling his knees to his chest. I stared in shock—when did he even learn that word? Forgetting, as usual, that he was not a child anymore.

"Talk to me, Galen... what are you feeling?"

Tears pounded down his cheeks, but he didn't let his soft innocence show this time as he jumped to his feet, "I don't want this anymore, Kayd! I don't want to see, because in reality, what can I do to change any of it? Every time I think I have affected anything, reality comes back to smile smugly in my face, reminding me that I can't control anything... starting with the oh-so-daunting 'my death!'" I could see Leon out of the corner of my eye, ready to meet us outside to check on Galen. I shook my head gently and raised my hand to him and he nodded, backing up into the kitchen. "I just don't know anything anymore." He fell back into his crumpled position on the cement bench.

"Galen, if there is one thing I am 100% sure about, it is that you know more than most people 20 years older than you. So, you see visions of the future, and then find out you can't control them, that is basically life." I said with a soft smile, tapping him on the shoulder. He dared to look back at me. I wiped away a few of his tears, "Life is thinking you have complete control, and then realizing that you never had control at all. You weren't given this Gift so you could change the future, Galen—you have it so that you can know what was coming." Galen nodded silently, sniffing as he wiped his nose.

Finally, he looked at me again and let his head fall softly on my shoulder. I smiled as I caressed his head, closing my eyes as we listened together to the orchestra of the forest as it played around us. I held my brother then, reminding me of a much simpler time, even if that time was made up of us running for our lives. Those days, now so long ago, were more peaceful.

After sitting with Galen for a while, I walked him back inside and put him to bed. Instantly I knew what I had to do. I went back to the kitchen and found Leon. He gave me a small grin, "Hey there, gorgeous." I didn't say another word as I practically lunged at him with a large hug. He seemed surprised at first, but tenderly embraced me back. "Are you ok?"

I stared at his neck, playing with his shirt as I continued to hold him, "There is something I need to tell you, actually..."

He pulled away slightly to look me in the eye, "What is it, sweetheart?"

I let out my breath, "Last week when I told you I had accidentally used a Gift?"

He nodded, "The Freezy Gift, right?"

I gave a single nod, "I lied..." He sat back in the chair, he seemed taken aback, but not angry yet, and I continued to sit on his lap. "There was actually a Freezy that came here."

"Why wouldn't you just tell me that?" he said with slight relief mixed with confusion. I got up and sat in the chair across from him. He watched me with concern.

"His name was Jeremiah." I said with a shaky voice, trying not to meet his eye.

Leon considered me cautiously, leaning forward, "Ok... Kayd I'm confused."

I sighed and finally met his eye, "He froze all of you for almost a half an hour..." Leon's eyes widened in shock as he mouthed a simple *Oh*...

"And..." he shifted uncomfortably in his chair, putting his hands on his knees, and closed his eyes, "And what happened..." he looked betrayed as he took in another breath, "during that half hour?"

"Nothing happened… we just talked." I quickly forced out the words.

I could tell he was trying very hard to stay calm, but it was easy to see he was drawing very close to the line between calmness and being crushed. "If you 'just talked' then why couldn't you tell me, Kayd? It was obviously more than that…" he pressed, his voice sharing his unease.

"It wasn't… it wasn't!" I said, almost as if I was convincing myself.

He laughed miserably, "You are doing a great job to convince me…" he said, putting his hands to his face.

"Truly, we only talked…" I urged, moving my chair closer to him.

"But—"

"But…?" tears filled my eyes.

"Why couldn't you tell me Kayd? Something happened, even if it is something that was said, that caused you to keep this from me!" I could feel his anger and worry swell, almost becoming a little unhinged.

"I saw into him!" I finally shouted back. He watched me with shocked confusion.

His eyes widened, "And what? You killed him because he was evil?" he said a little harsher than I think he meant to sound. He seemed to catch his words as he gave a slightly guilty look.

I scoffed back as agony filled my chest, "What is that supposed to mean, Leon? I have tried really hard to control my Gift!" I matched his anger, fierce tears flowing freely from my eyes now.

He shook his head, his voice taming a little, "I didn't mean for that to come out that way, Kayd... I just wondered if that was what happened since you usually don't let yourself even look people in the eye anymore."

I stared at the floor, "I didn't think he was bad when I used my Gift. And it turned out he wasn't..."

Leon's eyes shared his internal panic, "Wasn't, what?"

I sighed, "He wasn't bad, Leon. Honestly, he had the purest heart I had ever seen. When I told him that, he tried to prove to me he was bad. He knew I was with you, so he..."

"So he, what?!" Leon said in alarm.

"So, he went to kiss me, but before he did, I told him you were not just my boyfriend but my husband. Almost instantly he pulled away." Leon stared at me blankly, "So see? Nothing happened. Quickly after, he left and took his hold off of all of you." I said with as much of a reassuring smile as I could muster.

He sat down again, staring at his hands, "Why didn't you tell me, Kayd?" He said again with deep sorrow.

My chest is tight with words unsaid, "I don't understand why you are still so sad. I just told you that nothing happened." I said evasively.

He looked up at me, and a single tear lingered in his eyelashes, and that tear broke me, "Then why didn't you tell me?" my heart shattered at his expression, and I realized I was asking myself the same question...

"I just... didn't know how to say it. You were already so worried about me, and I didn't want you to worry anymore." I lied, not meeting his gaze.

Leon shook his head harshly and stood, watching me with pained eyes, "Kayd, *tell me!*" he said, his voice bellowing around the room like an echoing cave.

I felt it—the overwhelming urge to do what he asked—and I knew he was using his Gift on me as I said, "I might love him..." my mouth dropped as the words left my lips and tears swelled in my eyes. That couldn't be what I really thought, or could it? My hand flew to my mouth, though the damage had already been done. Leon was completely destroyed—his eyes showing the intense hurt my words had caused him. I don't think anyone could have caused him the sort of betrayal I had just caused by one simple thought: I *might* love him.

Leon nodded lightly and walked outside. Galen came running downstairs, and I knew he must've had a vision, "Don't let him go, Kayd!"

"He needs a moment alone, Galen." I force out, hiding my tears.

Galen shook his head adamantly, "You will never see him again if you let him leave, Kayd!" My body felt heavy as I nodded simply to him and went after Leon. He was just sitting outside where we had been married only two weeks ago. I sat across from him with my legs crossed.

We sat silently for a while, "I'm sorry I used my Gift on you." He muttered with a cracking voice.

"I'm sorry I didn't just tell you sooner. The longer I was left to my thoughts is what caused those feelings, I think." He nodded distantly.

He was quiet for a beat before sharing the ache on his heart, "Do you still want to be with me, Kayd?" I moved closer to him, taking his hand in mine,

"Of course, I do, Leon. I don't love you any less." I promised him, and in my heart, I knew that was true.

He stared at the wood planks of the gazebo, "Can I ask you a question?" he said quietly

"Of course."

He looked up to meet my gaze, "How could you have fallen in love with this guy after only a half hour?" the question caught me off guard.

"I didn't say I'd fallen in love with him…" I muttered quietly.

He nodded with a tired sigh, "I just need to know how you could think you might love him after so short a time."

I sighed, never feeling quite so out of place, "I felt like I already knew him, I guess... and there was something about when I saw him through my Gift. I don't know..."

Silence overtook us once more before he took my hand, "I'm sorry for yelling before. I've just never loved anyone the way I love you, and I don't want to lose what we have." He said, his voice cracking. He coughed and looked away.

"I will never even see him again, Leon. You don't have anything to worry about."

Leon became tense, "Oh but if you did see him again, I would have something to worry about?" his voice rose again.

I didn't know what to do, my eyes wide, "Leon, please stop all this. I am in love with you—my husband. Yes, I'll admit I was attracted to him, but that doesn't mean for one second that there is, or ever will be, anything between us." I never thought I would see Leon act so crazy, but would I be any different in the reverse situation?

He shook his head fiercely and rose to his feet. "Kayd, I just need a minute, ok?" he said, beginning to walk away. I had a bad feeling that I couldn't shake, and I didn't know how to stop the flashback. I became suddenly stuck in a moment that was not real.

I stared at my father, he was younger now, and so was I. I just stared at him, waiting for him to say something, but no words came.

He grabbed my hand from the ground, "Don't let people see that." He had said when I had tried to put those little flowers back in the ground when he had taken me to the waterfall. I now remembered… when I put the flowers back into the ground, they started growing again, gaining back the color that temporary death had stolen. "I'll protect you, always, Kaydy, but you have to protect yourself too. Don't get tied down ever—it is a weakness."

I was brought back to reality, staring at my husband, and suddenly my heart was more distant from him than I ever expected. I didn't like it, and I wondered how something I had forgotten, could suddenly impact me so much by remembering it for a single moment. I felt off, like something was suddenly missing inside me, yet I felt stronger than I'd ever felt before. I went away from him then, walking back to the place we temporarily called our home. I let my head fall to the bed, staring up at the wood paneling of the bed frame. I wanted to feel normal, whatever normal meant.

I hoped that our talk was enough for me not to lose my chance to see Leon again, but at that moment I knew there was nothing more for me to do. I pulled the blanket over my fully clothed body, not even having the energy to remove my shoes. I let the darkness crowd in as I fell into unconsciousness. As I wandered into sleep, I dreamt for what seemed like the first time in weeks.

I stared at Leon as he drifted from my side, pulled from me by an angry slap to the face. He turned away from me and walked away. I told my feet to move, to run after him, but my feet did not move. I watched as the love of my life drifted from my side, and I felt so lost and broken. I looked down at my hands, my arms feeling so heavy, realizing I was holding something large and wrapped in thick tarp. I set the package on the ground and opened it—inside was the body of my brother. I fell to my knees beside him, and my heart seemed to be pulled out of my chest. All I wanted was Leon to come back and be with me as I mourned my brother, but instead Jeremiah came to my side. He lifted my brother,

"I will protect him, Kayd. You have to go now, before someone catches you. Go!" He urged. I felt such joy and hope at seeing him, though at the same time I wanted to honor Leon, so I tried to push those feelings away.

I woke up feeling so disoriented in the now dark room. Though it had been morning when I fell asleep, it was already well past 9:00 pm. I looked around for Leon, but he was still gone. Panic overwhelmed me as I jumped out of bed, ready to search the woods for him. I ran down the stairs, grabbing my jacket as I went to venture into the night, but just as I opened the door, I saw something move out of the corner of my eye. I turned towards the movement with my guard up, but it was just Leon sitting at the small table in our cottage. I jumped when I saw him, and he smiled weakly through the dim candlelight.

"I didn't mean to scare you, sorry."

I cautiously sat in front of him, "No... *I* didn't mean to scare you." I said delicately to him, grabbing his hand, so thankful to see him.

He tilted his head at me, "You didn't, Kayd."

I shook my head, "I mean about Jeremiah. I thought about it even as I slept, and I had this dream... and it made me realize something—I could never, *never* love anyone the way I love you, Leon. You have my heart, and I am so sorry that I scared you to believe anything else."

He nodded, still apparently in thought, "I trust you Kayd, but I can' help but think about the possibilities. I trust you, but I'm not sure I trust him." Instead of pushing the idea further, I just smiled brightly and leaned over the table to kiss him.

"Thank you for trusting me, Leon. I love you." He smiled back and kissed me tenderly.

Chapter 14: Losing

I felt it before I heard the familiar snapping of twigs outside. My head shot up in bed and I quickly snuck over to the window. Leon sleepily looked over at me as he rubbed his eyes, "Kayd, what're you doing?" I waved my hand at him, but he simply stood up and walked over to me. The floor squeaked and I felt the glare come to my eyes as I stared at him, forgetting that he had not endured the same training my brother had from being with me for years. Where Galen knew all the usual protocols to stay safe from possible attackers, Leon's only instinct was running before any attackers could come.

"Get on the floor." I commanded, and he obliged, though his expression was filled with confusion. It had been a few days since Leon and my fight, but it felt like months as close as we had become again. But thinking about how much time we had been at Leon's grandfather's home reminded me that Galen had warned me that it would be at this home he'd be taken.

There were at least 5 men with guns scouring the lawn. I needed to get to Galen, but I didn't know how without being noticed, and usually the Soldiers were prepared for any kind of Gifted man or woman. My natural instinct, however, never seemed to care about what was technically right or not. I ran down the stairs, though being as quiet as I could be.

"Kayd, wait!" Leon said quietly, trying to grab my arm. He couldn't stop me though, as I walked into the yard, fearless as I froze the men to their spots without thought. I felt an odd fire shoot through my veins as I went to the man closest to the main house's back door. None of them were wearing the Soldiers' normal helmets that deflect Gifts. The man closest to me stared back, fear obvious in his eyes, but not a corrupted soul... it was so odd as my Gift began to take its usual course, I realized something wasn't right. I went to the next man in a hurry, and the same thing, and again with the third man, though I didn't let my Gift fully decide on the other men. Whoever had sent these men, sent them because they were innocents, probably prisoners they had been holding for this exact moment.

That's when I realized, these were not the men I should've been worried about. My heart dropped as I heard the muffled scream of my brother. I started running into the house, ready to fight if I had to, but instead, Leon was holding me back, his hand over my mouth as he pushed me quietly into the shed. I howled through his hand, trying so hard to break free, to save Galen.

I knew what this moment meant, but obviously Leon had forgotten... this was the moment before my brother was going to die. I don't think I could imagine ever being as furious at Leon as I was in this moment. I kept thrashing against him, when I felt the familiar ping I didn't like as Leon looked into my eyes, telling me to be sleep. I obeyed instantly.

I woke up later when the sun had risen high in the sky—probably 5 hours had passed. I shook with fury as I looked around to see I was in Leon's grandfather's house. I quickly stood, ready to get out of the house and look for my brother, also ready to take my husband down if he got in my way, but as I entered the living room, I only found Leon's grandfather. He was sitting so calmly in his reclining chair, and before even a sound could leave my lips, he spoke first, "Leon won't find him, Kayd."

Tears trickled out of my eyes as I listened in fear, "He went looking?"

He nodded, "He did. He left five minutes after you fell asleep."

"I didn't fall asleep! He *put* me to sleep!" I shouted.

He tilted his head at me, "Is that what matters right now, Kayd?" he was too calm. It hurt to have him be so calm when everything within me was being pulled apart. "Did you hear me, girl? Leon won't find him..."

I sat on the couch in front of him, "I know he won't... that's why he should have just let me go after Galen instead!"

He shook his head, "I'm sorry dear, but Galen told Leon that when the time came, that Leon would have to keep you back no matter what it took so you didn't follow."

I slammed my fist on the couch, "Dammit! If Galen would stop telling us what to do, I could save him!"

He watched me quietly for a moment before speaking, "He already told you, Kayd—he was always meant to die. But if you had followed, his pain and death would have been prolonged. This way, he dies quickly." I felt as if someone stabbed me in the stomach and ripped out my heart simultaneously. The room began to spin, but I held the cushions for balance. Had I really allowed myself to drift into a delusion that he would magically not die? He was never wrong, yet I kept comforting myself by saying he was this time. But this was the beginning of the end.

"You are a Prophet as well, right?" He nodded, "Then tell me… when does it happen? He never told me the day." I said sternly, my expression set.

He watched me with his cold blue eyes, "Look for yourself, Kayd. Your gifts well exceed my own, or even your brother's. Maybe you will find he was wrong all along?"

I couldn't tell if he was kidding or not, so I closed my eyes, and focused on my brother. My powers were more defined, more focused than ever before with my anger and devastation. I felt the world shift beneath me as I gazed into Galen's sad future. It was maybe one month from right now, maybe sooner, in one of the President's facilities in Montana. I could only see blurred moments and places, yet I knew at least what I wanted—when and where. I pulled out of the vision to see Paul watching me with care, "What did you see?"

I stood on shaking legs, "Montana, one month at most."

He nodded, "In the North Town Facility." He said like it was an old memory.

"How did you know that?"

He smiled sadly, "That's where they take Prophets for interrogation, but usually not where they kill them. I'm a little surprised at how he manages to die." I hated the way he was talking about Galen, like he was already dead... like it was his own fault he was dying. "It's a shame you will never get there in time." His eyes met mine for a moment before I jumped across the coffee table at him. I slapped him hard and he acted like it was nothing.

"You see what just happened?" he said calmly as he wiped a trickle of blood from his lip. I was somehow back on the couch, my hands still gripping the seat. I looked around in confusion, meeting his gaze once more to see the blood that should be on his lip was gone.

"What *did* just happen?" I said with my eyes wide in fear and shock.

He sighed, "I allowed you to see a potential future. I chose the most aggravating, and drastic, possibility I could think of for you to see."

"I don't understand... why would you do that?" I said as my body loosened slightly, but I was still on edge, suddenly wondering if I was really in the here and now or not.

He smirked sadly, sitting back in his chair, "Because Kayd, I want you to understand how your brother found he was going to die. I would never, ever, talk to you like that possibility insinuated, but I tested the possibility anyways. Your brother looked at not just likely things to happen, he looked at the most unlikely decisions you, or

Leon, or he would make, and yet every possibility still led to the same moment. When dealing with Prophecy, there is a lot of give and take on what you allow yourself to see, and what you realize you shouldn't toy with. Galen realized too late that he should never have looked at every possibility, because now he is left wondering: which way will I die? Who will try and save me? Instead of following the one path he should've watched. You are the one he should've been watching, Kayd… because, though you can't stop his death, you can get to him. You can see your brother before he dies."

I didn't know how to take anything he was saying, because he wasn't exactly saying anything positive, but he wasn't being negative either, "Will I see him die, Paul?" I whispered fearfully, my voice sounding small.

He considered me for a minute before nodding, "Yes, you will."

I held my breath for a moment, my tears pouring down my cheeks, and my head throbbing at the thought of my next question, "Am I the reason he dies?"

He watched me again with care, "Yes."

I nodded miserably, my entire body shaking as I let it sink in. "If I don't go though, he could last longer…"

He shook his head, "Kayd… one of the ways he could die is suicide." I looked back at him in pure horror.

"Excuse me?" I couldn't move…

"People who are taken by the Authority, especially Prophets, are used to find information, often about those they had traveled with before being caught. Your brother is strong, but even he knows his limit, and if you never come, he will kill himself to protect you and Leon."

I couldn't take this… I couldn't! My brother could *not* kill himself. I could not ever let that happen, but knowing he will die from me being there was almost as heartbreaking. Then another thought hit me: what if I was the one who killed him? *Oh God… that can't happen.*

"I need to go now. I can't waste another minute."

He gently touched my hand as I stood. "You need to wait for Leon." He urged.

I shook my head with instant panic, "That could be another 5 hours for all I know!"

He nodded. "It could, but you already have your answer of when and where, and you know it can't be avoided. It doesn't hurt to wait for Leon." I sighed and fell back into my seat. I tried waiting with Paul in the living room, but he was still so quiet, even when he tried to start conversation, the words felt empty and distant.

After I couldn't handle the forced chitchat any longer, I finally retreated back to mine and Leon's cabin. I sat on my bed, never feeling more alone as the sun began to set again, knowing that my brother had been gone now for almost a day. I felt so useless, like having all this power didn't really mean anything, and I felt myself drifting. I closed my eyes as I pulled my pillow close to my chest, breathing into it as I fell into slumber.

My mind focused on Galen, taking me back to when he was only 4 years old, right before the visions began, and before I started showing signs of being Gifted either. I was 8, but sometimes I felt like we were the same age, even though I was a good foot taller than him. He wore that old blue bowtie, and I wore the little red overall dress with my long braids hanging down my back. We would run through the smaller trees behind our house, weaving in and out as if we could trick the magical creatures to come out and play with us.

My thoughts moved forward to when Galen was 8 and he had *the* vision, the one of the Green-eyed Man—when I instantly felt my childhood sucked away from me. I wanted to cry at the memory of my brother's sweet naivety as he proclaimed his vision at a party my mother had thrown for some friends, thinking that everyone would want to know, not realizing that his vision was like committing treason to our dictator.

All I could focus on was his sweet smile and big eyes. Then I thought back to him now at 13 years old, with his eyes looking like a man much older and wiser—sadder. His thin chin had transformed into a strong jaw with light stubble wiping over his cheeks, and his knobby little legs had grown to be much stronger and longer now, pushing him at least three inches taller than me. I pictured his smile—trying to catalog every memory I had of those smiles, knowing that I would never see them again. Though Paul had told me

I would indeed see Galen once more, it would be the moment that he died... and I couldn't imagine another smile happening again.

I awoke later to the sound of pouring rain outside. When I looked around the room, I found Leon walking in, soaked to the bone, looking beyond troubled. He collapsed on the bed, covering his eyes with his hands. I laid next to him for a few minutes silently, but I could hear his quick breaths as he tried not to cry, "I'm sorry I couldn't get him..." He forced out finally.

I put my hand on his shoulder, "We weren't supposed to get him... but I know where we can find him."

He pulled his hands away from his face and looked at me with care, "We can leave now if you want."

I looked out the window, watching the moon as it began to rise and say goodnight to the sun. I shook my head, and closed my eyes, "We will leave in the morning." I felt his eyes on me, but I couldn't meet his gaze right now.

The distance between us overtook the room, but I wasn't sure anymore if the distance was just because I was angry about my brother or if it was something else... something deeper inside. The only thing I knew for sure about this rift was that it was because of me.

I stared out at the slowly lightening sky, with my heart pounding in my ears. My eyes unwilling to let me fall into slumber as I lay next to Leon. I found my feet moving me down the stairs without another thought before wandering out into the deserted lawn. My entire body was on fire, and my skin felt like someone was ripping it off of me. It was as if something was pulling me out here, yanking me by my soul. My knees hit the ground with a painful thud as the world began to scream out in my mind. I couldn't understand what was happening to me...

I tried so hard not to scream out in pain, but whatever was trying to get out of me, my body was putting up quite a fight. Suddenly my vision intensified and the entire forest around Paul's home seemed to glow. I stood, watching the odd illuminated world around me transform before my eyes. The glow disappeared, but in that moment, I felt my true strength bloom, almost as if someone else was lending me their strength, and I felt overwhelmingly powerful. I took in a deep breath wanting to see if what I was feeling was actually my power or if it was something else.

I closed my eyes and thought back through my treasured memories, and the one that stood out was when my father and I had gone to Westin Falls and picked those little flowers. "Grow." I whispered as I pictured the blue violets, the bright orange poppies, and the vibrant yellow daffodils. As I opened my eyes, looking towards a small, dead flower patch near Paul's home, I was saddened to see that not a single new flower had bloomed.

I shook my head with a small smile, "I should've known better..." But as I turned around to go back towards Leon and my cottage, my bare feet imprinted on a colorful field of flowers. I looked around again and realized the entire ground was covered in the budding beauties. My hand flew to my mouth as tears welled up in my eyes—I finally could control my Gifts. Exhilaration moved through me at the idea, but I couldn't help but feel a little unlike myself...

I didn't know where the understanding had finally come from, or why my body went through so much pain to tap into the power, but I didn't really want to question too much. I felt such exhilaration as I played in the flowers, rolling around in their soft embrace, forgetting entirely about all the pain, all the frustration, and all the dark reality that usually consumed my thoughts. This was my time to be a child one last time before journeying into the saddest stage of my entire life.

I lay in the flowers, staring at the last few stars lingering in the dawning light, and closed my eyes. I didn't dream or have visions, and it was so nice to have such a calming and restful sleep. When I finally awoke, it was to Leon touching my face and whispering gently to me. I smiled at his touch and he instantly breathed a sigh of relief, "I go to sleep with you next to me, and when I wake up you are gone, and then I find you sleeping in a mysterious field of flowers that was not here yesterday."

I smiled softly, "I couldn't sleep in there."

He watched me with care, "And the flowers were just already here?" he asked with a concerned eyebrow raise.

I stretched happily as the sun warmed my cheeks, "They were here when I came down." I lied, though I didn't know why I chose not to tell him. He nodded his head, pursing his lips slightly.

"Well we should probably get going." He said distantly, picking up the old black bag my brother and I had carried for almost four years. I expected more of a ping inside my heart at the thought of my brother, but little pain came. I tried not to linger on a possible answer to that, and just nodded at my husband. I grabbed a bag of food from Paul's kitchen, exchanged our goodbyes, and headed out the door.

As Leon and I began our journey to basically recover my brother's body, we were completely silent. I felt as though Galen and I were traveling together again—Galen always knew to stay as silent as possible when we were moving. But having Leon be the silent one felt wrong... Leon was the happy-go-lucky one that motivated us all forward when we felt low. Now Leon was the stern, quiet man beside me. After a few hours of walking, my feet couldn't handle walking anymore—our nearly three weeks of vacation had made my body weak.

"Leon, can we please stop?"

He looked back at me as if I had just appeared. He nodded lightly and sat down on a large rock shaped slightly like a boot. Leon tossed me a bottle of water, as he chugged one down as well, throwing the empty bottle into his bag. He reclined on the rock and covered his eyes with his hand. It hurt me deeply to see Leon so quiet and distant, even though I usually did the same—it wasn't in his nature to be so quiet.

"Leon, why are you being so distant?"

He sighed, "I love your brother too, Kayd… aren't I allowed to mourn the fact that there is nothing we can do to save him now?"

I nodded carefully, hesitating before I spoke. There was something nagging inside of me, telling me there was more to what had happened when Leon went looking for Galen, "Something happened when you went after him, didn't it?" I finally asked.

He took his hand away and looked at me with a deadly gaze, "Did you look into your crystal ball to figure that out?" he said through gritted teeth.

His ferocity cut me deeply. I stepped away, trying to hide the tears, "Why are you treating me like this?"

He closed his eyes and put his hand back over them, his lip quivering as he went to speak, "I had him, Kayd… I caught up to them." I watched him in shock as he stared up at the sky.

Pain pierced my heart deeply, "Did someone hurt you?"

He shook his head, "No… I caught up to them when they were taking a rest. Galen went by a stream to wash his hands, and I knocked out the guard watching him. I started taking the ropes off of Galen's hands…" He held his fists tightly together, "He told me I wasn't supposed to save him. He said I had to leave because I was too important…" He slammed his fist on the rock, a sliver of blood dripped from his hand.

I came closer to him, putting my hand on his gently. He looked at my hand with question, "Leon, Galen always has us in mind. He already knew there was nothing for us to do."

Leon laughed darkly, "He told me this would happen…."

"Told you what would happen?"

He watched a yellow bird jumping from branch to branch above him, "That you would lie to me…"

"What could I be lying to you about?"

"He told me about the visions of the Green-eyed Man… he told me how he had warned you that you would help him to defeat our Dictator."

My eyes widened, more at the harshness behind Leon's tone, "So? I'm not lying to you about that…"

He watched me with an almost unhinged agony in his gaze, "I thought it was fate that brought us together, Kayd, but it was Galen. He told me that originally you and I were never going to meet. He guided the two of you to me…"

I shook my head in disbelief, laughing uncertainly, "No… no… he was surprised when we found you!"

Leon laughed again, "Was he? I remember him being pretty excited about meeting me… about *you* meeting me."

Tears dropped from my eyes, "What are you trying to say, Leon?"

"We were never meant to be together, Kayd. Galen guided you to me because he thought it would protect both of you... and instead it meant that he would die. He is going to die because you are with me. That's what he told me when I found him... when he told me I had to go back to protect you."

My entire body shook as I thought back to all the times Galen had subtly pushed us in different directions, the times he assured me that Leon and I would meet, the times I thought he was crazy. Galen had forced Leon and I onto a path we never would have taken, and almost as a twist of fate, Galen was now being punished for taking us on this path. Galen had urged us to get married, saying that it didn't change whether he died or not... but what if it had? He wanted us together so badly that he pushed himself into a corner. I stumbled backwards, my back slamming against a large tree.

"He didn't want me to join my father..." I whispered painfully, shaking my head as tears poured to the ground.

"What?"

I threw my head back and stared into the sky, "Galen's first vision was of me against the President, Leon... what if you were never meant to be the 'Green-eyed Man', but Galen was trying to protect me? He said before that my father wanted me to join him someday, so what if Galen was trying to keep that vision from coming true? He was trying to have you go against the President instead...."

Leon put his feet back on the ground, "So you didn't know about any of this before?"

I shook my head, "No… when he told me I was going to be with you, I never dreamed it could be true. You were this amazingly handsome, sweet man that was apparently going to be the next leader of our world. I thought he had lost his mind, but instead he was planning for us to be together…"

Leon came over to me and took me in his arms gently. His anger seemed to melt away entirely, "Kayd, he didn't make us fall in love. He may have guided you to me, but I fell in love with you all on my own, and you fell in love with me on your own too. Even if he was just trying to protect you, he must've seen a much brighter future for everyone if we were together." He took in a deep breath, "I'm sorry I blamed you." He whispered softly in my ear.

"But he told you I would lie?" I whispered.

Leon stiffened for a moment, "I probably just inferred that you were lying about your brother's prophecies?" he said with an uncomfortable laugh. He pulled me closer, "Kayd, we shouldn't be mad that Galen brought us together. He obviously didn't know it would mean losing his life, and even if he did, this was his last wish—for us to be together." I watched him with care, sensing he must be right, but it was just too hard to think of my brother being so strategic, just like my father always was. I always had seen my brother as being vulnerable and innocent, but I often forgot about how my mother had abandoned him, and my father only spent time with me. Galen was an orphan long before I was...

Even though everything within me wanted to sob about this discovery, there was something else inside of me that seemed to put a lid on any desperate emotions I had. "I am so sorry for how I treated you." Leon whispered.

I dared to look in his eyes, "It's ok. I'm sorry for how distant I've been." I whispered back. There was so much about what Leon had told me about Galen's push for us to be together that didn't sit right. I of course loved Leon, but when I had met Jeremiah, I had felt so close to him too as if we were always meant to meet... always meant to touch.

Had Galen seen both possibilities? Had he known that I could've been with Jeremiah instead? Could it be possible that my entire future had been altered because of Galen? Galen would still be alive, I could be with Jeremiah, and he could've taught me how to control my abilities sooner... Leon's mom would still be alive, and all those people in our old camp would be alive.

Everything would be different... but then I would never have met Leon. And as I stared at Leon now, the man I loved enough to marry a week before I had even turned 17, I realized no other future was worth the thought. I cuddled close to him then, trying only to think of him and I. I was in love with Leon, and nothing could ever change that... nothing.

Chapter 15: Tense

I was losing count of how many days had passed, or how many times I had seen that rock shaped like the boot. No matter what path Leon and I took, we always ended up right back in this spot, desperately trying to get out. I started losing track of my thoughts as we wandered around and around, while Leon refused to admit that we were stuck in this little patch of forest. I wasn't letting myself drift into the past anymore, but every day I found myself trying to tap into the future. I usually wouldn't allow myself to wander into that hidden place when Leon was around, but the more monotonous our path, the easier it was for my mind to fall back once again.

"Dammit!" Leon finally said slamming his fist against that same rock we had sat on nearly four days before. He pulled me back to the moment too quickly, causing my mind to quickly forget whatever future I had looked into. I had never realized how hard it was to use the Prophetic Gift considering how easy Galen always made it seem. The future is filled with holes, and minor paths you have to take to even peek into it by yourself without the natural push the visions bring.

"What is it?" I said, only slightly aggravated.

He let himself fall to the ground, his back against the rock, and covered his face with his hand again, "We're going in circles!" he shouted.

I rolled my eyes and continued pacing, "Yeah, I've said that since the second time we passed this rock," I whispered.

"What did you say?" he said with a bite to his tone. We were both tired, both overly irritated, and both completely annoyed by each other.

I let out a low breath as I turned to him, "I said I told you we were going in circles two days ago when we passed this rock again."

Leon sighed angrily, pushing his hands into his hair before letting out a calmer breath, "Ok… I'm sorry I didn't listen to you. How do we get out of here?"

All of a sudden, an odd feeling poured over me, a tingling rushing through my fingers as my eyes focused on a small path in front of me. I went forward like someone was pulling me by an invisible rope.

"Kayd?" Leon said with worry, coming to his feet protectively. My mouth moved, but I couldn't hear the words that came out. I offered my hand to him and he took it cautiously.

I didn't know what Gift was possibly guiding me, but whatever it was, it knew what it was doing. "Kayd… where are we going? This isn't even a path." He said apprehensively.

As I stared into the distance it was almost as if I could see the opening to the outside world. The further we trudged through the thick foliage, the harder it became to get through, so without hesitation I raised my hands and the trees bent to my will. Leon watched me with almost an envious gaze, though I could feel an overwhelming fear from him too, but I chose to ignore the sudden and unwarranted impulse to look into his thoughts. I felt amazing as I used my different abilities by my own choice, and the power was exhilarating.

Without saying another word, I led us to the edge of the forest, staring out across an open field filled with wheat and drying leaves. An occasional purple flower poked out of the ground, creating a perfect picture of early fall. I had not realized it, but Leon was no longer holding my hand. I looked back at him with a joyful grin, anticipating something similar, but instead, he looked petrified.

"What?" I asked softly, trying to take his hand once more.

He considered me for a moment unblinkingly, his body completely rigid as he pondered what to do with me, "You lied to me..." he whispered.

I looked around in confusion, "What are you talking about?"

He shook his head, taking a step away from me, "Galen told me you would lie to me about your Gifts... that you would deny the truth. When I asked you about the flowers at my grandpa's house, you said they came on their own... but I watched you speak them into being, Kayd..."

I stared at him in shock, "Why wouldn't you have just called me on it?" my chest was tight with the guilt.

He shook his head again, his exasperation growing by the minute, "Because I shouldn't have had to, Kayd! I hoped you would just admit it, at least in your own time. But instead of telling me, you go into another one of your trances and use your powers as if it were the easiest thing in your life!"

Where was this coming from? I was slightly aware of why he might be upset, but inside of me I almost resented the fact he wasn't excited for me.

I tried to reach for him calmly, "Leon… I may not have told you, but it was just because I wanted to see if it was really true before I said anything…"

His eyes watered with anger as he looked at me, "Kayd… we've known each other over a year now, and in all that time, you never kept anything from me about your Gifts. We were a team in your discoveries, yet now you are constantly keeping secrets from me… and what's worse is the fact it didn't start until we got married."

I stared on in horror, but he was right… more specifically, it was since I had met Jeremiah. Suddenly everything new I kept secret, and we never truly bounced back after the Jeremiah debacle. Our distance had all grown to this moment now, getting out of a never-ending spiral of trees. I didn't know what to say or what to do. Leon and I had fallen in love so quickly, so effortlessly, but ever since that moment we knew we wanted to be with each other, it has been trouble and pain ever since.

"Kayd... I can't live with all these secrets..." He said, tears trickling down his cheek, causing tears to pour down mine.

"This doesn't have to go this way, Leon... I want to be with you one hundred percent! Maybe I've kept some secrets, but I do always eventually tell you." His eyebrow lifted at the 'eventually', and I realized that was the wrong thing to say, "I kept secrets from my brother every day for four years—it's what I was used to doing. I didn't like sharing without knowing it was the right time. I'm trying not to keep the secrets... please give me another chance." I said, pulling his hands into my own.

He considered me carefully, though ever distant, but just as he opened his mouth to answer, we heard a crack of thunder. Both of our heads snapped towards the sound just as a bolt of lightning snapped to the ground in front of us. I felt the ground tremble as a huge man came thundering towards us—a Colossal—and I quickly found the Shockie who had tried to strike us.

Leon grabbed my hand tightly, "Run!" He said powerfully and we ran. I felt the ground shake and tear apart as the Colossal got closer to us. I looked back only once as he stopped, pounding his foot to the ground.

My eyes widened as I saw the rift in the ground created, expanding towards Leon. "Leon, look out!" I shouted, pushing him out of the way, "Stay down!" I shouted again, and he listened, ducking beneath the tall wheat stalks. I turned all my attention to our pursuers—the Shockie was an odd-looking woman with bright pink hair shaped like a lit flame, and the Colossal was a thick-muscled man with dark brown skin, though his eyes were an eerie red color. They smiled as we watched each other, analyzing our opponents.

I had a feeling deep down that they knew how to dodge most of the natural Decider Gifts—President Reece wouldn't have sent them after us without being prepared. So instead of trying anything, I walked towards them with caution, my hands up. They looked at each other curiously for a moment, "Stop there." Called out the woman, her voice coming out too sweet for such an obviously dark woman. I obliged. They decided to approach carefully, "Now don't you go using that eye trick, reading my insides and then decidin'." She said with a slight accent.

I nodded, "So you know about my powers?" I asked wisely.

The Colossal folded his arms over his chest, "Not much we need to know to get you to the President." He said with a low, strong voice.

I smiled simply, feeling something dark growing inside my chest the closer they got, and whatever it was seemed to understand exactly what to say, and exactly what to do. "Of course. Just the necessities to know about the Most Dangerous Gift." I said, tilting my head with a knowing smirk. The Colossal recognized it, but the Shockie didn't stop her approach.

"Wait!" The Colossal said, grabbing for her, but it was too late as I whispered the simple word,

"Sleep." The girl fell to the ground instantly, and I hoped she stayed asleep for at least a few hours.

The Colossal took a step back, "The Speaker Gift? How in the Hell do you have that?" He asked, his eyes fearful, though his stance didn't show it for a moment.

"It's more than just the Speaker Gift, Colossal... shall I match your ability too?" I said too sweetly, and he flinched.

He looked truly scared now, which was probably very new to this monster of a man, "Colossals can't match each other... and you should know those mind tricks don't work on me either." I nodded watchfully, now approaching him again. He didn't move, "They don't..." I nodded again, my steps continuing until I was only a foot from him. "Others will come for us, you know..." he urged.

I tilted my head at him again, reaching out a hand to touch his large arm, "Will they? Does he really care enough, or was it just about me?" He seemed to think about this, and his answer was apparently not a happy consensus, as his face lost a bit of his color. "So how about we make a deal?" I felt the pull to meet his gaze, my Decider Gift eager to get a crack at him while the others probed at him from here, testing his limits.

"A deal?" he asked with intense hesitation, his gaze briefly going over my shoulder.

"Kayd!" I could hear Leon calling out to me distantly, but it sounded urgent. I didn't look back to him though.

"If you promise not to come after my husband and I, I promise not use any other Gifts on you…" I whisper with promise.

He looked past me again though, and he started to look a little smug, "I told you, those mind tricks don't work on me." He said, switching his vulnerable expression to one that spoke death. He grabbed my arm painfully, nearly crushing my bone in a moment. I watched him, trying to keep the pain from my face, allowing only a single tear to leave my eyes.

I finally decided to look around, realizing the entire field was surrounded by at least a hundred Shockies and Colossals. Leon had tried to warn me, but I decided to teach this man a lesson and ignore Leon when his guidance could've helped us get away. I nodded simply as I met the man's gaze in front of me, smiling through the terror in my arm. "I've heard that Colossals have a hierarchy… with their champion acting basically as their leader." He grinned with cockiness, "I'm getting the feeling that *you* are their champion or something?"

He smiled with a proud grin, "I am." I feigned fear, "You don't have a chance against any of us."

Something inside of me felt so wild, so stupidly fearless, but it seemed to be guiding everything inside of me. I laughed, causing a worry line to show on his brow, still managing to hide the blinding pain, my arm is feeling as though it had been pulled off of me, "That's where you are wrong." I finished. Grabbing his face in my strong hand and looking into his eyes without hesitation. At first, all the other Colossals and Shockies moved towards us, but I raised one hand to them, "Stop!" I shouted to them all, and they were all frozen instantly. My eyes didn't leave the Colossal's terrified gaze, "You should've taken the deal." I whispered to him.

I looked into his eyes with my Gift, and no light surrounded him as I Decided instantly, "Death." I spoke loud enough for everyone to hear me—I didn't want any of them to doubt for a moment that it was me that destroyed this mammoth of a man.

His eyes turned dark, as a brief, "I'm sorry..." left his lips before he fell to the ground with a powerful thud. One hundred gasps came out at once as I looked back at them. Each face spoke for all of them—no one could stop me.

"When the frost wears off, don't come after us, or the same thing happens to all of you." I said forcefully. I jumped across the small chasm the Colossal had created, and pulled Leon to his feet. He watched me in awe as we walked by the army that had been meant to capture us. I had never heard the forest so silent as we pushed through the next thin layer of trees.

I felt unstoppable as Leon and I held hands without worry. I felt like I was on top of the world until the adrenaline started to wear off, and I remembered the searing pain in my arm. Once we had gotten a little way into the woods, I found myself wincing from the pain. Leon looked at my arm gently and stopped, pulling some bandages out of his bag, "We should fix that up." He said lightly. He brought out a bottle of water first to pour over my hot swollen flesh, and I realized I had never tried to use my Healer Gift. I focused on the water, trying to remember how the other Healers used liquid as if it were medicine.

"Let me try." I said hopefully as I slowly poured the water over my hand and closed my eyes, willing the water to transform into my cure. The pain began to disappear, and within a few minutes the pain was completely gone. I looked down at my arm, and the swelling was entirely gone. I smiled at my accomplishment, "I did it!" I proclaimed with utter excitement, the freedom so strong inside of me, running through my veins like a drug. When I glanced back at Leon, he looked sick. "Are you ok?" I asked, "There's no reason to be upset, my arm is fine!" I said happily, twisting my arm back and forth to show how well it worked now.

He stayed quiet at first, "I was once excited about seeing your power... about how it could be used for such good," he took in a deep breath, "But I'm not so sure anymore if it is a good thing."

It felt as though cold water had been thrown over me as I looked at him in utter surprise, "I'm confused... I just saved our lives, and only had to kill one man."

A slight look of disgust passed over his face before he shook his head, letting go of my hand, "Kayd... remember when it broke your heart to kill someone?" he asked beseechingly, "Now you killed not just a man, but a man you knew was a champion, just to show your strength. It wasn't to save us... it was for you."

He's just jealous… a voice inside my head whispered, and I felt the bitterness touch my surface at the thought. I decided to break my old vow as I touched his hand again and peeked into his mind, *I don't recognize you, Kayd…. God, what happened to her?* My heart suddenly broke at those words, and knowing I had thought selfishly, just like he had told me I was acting.

"Everything I do is to protect us… you are important, Leon, and I won't let anything happen to you."

He shook his head, pushing my hand again once more with a disappointed look on his face mixed with fear and distaste, "No Kayd, I don't think it's about me. You could've used my Gift to just make them forget us, like you did with my group of Gifted when they had been attacked… I don't think anything you do anymore is for good."

"Leon… no…" Tears trickled from my stunned eyes.

He looked so heartbroken as he watched me now, not with loving eyes, but with the eyes of a stranger. He let out a long, devastated breath, "I think we need to go our separate ways, Kayd."

Four weeks… that's as long as our marriage lasted before we lost our way. Four weeks before my husband left me alone. Four weeks before I realized that if I looked at my reflection with my Gift that I would not see someone worth living. "I need you, Leon!" I begged, sobbing as I fell to my knees in front of him.

Tears poured down both of our faces, and he kissed my hands, "I don't think you do Kayd. You've made that unmistakably clear."

"Leon..." I whispered desperately, still clinging to his hand.

He turned back to me, defeat covering his entire body as he looked into my eyes, "Maybe it was a mistake for your brother to bring us together after all?" He said, shaking his head as he walked out of my life.

Chapter 16: Lost

I watched every single step he took away from me, and even when I couldn't see him anymore, I could still feel his distance away from me. With every step, a new dagger pierced my heart, and with every step I realized how lost I was without him already. How had I fallen this far from the path Galen had helped lay out before he had been taken? Or had Galen known this would always happen? I couldn't imagine Galen would've guided me to this moment... my choices had left me utterly alone, not Galen's.

The night had come and gone without me moving a muscle forward as I stayed on my knees, gazing into the dark trees. I had not been truly alone in four years, and I didn't like the feeling. I finally stood, forcing my body forward though I wondered why I should even keep moving. I didn't walk far before collapsing near a small rock structure that could hide me as I slept. I curled into a little ball, barely pulling the sleeping bag from my backpack, and cuddling as close to it as I could.

Dreamland grabbed me by the shoulders harshly as I fell into all the possibilities that were waiting for me. The first vision that caught me was of me walking to the Fortress alone, managing to walk inside without a single person to stop me. Galen would wait for me at the end of the hallway with open arms, and we could journey on once again together like we used to. Nothing would've gone wrong, and Galen would be able to live a long and happy life.

I woke up with fresh tears in my eyes. And though the sun had risen once more, a new day ushering me forward, I knew I preferred to stay back in my yesterdays. My heart had fresh cuts as well when I realized my brother's sacrifice was useless now that Leon had left me...

I wiped away my tears and tried to go back to the professional, seemingly emotionless self. I packed away my few belongings and started back on my path towards Montana to find my brother. A near week had been wasted walking in circles, allowing Leon to fall further out of love with me, and I had to make up the time as quickly as possible. Though my vision had shown myself getting to Galen in a month, it was hard to know any more if that timing would be right.

I pushed myself forward, reminding myself that I could never fall into my memories like I did before, because now there was no one to remind me to wake up. I didn't let myself cry—no more time for tears. I would be Strong Kayd again, even if it was only for myself now. After a few days walking on my own in complete silence, I started wondering if I would even get to Galen in time... I didn't want him to ever think I didn't try. One of the other things that kept circling in my mind was the fact that Leon was not deserting me, but Galen too. Galen would never see Leon again... and then it hit me— maybe I would never see Leon again either.

The thought stopped me dead in my tracks, and those tears found me again. Even when I shook my head, telling them desperately to leave me alone, they didn't. I slumped against a lonesome tree, and suddenly it was Leon's turn to consume my thoughts.

I remembered the first time he hugged me. The first time he told me I was beautiful. The first time he kissed me... and said he had fallen in love with me. I remembered how sweet and affectionate he had been, and I tried to solve the problem in my head—what happened? It had to have started sooner than Jeremiah, because the distance had started sooner. Why was I becoming so unlike myself? I had always been strong, careful, and quiet... but Leon changed me. He made me suddenly confident and happy and vulnerable.

As I looked back to the moment I had met Leon, and he had walked me to Westin Falls, I realized that the first kiss he gave me was the moment my life finally began. I had just been wandering aimlessly before that, believing I was just my brother's protector... but he made me see that I had something to offer the world. We had a love story that others would envy and yet now it was gone. Maybe 17-year-olds were just not meant to get married... at least that's what I kept telling myself. I wanted to believe that the problems between Leon and I could be pegged simply on my age rather than the fact that I was spiraling out of control with my Gifts.

I forced myself to my feet and pushed on, trying so hard not to think about Leon. But with every turn, his face kept popping up all around me. The harder I tried to push his face from my thoughts, the more he appeared. I started running, trying desperately to get away from his taunting, when finally, I stopped, falling to my knees and shouting up to the sky, "Stop!" I screamed at him. The ghosts disappeared, but I still felt him there with me.

I knew then, I had to become better for Leon. I needed to be the girl he had always believed I was, and could be. "Leon... please come back." I whispered as I finally let my tears have their way. The sky had darkened so quickly today that I could barely see where I had fallen, and though it seemed fairly in the open, I just didn't care as I curled into a ball and fell asleep.

The next morning, I felt painful pokes to my sides, and odd laughter. My eyes popped open as I tried to assess my whereabouts—I was in the middle of a cobblestoned street covered in harvest-time décor. Two little children, a boy and a girl, giggled as they ran away from me when I sat up, "Milly, John, where are you?" their mother called, and they sprinted towards her, obviously making it a race.

I smiled at them, but my expression felt stiff. I wiped my eyes and came to my feet trying to act as if I had not just been sleeping in the middle of a town street. I tried to assess my surroundings—I was in a small town just outside of the town square. Just as I was trying to figure out what direction to take, I heard the footsteps of someone I had never wanted to see again...

"My daughter-in law!" Leon's father said cordially, but I had a foreboding feeling even quicker than the last time I'd see him. As he approached, I held my hand up to him. "Where is Leon?"

"Don't take another step, Mr. Hensley..." I said through clenched teeth. He looked around before approaching once more. Something about seeing him set my skin on fire. "Mr. Hensley... *please* leave me alone."

He looked stricken, but as I really looked him over, I realized he looked aged today... like even just the last few weeks had stolen some of his life away. I truly turned to him then.

"Please, just tell me where Leon is." He says as if he's being fatherly, loving, concerned... but I see a different kind of worry as I looked back at him. I was overwhelmed with a vision of Mr. Hensley offering information to a soldier. He smiled at the soldier, nodding as they spoke. Though I couldn't hear their words, I knew it in my gut that they were talking about me and Leon.

I couldn't stop myself as I went at him with all my anger. I pinned him against a tree before he could take a breath, or I could figure out how we had gotten back to the trees. He watched me in astonishment, "Kayd... what are you doing?" he asked with fear. I could tell he had noticed I was meeting his eye now, but I was willfully choosing not to use my Gift yet.

"I saw something, and whether it already happened, or it is going to happen if I told you where Leon was, I need to stop you." I said earnestly, though not relaxing my grip.

"What are you talking about, Kayd?" feigning innocence yet again, but it was less contrived now. I think it was more from practice than actually thinking he would fool me.

I came in close to his face, "I swear Jonathan, if I find out you turned in Leon or anyone else I love, I will kill you in an instant. Do you understand that?" I spat out through clenched teeth.

He considered me as he tried to hide the fear transparently wiped all over his face, "How do you know so much? You haven't used your Decider gift on me yet..." he tried to sound more certain, but I think the idea actually pulled more fear from him.

"If you send anyone else after me, more people are going to die, and their blood will be on your hands." I said, letting him fall to the ground. He looked back up at me in terror,

"What could you mean?" He spoke in that sweet tone he used when he tried to get what he wanted.

"I may be married to your son, but don't mistake that to mean you are safe... because I don't take well to lies or betrayal." I growled.

He didn't try to follow as I began to walk away, but before I was too far away, he said desperately, "Please protect Leon..."

I met his gaze once more, and I could see the sad honesty, "He left me." I muttered simply. His eyes showed his grief and shock, but he said nothing else as he let me leave.

I pulled out a small hand mirror Paul had given me as a wedding gift, and checked my face and hair. I wiped away all dirt smudges, and drenched my hair with water as I pushed it into a high bun. I pulled out a small tube of mascara I had snatched soon after Paul had married Leon and I, and then I added a touch of pink gloss to my lips before walking back into the town.

I walked proud and confident, ready for anything the Authority had in store. One week and two days were gone, and I needed to make up the time. Maybe if I was lucky, I could get to Galen sooner than I had seen. I saw a man with an old car he had preserved with a new coat of paint and the new fuel system used in all cars in our time. He wiped an imaginary smudge off of the hood and stood happily next to his masterpiece.

"Good morning, sir." I began sweetly.

He looked at me with brief acknowledgement, before giving me a second more approving nod. He had dark brown hair, brown eyes, and a thin face—he looked to be almost 40, "Well hello miss." He said with a bow of his head. "Can I help you with something?" he wiped his hands off on the white rag in his hands, and tossed it into his open car window.

I smiled as I took a few steps closer to him, "I need a ride somewhere, but someone stole my car—a runaway I think." He nodded his head with a repulsed look.

"Those damned runaways have no respect!" He said with irritation, touching my arm gently, "And to such a sweet girl." He caressed my hand for a moment, and I briefly saw his intent. I pulled my hand and looked away for a second, trying to pull myself back together. He couldn't know about my Gifts.

"Yes… I found myself laying in the middle of town completely confused this morning. It must have been one of those… *Gifted* people." I whispered to him with feigned horror. He gasped.

"You mean… there's Gifted people around this town?" He looked around fearfully.

I touched his arm, "No, I think they were just runners. I'm sure we are ok." I said with a reassuring grin, "But I do need a ride desperately. I need to get to my brother…" I realized I had not come up with a cover story yet for why I needed to get to Montana, "He was put into the hospital while he was visiting our father in Montana." The man watched me with concern, but I tried to act as conversational as possible, "He was riding an old motorcycle, and lost control." I said with a sisterly shrug, "He always got himself into trouble." I said with a laugh. He laughed with me and nodded—I got him.

"Of course, sweetheart. I just have to get a few things, and I'll be right back." I looked at him carefully as he scratched his head nervously. "To travel you have to have papers now… so I have to go get them." I touched his arm seductively, pulling him closer,

"You don't need anything. We should get going now." I pushed into his mind the words, and they came out of his mouth.

"Let's go miss, I know some of the back highways so we won't need the papers." He said with a kind grin as he opened the passenger door for me.

We drove for a little while before the man began to speak again as if he was breaking out of a daze, "So I just realized I didn't tell you my name. I'm Wesley Polk."

I smirked at him, "I'm Alex Weaver." It was girl I had known years ago who was in a good family, and had always been considered the most prestigious girl in my school. She was about three years older than me and not Gifted as far as anyone knew.

He offered me his right hand while keeping his eyes on the road, and I shook it cordially before sitting with my hands in my lap. "So where exactly in Montana do we need to go, Alex?"

I closed my eyes for a moment to focus on the place exactly in my memory. "Near the border of Canada on the western border." He nodded at my explanation.

"You are awfully trusting to have a stranger take you so far— you being such a beautiful young lady and all." He said in a tone I didn't like, as he briefly looked me over. I pulled my jacket tightly over my chest.

"I know for a fact you wouldn't do anything to me, Wesley." I hurried out, trying to sound as confident as my words appeared.

He smiled genuinely, "What makes you say that?"

I forced a soft grin, "Because you are a good man." I muttered, hoping that would get him to keep his intentions honorable on our journey.

"Well thank you." He said, ending our conversation for the time.

It had been so long since I had been in a car that I had forgotten how dizzying it was to look out the window and see all the trees fly by. I fell asleep without even realizing it, and my dreams were sadly not pleasant. First, I saw Leon fighting for his life against a group of Colossals who were thirsty for blood after I had killed their champion. Leon got away in the nick of time, but he was limping harshly as he tried to find cover away from the Colossals who could feel any person's footsteps echo on the ground.

Next, I dreamt of Jeremiah. He was at the fortress with Galen, in total surprise as he looked in at him through the thick bars the Authority had for all their priority cases. *"Galen... where is your sister? Is she safe?"* he asked Galen in the softest whisper.

Galen peered at Jeremiah sadly through the electric blue of the cell holding him, *"She's coming here... now..."*

I woke up soaking wet, my breath harsh and staccato, "You okay, missy?" Wesley asked a little too brightly for my liking. The light was completely gone from the sky, and the moon was hiding behind a black cloud high above.

I wiped my eyes—they were wet and puffy, "Yeah... just a bad dream."

I felt his gaze on me again, "So I see you have a ring on your finger... ya married?"

I looked at my hand, "Yes... well... I was. I mean... I am, but..."

He put a comforting hand on mine, "Hey, I know how it goes when you are young. You leave him or the other way around?" he was actually being a kind companion.

I sighed, "He left me... he said I wasn't the same woman he had fallen in love with."

He barked out a frustrated laugh, "Those young kids never realize that people change—that doesn't mean you are a different person. You hear me, Alex?" He said reassuringly, patting my hand again before putting his hands back on the wheel. I smiled thankfully.

"I hear you, Wesley."

He looked back at me again, "You were calling out for him in your sleep I think..." he whispered.

My head whipped back towards him, "And you didn't wake me up?"

He shook his head with a smile, "No... I figured maybe you needed to yell at him a little bit, even if it was in your sleep."

We laughed together for a minute, "Well that's probably true." I took in a deep breath, "So Wesley, where are we?"

He stared on at the dark road, "Shockingly not as far as I thought we'd be. There was a horrible accident about two hours ago, and kept us held up for quite some time. We only just entered Idaho." I knew that to him that wasn't far, but to me that was a distance that would've taken me days without this vehicle.

"Oh, don't worry about it."

He nodded, "So, I'm getting awfully tired. Do you mind if we stop off for a few hours?" He said with something behind his voice that made me uneasy.

I cleared my throat uncomfortably, "Do you want me to drive? I'm pretty sure I've been asleep for basically a day." I laughed.

He turned his attention to me for a moment, "You don't trust me, do you?"

I sighed, "I just don't want to be put into the kind of situation where I would need to worry about trusting you or not." I explained.

He nodded, still looking forward, "Sweet girl like you really shouldn't travel alone with a stranger." He urged once again, and I didn't like his tone as he pulled to the side of the road. He turned his body to me, but I was waiting for the kill-strike. He locked the doors and then made it to where I could not get out. I pushed myself as far to my window as possible, but he didn't come any closer. He smiled carefully and just watched me.

"Why aren't we moving? Can't we just keep going? Like I said, I can drive if you are tired."

He shook his head, "Alex, I know you are Gifted." I stared in horror, "You talked about it in your sleep. I called the Authority while you slept, and they should be reaching us soon." He said too securely for my liking.

I calmed my mind as much as I could, but knowing that the Authority would be coming soon was not helping. Though it was lucky Wesley didn't know who I really was, the Authority would know as soon as they saw me. I looked into his eyes with a content smile that made him flinch,

"So you think you know so much about me?" I offered as I tilted my head.

"Well Missy, I know you are Gifted, and that is all that matters." He scoffed, turning his head.

"And here I thought we were having such a good trip... you seemed so nice." I said, truly disappointed.

He sighed sadly as he looked out the window, "Why did you have to be Gifted?" He whispered.

"Why did you have to be a traitor?" I threw back at him coolly.

He glanced back at me with wide, fearful eyes. "They would've found out that I had been consorting with a terrorist. You would've hurt me... or killed my family... or..." he looked so terrified.

I watched with concern, "Is that what the Authority has been telling everyone?" He nodded, "Well you should know, I didn't even know I was Gifted until a few months ago. I was protecting my brother, who was just a Prophet, for the past four years."

His eyes widened in confusion, "Why are you still telling me things? I'm turning you in... telling me any information would just be giving the Authority more information." He said in surprise.

I smiled, "Because I want you to realize who you are turning in. They are torturing my brother right now in Montana, and it's not because he is Gifted, but because he has information, and he is an incredibly powerful Prophet. He is only 13 years old. All I wanted was to get him out of there… I wanted to see him one more time before he dies…"

He considered me with compassion, "You don't know he will die…" he offered gently.

I laughed darkly, continuing to look him in the eye so he could feel the full amount of guilt, "Yes I do. He had a vision about it… and apparently he will die whether I get to him or not, but if I don't get to him, he will kill himself, so he won't be made to give me or my husband up."

Wesley stared at his hands miserably, "I don't know what Gift you have… but if you could make me forget, then you could get away with my car and I'd be none the wiser." He said compassionately, tears lingering at the corners of his eyes.

"You mean you don't consider me a 'damned runaway'?" I said with my eyebrows raised.

He looked out the window regretfully, "The Authority tells us such awful things about the Gifted, and if we don't believe them, then we are considered traitors." He brought his attention back to me, "Please Alex, just use whatever Gift you have on me and take my car."

"Won't you miss it?"

He shrugged, "I think you need it more than I do." I considered Wesley with care. Though I could've used my powers on him at any time, I hadn't… and obviously it had been the right choice.

"I'm not going to take your car Wesley… but I will take your map if you will let me."

He watched me for a moment before nodding. He pulled out a thinly folded paper, unfolding it carefully as he pulled a pen from his glove box. He marked a spot on the map with a big 'O' and then another point with a large 'X'. "Okay, this is where we are, and this is where you'll want to go." He handed the paper to me and took in a deep breath with his eyes closed, "Alright… I'm ready."

I shook my head, "If you tell them about me, so be it. If you don't then that's fantastic. I'm not going to make this easy for you though, Wesley. I am a Speaker, but I'm not going to use my Gift on you. That's the whole reason my husband left me… I was using my Gift when it wasn't necessary."

He became panicked, "But they will be able to tell I'm lying… they could interrogate me Alex!"

I nodded, "That's not my real name." I said delicately. He offered a look of confusion, "That's why its ok if you end up telling them. Thank you for all your help though, Wesley." I said, leaning over and kissing his cheek before making the door unlock. I quickly ran into the woods, making sure to get as far into the forest as I could before the Authority got to Wesley. I was glad he had not quite been what I expected—even with him trying to turn me into the Authority was not hard to understand… after all, the Authority made people truly believe that all Gifted people, even those who were not the Dangerous Ones, are monsters.

Chapter 17: Destination

I walked for days and days, suddenly wishing I had taken Wesley's offer of using his car. My feet were weary and tired, but I didn't dare stop in fear that any moment wasted not walking was a moment I could've used to get to Galen sooner. I couldn't understand how my vision had seemed so far in the future considering I was at the 2-week mark and I was almost there. Maybe had Leon still been with me we would have lollygagged about and wasted too much of our precious time? None-the-less, I felt as if something was pulling me forward, though not necessarily towards Galen.

I had basically been walking for three days without stopping except for an occasional nap when I couldn't move any longer. But I had stopped eating, practically stopped drinking water, and my body was painfully paying the toll. My limbs felt as though they were ready to break off of me like a dying tree's branches break at the slightest pressure. My eyes felt overly heavy, and my feet were unhappily sore and tired—even the arm I had healed almost a week ago seemed to be losing its healing. I was a shadow of myself, but I couldn't stop... not now.

It was on the fourth day of walking that I lost control of my body when it flopped forward as if I had no bones. I fell to the ground in agonizing pain screaming at my body to stand again, but my body did not listen. "Get up!" I yelled, but it still did not listen. I turned myself over so I could look at the sky—if I was going to be stuck here awhile, I at least wanted a decent view of the forest.

At first, I just watched the clouds fly through the sky as I let my heartbeat join the soft rhythm of the forest. My eyes began to close before I could stop them, and within a few minutes I had drifted into slumber.

"Where is she?" a woman with pitch-black hair asked. She was beautiful with light eyes and white skin standing at almost six feet. As I watched her in my dream, I could not see whom she was speaking to at first, *"The little boy said she was in these woods! I'm sure she is somewhere around here."* The woman continued in a high whiny voice.

I could hear a man sigh, *"Darcy... she will come to the Fortress no matter what, so why look for her now?"*

The woman let out a single note laugh, *"Because! Can you just imagine how Lee would reward us for bringing her in?"*

"Darcy..." The man said softly, touching her shoulder. She turned to him with a sweetly feminine glance. Suddenly I saw the man as he pulled her into his arms, *"Why don't we just take this time for ourselves?"* Jeremiah said to her affectionately. She looked at him lovingly as she traced her finger over his chest. His eyes were disconnected, but the woman obviously didn't notice as she kissed him passionately. She pushed him against a tree, and I could see a large branch snap.

That's when I heard the distant voices, no longer only part of my dream but moving into my reality, and I opened my eyes to see them only a few yards away. Brief panic moved through my body, but I forced myself to be calm. I pushed myself as low to the ground as I possibly could, suddenly thankful I had kept my darker clothes on even when I had gone into town. The conversation began between them the same as my dream had suggested with Jeremiah saying, "Darcy... she will come to the Fortress no matter what, so why look for her now?"

It was then, as Darcy was talking to him, that I saw him catch a glimpse of me. His eyes glazed for a moment as he caught my eye, but he showed no panic on his face. That was when he touched her gently, bringing her into a tender embrace. Though she did not realize it, Jeremiah was freezing her to her spot. Once she was motionless, their lips parted, he hurried over to me with concern, "Kayd, what are you doing out here alone?" he whispered softly as he offered me a hand. I took it thankfully as he helped me to my feet.

"Sort of a long story..." I said in a weak voice, and in my weakness, he was even more intoxicating than the last time we had seen each other. I staggered forward when he held my hand and he caught me in his arms with worry covering his face.

"Kayd, are you alright?" he said with concern, touching my cheek softly. I looked into his eyes longingly, though I tried to remind myself I was trying to change for Leon.

I finally looked away from his tauntingly perfect gaze, "I need to get to Galen..."

He looked around with confusion, "Where is Leon? If he is getting firewood or something, tell him to take you with him. It isn't good to be alone out here—you are so close to one of the Authority Fortresses."

I felt weak again at the mention of Leon's name, "He's gone..."

Jeremiah hesitated, "What do you mean 'gone'?"

I sighed, trying to hold back the tears, or the wavering in my tone, "He left me..." He stared at me in shock.

"You're alone?" he almost whispered. I nodded. He looked back at his frozen companion and back to me, "You can't go after Galen, Kayd... it is better for you to just stay safe somewhere. The President has Soldiers, and Dangerous Ones, scouring the area for you. They know how to capture you... and if you go right into their hands, just like they want you to, you will be stuck in their grasp."

"I'm going to him... I have to." I muttered as if it should be obvious.

He smiled sadly, "He told me you would say that..."

I perked up knowing Galen had spoken to him, "What did he say?"

He shrugged, "He tries not to say much since he is monitored at all times, but he told me he misses you." I nodded with a happy grin, tears blurring my vision. "I wish I could come with you... but Darcy will wake up soon since she is also a Freezy. But I can tell you where to go to be safe for the next few days." He offered, squeezing my hand with affection. "There is an old guard post less than a mile from here to the North. The guards at the Fortress take a break from 2 am to 5 am, so you can head to the Fortress around then. If you get out before 5, they will only know you had been there by the tapes, but it will be too late for them to care." He said, helping me forward towards a low-hanging tree branch. "Darcy and I will head back to the fort..."

"When she unfreezes, won't she still think you were kissing her?" I asked, trying to make it sound like it didn't matter though inside I was jealous.

He smirks sadly with a shrug, "Yeah... Darcy's been waiting for it forever. She's always had quite the crush on me. It's the best distraction I could think of."

I give a single nod, looking towards him carefully, "I could always tell her mind there is an emergency back at the fort, and then she would still be quick to head back."

Jeremiah considered me with an interested smile, "Have you gotten to the point where you can use your Gifts so easily now?" I nodded, "Well that is awesome, but I don't think it is really necessary. This is the sort of distraction I can use anytime I need to throw her off." I forced a smile as I nodded again, looking away. He looked at me with a shocked grin, "Oh my God—you're jealous..." he said with a hearty laugh.

I pushed him weakly, "No I'm not... I just figured that you might want an out so you didn't have to kiss her..." I lied badly.

He nodded with an unbelieving smirk, "So I wouldn't have to kiss a gorgeous girl who's been in love with me for years?"

I shrugged my shoulders with frustration as I tried to walk forward without his help again, "Fine, kiss her. I don't care... I was just..." I fell again, but he caught me with ease, holding me in a dancer's dip suavely. His face was only inches from mine—I was breathless as my eyes went to his perfect lips. I told myself to stop looking, but I couldn't. He came in closer, our lips nearly touching when he pulled away. He had a very tender look on his face as he helped me back to my feet, though still holding my waist, "I don't care about her that way, Kayd... but in our world, you do what you need to do. I'm able to keep my emotions out of most things."

I watched him with understanding, "Ok... you better show me where I should go." I said hurriedly, realizing we probably only had a few minutes before Darcy unfroze. He nodded kindly and took me about 30 feet away.

"Are you sure you can get there without help? I could easily tell her to go back and I would meet her there." He continued, softly touching my shoulder.

"I can always climb a tree or hide behind a rock." I said with a laugh. He considered me.

"Kayd..." he began in a sweet voice, "You look awful." He finished.

I laughed, "What every girl wants to hear."

He shook his head, coming closer to me again, "You've been crying." He said, touching my cheek. My eyes closed at his caress, and suddenly I realized how relaxing it was to have him touch me—for him to be close. "Why did he leave you?" he finally asked.

My eyes popped open and I looked back to him, letting out my breath, "Because I wasn't being me anymore. Everything I did was selfish... I was out of control." My face suddenly felt wet and I realized I was crying... again. I angrily wiped the tears away, and pushed a small smile onto my face, "It was my own fault."

He shook his head, wiping away a few of my larger tears, "No it's not, Kayd. If he left you, it was his own mistake." He pulled me into a hug, "I would never leave you..." he whispered in my ear, and I knew he was telling the truth. I didn't want him to let go of me, but I knew our time was fading quickly. I knew my place wasn't beside him, or that would mean I would be with the Authority.

I finally pushed him away, "You better get back to Darcy before she wakes up and realizes you aren't there."

He looked into my eyes affectionately, tucking a loose hair behind my ear, "I have wanted to spend time with you every moment since we last saw each other." He admitted, his fingers lingering in my hair as he ran them gently through the strands.

"So have I..." I accidentally said out loud. But it was true—I'd never stopped thinking about him.

He smiled at my words, "I wish I never had to say goodbye, Kayd." I dared to meet his gaze, and his soul told me his love story with me. My brother had altered my future, and I was now looking into the eyes of the man I could've been with. I couldn't leave his side, yet I had no choice but to move on.

"I..." I took in a staggered breath as he moved gently towards me, pulling my body closer to his as if he would never let me go. His lips parted a little as he closed his eyes and carefully allowed his lips to touch mine. Our kiss was soft and gentle, yet there was more passion behind it than I thought was possible to experience. I pulled away quickly, pushing him away as I held my lips. Tears welled in my eyes as I looked back to him, "I have to go now..." I forced out, making my legs move as quickly as possible. I tried not to think about the aweing look he had given me as our lips parted, knowing that he felt that unyielding fire as well.

I found the guard station quicker than I expected to and forced the door open, pushing myself inside. There was a bed on the second-floor landing, and I practically ran to it as I pulled the blanket around my shoulders. I stared into the dark room with wide eyes, trying to understand what had just happened. Though Leon was gone, I had wanted to be with Leon still if he would take me, but as I thought back to my kiss with Jeremiah, I couldn't help but desire him instead.

I let my head fall to the pillow as I stared at the cement ceiling. I let myself fall to sleep in hopes I could escape my confusion and pain. When I awoke, I heard voices outside the window. My body was still tired and starved, but it was more well rested than usual. I carefully peeked out the window to see who was talking—it was two Soldiers. I flattened myself against the wall and suddenly saw a little plaque on the wall on the stairwell that read: "West Tower—Dedicated to General Barn of the West Branch"

I was at the wrong tower... I wanted to shout in fury as I realized my mistake, but that would make me even more obvious. I could hear the men's feet clomping loudly on the loud cement. A man laughed, and his laugh echoed up the stairs with his slowly approaching footsteps.

My entire body froze as I watched the stairs in terror. Though I could use my Gifts on this man, it was unlikely I would get away without being seen by someone. These are men and women who are trained intently on how to deal with Gifted people... and in particular, me. Jeremiah had told me that Soldiers were looking for me high and low, though they were unlikely to have expected me right under their noses in one of their beds. I inched towards a door at the far side of the room, careful not to show myself to my approaching enemy. Luckily the man was not paying any attention to the room he believed to be empty.

I pushed my way through the little door and breathed a deep sigh of relief. I looked around and found a Soldier uniform. I quickly put on the black leather riding pants, the large blackened coal jacket, and the large colored glasses they always wore to be protected from

Speakers. I was just about to take a step out of the room when I realized my red hair would stand out too easily in a group of trained men with senses like a hound dog.

I found an easel with paint of every color sitting out around it with little organization. I found a tube of black paint and took in a deep breath as I quickly squeezed a large amount into my hand and massaged it into my hair. I spotted a sink I could wash my hands in, and then ran a bit of water through the strands to make it look more realistic. I pushed an army cap onto my head, and folded my hair into a strong braid down my back. I didn't have time to track down a mirror to check out my disguise, so I simply took the risk and came out of the room.

The man's boot had just hit the second floor landing as I came out of the little room, "Hey... who are you?" the man asked, suddenly cautious. His hand instantly went to his belt for security. His blue eyes were surprisingly kind for a Soldier, and he looked much younger than most of the other Soldiers I had ever seen.

I offered a polite smile, "I'm Indra Collins, the new recruit. They told you I was coming, didn't they?"

The man's eyes widened as he looked back down the stairs and rubbed his fingers through his hair, "Actually no... are you sure they sent you the West Tower? We don't usually have women here." He explained courteously.

I laughed, "Well that would explain why no one was here when I first arrived! I was told my commanding officer would meet me here at 0'600. When no one was here, I decided to take a brief nap…" I pretended I had said some horrible secret as I covered my mouth, "Oh please don't tell anyone I was sleeping on the job!"

He smiled lightly, "No need to be ashamed—we Soldiers often go days without sleep, so no harm taking a brief shut-eye when the opportunity presents itself." He offered his hand to me, "I'm Jameson Lee." He had a firm handshake.

"Well you may need to point me in the right direction, Jameson Lee." I smiled sweetly to him and he blushed.

"I think I could do that." He nodded to me and we headed down the stairs. I felt my fear rise to my surface as I realized the room was packed full of Soldiers eating breakfast and filling their weapons with new ammunition. The slightest flinch from me could give me away to these men. Jameson smiled as we hit the main floor, "Hey Commander Lion, I have a new recruit for you to meet."

A much older man, probably in his fifties, stood up with perfect posture and a deadly looking expression. For being in his fifties, he certainly was very tone and powerful looking. I gulped quietly as the man approached us, most of the other Soldiers suddenly going silent. He stopped in front of me, towering from at least six foot five. "I have no new recruits." He said in a harsh voice as he spit out something black from his mouth.

"She was supposed to go to the new North Tower but mixed up the directions. May I take her to her tower, Sir?" Jameson asked a little too conversationally, but he fixed it by adding the 'Sir'.

Commander Lion considered the young man's words, eyeing me with a meticulous gaze as he circled me. That's when I felt the drops falling from my still wet hair—the paint was dropping. I cringed as I heard it slide down my jacket, and I hoped no one else was noticing. "Not many girls take on a position like this, miss…"

"Collins, Sir!" I said as powerfully as I could, trying to stand tall and act the part like I had seen so many other Soldiers do.

He smirked with slight humor, "Collins? Your father must be Edward Collins of Fort Hamilton." I held in my breath,

"No Sir. My dad was Thomas Collins… he was killed by one of those Gifted people. I wanted to join the Authority so I could be on the right side." I said, surprising myself at the validity of the story, or at least how real it sounded.

He nodded, putting a hand on my shoulder, luckily missing the small puddle of black paint that had collected on the back of my shoulder, "Good woman." He stayed silent for a moment before looking back at Jameson, "Go ahead and take her to the North Tower, but don't forget your gear this time, Lee. I don't want to have to explain to your father that his only son was too stupid to protect himself."

Jameson nodded, trying to wear a more somber expression. He ran up the stairs and pulled his large black gloves over his hands, and covered his eyes with the large glasses. He smiled at me as we started walking outside, "Usually Commander Lion would have radioed ahead to the North Camp, but all our radios are down for some reason." He said with a laugh.

"Oh, it's ok. This way I'm able to be escorted by a handsome man." I said bashfully. He blushed profusely with a large grin. It was funny to me that just last year I believed myself to be ugly and unable to flirt even by accident, but now I was acting like a professional flirt whenever I needed to use my womanly wiles.

"Well it is certainly nicer to be escorting a beautiful woman than to catalog supplies." He said, looking down at my hand carefully. "You forgot to grab gloves." He said with worry, touching my hand awkwardly with his overly gloved fist.

"It's ok. I doubt we would run into any Gifted on such a short walk... or is it not that short?"

He laughed, "It's about an hour from here. We don't use any sort of transportation between towers, so we don't give our position away to possible Runners." I nodded with a small smile, "Ya know what's funny? They just put in a new North Tower because the old one had a small fire. The place is made of cement just like ours, but a few scorch marks is apparently too much for some people."

I smiled again with a polite chuckle, "So where is the older one?" I asked curiously.

He shrugged his shoulders, pointing forward but slightly to the left of the direction we were heading, "It's more directly North than the new tower. It is one of the closest towers to the North Town Facility."

A genuine grin came to my lips at this new information—Jeremiah had sent me to the safest place closest to where Galen was. We were fairly far from the West Tower now, and I didn't want to get too far from the tower I actually needed to get to. I suddenly remembered what Jeremiah had said, "*You do what you need to do. I'm able to keep my emotions out of things...*" I turned to Jameson carefully,

"Listen... this may sound really forward, but I think you are really hot." I said with blushing cheeks, and his face turned beet red as he looked around as if to see if anyone else heard me call him hot.

He laughed oddly, "You're kidding..."

I shook my head, "No I'm not. Can't you feel the chemistry here..." I said, putting one of my hands on his covered shoulder. He smiled like a fool,

"But... you are so gorgeous—how could you possibly be attracted to me?" This question actually surprised me, considering he was actually a very attractive man.

"Jameson..." I put my hand on his face, "You are truly handsome—don't let anyone else tell you anything differently." I felt my Speaker Gift leak out with the command by accident. Jameson smiled, taking off his glasses carefully. He guided me over to a large tree and sat down, patting the ground next to him. I felt jitters running through me—what did he think I was suggesting?

I sat down beside him and he nervously put his hand around my waist, "You know… I've never actually kissed anyone before." He admitted, "So I'm sorry if I'm not any good." He said apologetically.

I stroked his face gently and he smiled brightly, "Well luckily I'm pretty good." I said with a smirk that made him laugh. I took off my glasses and moved towards his face to kiss him, but Leon's face popped into my head, and I couldn't do this. I looked into Jameson's eyes for a moment, and I shook my head.

"What? What's wrong? Does my breath smell bad? I'm so sorry…" He said so regretfully.

I shook my head, keeping my hand on his face, "I need you to go back to the Tower. And I need you to tell them that Colossals attacked us. Tell the Commander that they ripped me in half…" I explained carefully, "Tell them I died."

He watched me in confusion, "I don't understand… why?"

I didn't want to use my Gift unless I had to, and I hoped maybe I would get lucky with Jameson, "I'm not who you think I am." He put a hand on my arm, "I'm Gifted…" I admitted sadly.

He watched me in shock, but he didn't move his hand away, "Oh my God… are you serious." I tried to make tears come as I nodded, but few called to arms. Suddenly he smiled, "So am I!" He said excitedly, suddenly relaxing even more.

It was my turn to be surprised, "But you're a Soldier…"

He nodded with a forced laugh, "Yeah, because my dad is a Commander. He doesn't know either… but that's why I just agreed to be a Soldier because I figured no one would expect a Soldier to be Gifted."

I smiled, "That's kind of brilliant. That's why I hoped disguising as one would help…"

"So, you are not really a Soldier?"

I shook my head, "No… I made up all that stuff I said to Commander Lion."

He laughed, "Yeah, I'm a Healer. Nothing too serious, but still enough to be taken by the Authority in most circumstances." He continued sadly. "What are you?"

"I'm a Speaker." I said softly.

His eyes widened, "So you could've just used your Gift on me, but you told me the truth instead?" He said in surprise. I nodded, "Wow… that is amazing. So why are you out here anyways?"

I closed my eyes, "I have to save my brother. He is at the North Town Facility. So, I was told to hide at the North Tower until the right moment."

Jameson nodded carefully, "If you go to the Old Tower, it would be best. They go by the tower every three days to check and make sure no one is hiding there. They just checked last night, so you have at least two more days. I can tell them the story you wanted me to tell them, but they will probably think you just used a Gift on me."

I nodded, pulling his knife out of his pocket and slicing my wrist. Blood splattered over his jacket, and a little on his face. He stared in horror and confusion, "Now they will think something really happened."

His eyes widened, "I guess so… don't use your Gift on any Soldiers, by the way, unless you don't mind giving away your position. They have special tools to check a body to see if it has been tainted by a Gift."

"Does that mean you never use your Gift?"

He shook his head with a smile, "No. They just don't usually check us unless we come off of a mission. And it only works that way if someone else used the Gift on you." He stood, helping me to my feet, "Well you should get going before someone is sent after us." I started walking away when I came back to him quickly and kissed his lips. He smiled happily, "I was starting to think you were only pretending to like me."

"You have plenty to offer." I said with a wink and continued on. I hoped he would be ok going back without me, and acting as though I was gone for good. Once I got to the North Tower, and made sure it really was the right tower this time, I went up the stairs to the second floor, and, once again, a few beds were lined up meticulously along the wall. I went into the next room and I found a sink with the bathroom door right beside it.

I quickly took a shower and washed as much of the dark paint from the strands, but my hair still kept the slightly darkened tint. I wiped off the condensation-covered mirror and said hello to my newest form—woman. It's funny how when you are young, how quickly you transform from a child to a young adult... yet you don't even realize it until you really get a good look.

I liked the look of my slightly darkened hair, it made me feel older and more mature somehow. I pulled on a pair of thin dark pants stored in the smoke-filled cupboard, and put on a crisp black t-shirt over my chest. I pulled my hair into a loose bun hanging at my neck, and decided to see if there was any food downstairs. Luckily the metal cabinets still had a few cans stored at the back where few hands could reach. When the Soldiers had left this tower it was obviously in a hurry considering how few things were really taken. It seemed odd that a fire would scare the Soldiers away so easily. That's when it hit me... a simple fire was not enough to keep them away.

I shoveled the last bit of chili from my can and ran upstairs. I packed my clothes back into my bag and threw in the last few cans lying around, as well as a can opener. After I'd gathered the few things I wanted to bring with me, I put my hand on the door, ready to push it open, when I heard the voices outside.

"Rana, I'm positive I saw a Soldier come in here!" an overly excited young voice said. My heart jumped into my throat as I let my back slide down the wall so I could look as small as possible.

"Len, there is no Soldier stupid enough to come back here after we claimed it."

It was moments like this when I could see that the President's Soldiers only preyed on the weak... they did not go after groups because there was little point. He only sent his Soldiers after groups if he needed something from them. And though I could tell the fire had been started by one of these Gifted people, who I assumed were Shockies, they still were no match for me. I focused on the Shockie Gift, which of course I had yet to use, and tried my hardest to create a spark in my hand.

"I don't care if you think they would or wouldn't come. Someone is here!" the young voice repeated.

I went back to the door and opened it quickly. Both women put their guard up instantly, and I realized if these women were Shockies, they could not be very powerful considering the older one was maybe 11. The younger girl was very tall for her age, which might have been 8, and she had a short bob haircut, her eyes were a light blue that almost looked white. She smirked smugly at the other girl, "Told ya so." She whispered and the other girl raised her free hand at her.

"You should know—we are Gifted!" The older girl shouted to me, her hand holding something that I couldn't see. The older girl had white hair with dark brown eyes, and she was only a little taller than the other girl.

I smiled at them as I approached with my hands up, "You should know, so am I." I said gently to them.

The elder girl raised an eyebrow at me, "Doubtful... unless you have others with you. No Gifted person travels alone." She said as if it were an ultimate fact, which it almost always was.

I nodded, "I'm alone, but not by choice. My brother was taken from me in the night about two weeks ago, and the other man I traveled with left me. I've come all this way to save my brother, and I was told this was the place to stay safely until I could get into the Fortress." I decided telling the truth was the best course of action here.

The two girls exchanged a look before lowering their hands slightly, though not completely, "Prove you are Gifted... what's your Gift?"

"What's yours first?"

The older girl smiled as she lifted her hand towards the sky and suddenly rain began to pour around them from the dark clouds above. I was shocked as I looked at her, because this was the exact method Leon had used to show me his Gift as well—Speaker.

"You're both Speakers?" The girls nodded. At least they were using a Gift I knew well, but the problem with Speakers was that their Gift could be used so sporadically if they didn't know how to use it. This at least made more sense as to why the Soldiers would stay clear of the young girls. I nodded, whispering gently on the wind, "Jump." And suddenly the two girls started jumping, looking at their feet in surprise.

"Hey... what are you doing?" the younger girl asked with confusion, her voice fluctuating with each jump in the air.

I smiled, "Stop." I said loud enough for them to hear as I came over to them. The two girls excitedly came over to me when they realized I also possessed their Gift, even if they had no clue it was only one of my many Gifts.

"That was amazing!" The younger girl said, pulling at my hand as if she would be able to find something hidden there.

"We aren't able to control what even one person does, let alone two people at once!" the older girl said excitedly. "You must have been training for a long time!"

I smiled, "I actually only just found out I was Gifted about a year ago now. My husband was also a Speaker, and he taught me how to use the Gift. He was incredibly talented."

"Husband?" The older girl asked, "Are you really that old?"

I laughed, "No, I'm only 17, but I'm an orphan so we decided to just go for it anyways." The girls smiled.

"I'm Rana, I'm 12."

"And I'm Lenka, but I go by Len. I'm 8 and a half!"

"Well I'm K..." I almost said my real name, and I caught myself, but not quick enough. Now the girls knew my name started with a K, "I'm Kendra. You girls must be pretty strong to have made an entire troop of guards leave so much behind."

Rana smiled, "We made it seem like there was a large group of us. And Len created a small fire on their stove and made it spread to their table. They were terrified! It was great."

"Well do you mind if I stay here for just tonight. I'll leave your hair early in the morning." The girls exchanged an almost disappointed look.

"We could help you..." Len said with a hopeful smile on her face.

"Yes, though we can't affect people, we have learned a lot about controlling our surroundings!" Rana exclaimed with passion, grabbing my hand. "Really... we could." That's when I realized these girls were a lot like me when I first left home: desperate for someone like a parent to protect me, to teach me, to love me.

"How long have you girls been out here by yourselves?" Rana shrugged her shoulders, taking on the air of a more mature teenager.

"About seven months." She said delicately.

I nodded, "My brother and I wandered for four years by ourselves before a group of Gifted people took us in. That group had been together for over five years..." I took a deep breath, "Within about a month of having me and my brother with them, they were attacked by the Authority. Though the few Soldiers were pushed away, within another month the Dangerous Ones came after the group." The girl's eyes widened at the name, "It's not good to have me around... the Authority wants me desperately, and they won't stop until they take out anyone I care about. You girls have managed to do well for seven months without help—just trust yourselves. It is better to be without me than with me."

Len gave a sad look, "But Kendra..."

"And you should know, Kendra isn't my real name... but I don't want you to get into trouble by knowing who I really am."

Rana's eyes widened as her hand went to her lips, "You're the Decider... aren't you." I watched her carefully before nodding, and Len came closer to me, tugging my shirt so I would kneel down to her height. She put her hand on my face and looked into my eyes. My Gift took over as I looked into her soul—she was innocent, yet she was guilty for something she had done.

"What did you have to do to escape?" I asked Len gently.

Rana's eyes glazed over protectively as she put her hand in front of Len, "We had to run away. That's all..."

I shook my head as I lightly pushed Rana's hand away and looked at Len's teary eyes carefully, "Tell me, Len."

Len stared at my feet with a frozen frame, "We had an older brother... Connor." She began as Rana tried to hold me off, "The Soldiers came for Rana and me... but Connor wouldn't let them take us." Tears ran down her cheeks.

"It's okay, Len, I can tell the story." Rana said, touching her shoulder.

I raised my hand to her, "It's Len's story to tell," I began to her, "Isn't it Len?"

Len looked into my eyes with such fear and pain as she nodded, "But Connor was Gifted too... he also was a Speaker—he was teaching us how to use the Gift—but he knew how to hurt people..." Tears poured down her face as Rana put her arms around her protectively. "So, when the Soldiers came to take Rana and me,

Connor put up a fight… hurting them with his Gift by making them shoot each other.

"I kept calling out to him to stop, but he wouldn't. So, I had to stop him." Len began to tremble, barely able to speak through the wavering in her voice, "I used my Gift trying to stop him… I just told him to stop… but when I looked into his eyes… there was this weird red color and he died right there…"

I stared at her in surprise—she was a Decider too. I had never known there was even another Decider anywhere else in the world, so sure I was the only one. Now knowing what I was becoming after using all the different Gifts, I wanted to help Len. I realized I had three choices. In the first choice I told her about being a Decider, and showed her how to control all her Gifts. In the second choice, I would warn her about only using the Decider Gift and the Speaker Gift. I would warn her not to dabble in the other Gifts, no matter how enticing they seem… I would warn her of how lonely being a Decider is. And then the third choice—don't tell her what she is.

I knelt in front of her and took her hands in mine, knowing that whatever words came out of my mouth next would decide the fate of this little girl. So instead, I tried something else, "You're a Decider, Len." Len's eyes widened fearfully, "But being a Decider is a lonely, terrifying Gift… and honestly if I could get rid of it, I would. But I can already tell that it has seeped its claws into me."

"No… I don't want to be a Decider… I don't!" She began to shake again in sorrow, "Please help me! I don't want that to happen again! Please don't let me hurt someone again!" She begged, falling to her knees as she grabbed my shirt.

I felt her pain, knowing what a burden it was to be the Decider, so I tried something that I wasn't sure would work, "Look me in the eye..." she listened and I peered into her heart, into her soul, and into her mind. I can't explain how I managed to do it, but as I looked into this 8-year-old's soul, I found a spot inside her, behind her eyes, and I willed it to go away. As I pulled my gaze away from hers, I saw the innocence and purity of a child untainted by guilt, death, or a Gift...

She smiled at me softly with a confused gleam in her eyes, "I forget... why was I looking you in the eye?" Len asked, suddenly happily herself once more. Rana watched us in confusion, obviously noticing the change in her sister as well.

"I was helping you get something out of your eye." I said with a simple smile.

Len smiled joyfully as she giggled, twirling around Rana and I like a normal 8-year-old girl would, "Gosh, I just feel so good!"

"What did you do to her?" Rana asked me softly so Len wouldn't hear.

"She isn't Gifted anymore..." I murmured gently.

Rana turned to me in horror, "How could you do that?" she whispered through clenched teeth.

We watched Len together, "Because... she was a Decider..." Rana turned to me with wide eyes,

"Why couldn't you have just taught her how to use the Gift then? We could've been safe forever!" she said, startling Len from play.

I smiled at Len, "Go ahead and play inside for a moment Len. I'll try and find you in a minute." Len ran off happily, laughing loudly.

Rana became furious at me as she watched her sister run away, "How dare you speak to my sister at all! We shouldn't have trusted you!" she said, shaking in fury.

She raised her hand to slap me, but I caught it with a thought before her fingers could even brush my skin, "She was in physical pain inside because of what she had done… I understand what she was going through. I killed two men before I realized what was happening. I carried that burden on my shoulders… and then it doesn't help once you realize what you can do. I'm ruined because of my Gift… because of the thirst for power… it doesn't matter how innocent you are when you start using the Gift. It consumes you… and she begged me to get rid of it."

Rana shook her head, though she was now calm, "I didn't hear her beg."

I smirked, "It was in her mind. So, I took it away. I gave her the real gift, Rana—freedom." I said, trying to hide the shaking in my voice.

Rana looked back towards the building behind us, "But she was special… now she's not."

I let out a sigh… the same sigh that I had let out many times when I had believed the same thing about myself when I believed I was not Gifted. "Your sister is special because she is Len… being Gifted doesn't make her special. Remember that."

Rana considered me for a moment before nodding. She was silent for a while before saying, "Does she remember what happened?"

"She can't remember though she knows your brother died. Don't tell her the truth. Save her from the grief… because that grief is crippling."

"Well it's getting dark, Kendra. We should get inside… the really scary Gifted people come out at night." She said with a shiver. We went into the guard tower and played with Len. I was proud for what I had done for Len, but it made me wonder if it was that easy for everyone? Granted, I had to look into her eyes for at least thirty seconds before finally finding the essence of her power… but what if I had the ability to remove anyone's Gift? It would certainly be handy when I had to fight other Dangerous Ones, but was that too cruel? For most Gifted people, our Gifts are the definition of who we are, and to take that away would be stealing their entire life in their eyes. Could I truly be that ruthless? Though to some literally killing someone would be worse, but if you had to live without the very thing that kept you living—would it be worth living?

I finally went up to one of the beds and slept, leaving Len and Rana downstairs playing and laughing. Though I dreamt, they were only of pictures flashing by in a single moment. As if an alarm clock was going off in my head, I awoke early: 2 am on the dot. I let my feet hit the cold floor before sliding them into my shoes. This was the day...

The last day I would see my brother...

The last day I would hug him...

The last day he would be alive.

I tried to shake off those thoughts as I packed my things back into my bag and went down the stairs. Len and Rana were asleep, and I didn't want to wake them, so I said a simple, "Goodbye," to the air, and went out the door.

Luckily the Fortress was not too far, but I still ran there to make sure I didn't lose any time. No one stopped me as I got to the large, daunting steps leading into the building my brother would most likely die in.

I took in one last breath before starting up the steps, but before my feet had even gone up two steps, a warmly familiar voice caught me, "Kayd, wait!"

I felt frozen as I turned my head towards the voice, towards the beautiful man that ran towards me, "Leon..." I said, but in a barely audible whisper. He didn't look happy to see me, but he still had a tender look on his face. "What are you doing here?" I wanted to sound strong, so he didn't know how much he had hurt me, but my voice told the truth as it shook with fear.

"I love your brother too, Kayd..." he began with distance before shaking his head and touching my hand, "And because I couldn't let you do this alone."

My throat had a large lump that I just could not swallow, my tears threatening to erupt from my eyes, "How did you know to find me right now?"

The distant look returned to his face, "A guy named Jeremiah told me..." I felt my body stiffen at the name knowing it was coming from Leon's lips. "He told me that you would be here anytime in the next three days around 2-5 am."

"So, you were just going to wait for me for the three days?"

He shook his head, "No, I figured I would just go in and try and save your brother whether you were here or not." He admitted honestly.

"Ah." I replied, forcing my body to stand a little taller, "Well we should get in before we run out of time." I said, looking at my watch and realizing it was already 2:45 am. I didn't like that it had taken me so long to get here. There was so much for us to say, but now wasn't the time to say it. I had to be distant, like Jeremiah told me he could be... I could be like that too right now.

He nodded and we started up the stairs and went to open the main door. The building looked almost like a normal office building with a beautiful exterior, and glass doors. I figured this was the Authority's way of saying, "See? We have no secrets," even though the real secrets were most likely below the main floor. We peeked through the glass to see that there were no guards at the front desk, just like Jeremiah had told me.

The door was locked, but that was easy enough to change with Leon or me using our gifts, "Unlock." Leon said, but the door didn't unlock. It is funny how it never occurred to either of us that a Fortress for the Authority—the very people who kill and capture Gifted people every day—would have defenses against Gifts. I shook my head
as I pulled a bobby-pin from my hair and pushed it into the lock. Luckily the lock gave pretty easily, but I still felt Leon's eyes on me like they were drilling a hole into my skull.

"What?" I finally whispered to him as we opened the door.

He shook his head, "I'm just a little surprised you didn't try to use your Gift..." his voice was hard, but his eyes were gentle.

I felt so annoyed as I shook my head and walked inside, scoffing back at him, "You know Leon, I didn't know I was Gifted until about a year ago, if you will remember correctly." I threw at him spitefully, "I went 16 years doing everything like any other non-Gifted person. I'm not inept without my Gift."

He nodded his head again quietly with a regretful sigh, "I guess I just forgot." He offered guiltily, following close behind me. It was so odd to be walking with Leon again, especially since neither of us were acting like ourselves. Had I truly ruined him so badly that he could be this unrecognizable compared to the happy, confident man I originally met? Then I had to remind myself that he had just lost his mother and all his friends only 1 month ago. And now he was losing Galen... he had chosen to lose me, so I didn't really count it. But, in two months, he had lost everyone he loved except his father and his grandpa. I found myself looking at Leon with a pitying glance before he met my gaze and made me look away.

"Did Jeremiah tell you what floor we were supposed to go to?" I asked him.

He looked at me with surprise, "No, I thought he would have told you that."

I sighed with a fresh wave of irritation. I guess Jeremiah couldn't tell me everything... but I do wish he had told me a little more, but I guess we had gotten a little distracted. Suddenly my mind was taken back to the kiss, and guilt overwhelmed me as my cheeks flushed red. I pushed the thoughts from my mind. "Well I suppose we will just have to guess." I said as we entered the elevator. I closed my eyes and tried to feel my brother's presence in hopes of finding him, but before the elevator doors closed, I realized Leon had not entered with me. "Come on, we need to get moving."

He shook his head, "I'm not going in that. What if the guards come back? They could easily stop the elevator and then they'd have us. If we can't use our Gifts in here, then we wouldn't have much chance. We can take the stairs." He said, grabbing my hand to pull me out of the elevator before I could decide for myself. It was nice having him touch my hand again, but even his touch didn't inspire the same sort of passion he had once inspired within me. Were we really over? Though this was not the time or place to even think about that, I couldn't help but wonder.

We started down the stairs, and as we went three floors down, suddenly my thoughts decided they couldn't stay in my head a moment longer. "Leon, do you even love me anymore?"

He stopped in his tracks and turned to me with a look of pain, "What kind of question is that, Kayd?" his voice cracked on my name.

"The kind of question that comes from a woman who was completely confused and heartbroken when you left her in the middle of a forest alone." I said with an aching in my heart.

I caught his tender gaze as he came a step closer, "I still love you, Kayd... but I feel like having me around is what pushed you to the point you had gotten to. You wouldn't have even tried to push your abilities if it hadn't been for me telling you to control them." He confessed with obvious regret.

I shook my head in shock, "You were afraid of me a long time before that final moment, Leon."

He watched me in surprise, "Is this really the time to talk about this, Kayd? It is already 3:00. We only have a two hour window left to find your brother, and we don't know how expansive this place is."

"This needs to be said right now, Leon... because just in case we die here today, I need to know the truth."

His head fell and he met my gaze with a long, exhausted sigh, "I'm lost, Kayd. I had just found out that your brother had brought us together, and I got thinking about how it all could've been so different," Well I knew how he felt there, "I thought about all the people who would still be alive, and the people each of us could have helped had we not met…" my heart was breaking all over again, even if these had been my exact same thoughts, "And I just realized that maybe you and I really shouldn't be together. What if separate we can help more people?" he finishes, and those words were the final knife to my heart.

Those words gave me no closure, only anger, "So the vows you said to me only a month ago suddenly mean nothing? You learn one tiny piece of information and suddenly you won't stand by my side anymore?" I fume.

"Kayd…" he reached for me, but I slapped his hand away.

"No!" I shouted, my voice echoing across the staircase. "You don't think I haven't considered those same things you had thought? But the point isn't what could have been—it already is *this* way! But you chose to take the easy path…"

"You think leaving you was easy?" He said miserably, his words catching in his throat as he spoke.

I glowered at him, fire nearly exploding from my fingertips, "Damn right, I do! Leaving me was *way* easier than staying, and figuring out how to help each other. Leaving is always easier than staying it out, Leon. So, I just have one more question." I fire back at him.

"What?" he forced out, and I swear I could see how broken his heart was.

"Knowing all this now—being apart for a month, and realizing that we can't change the past—do you regret leaving?"

He looked away, brushing his fingers through his hair to hide his nerves, "It's not that easy…"

I felt the disgust come to my face, "I think it is, Leon. Are you glad you left me?" I growl out.

He ran his hand down his face, "Come on, Kayd…"

My eyes widened as I realized he and I really couldn't come back from this. "Jeremiah was right…"

His eyes gave an incredibly pained look, "Jeremiah? About what?"

"When I told him that you left me because I had been selfish… he said that it wasn't my mistake, but *yours* for leaving me when I needed you the most." I spat the words at him.

"When did you talk to him again?" he was completely abashed.

I felt my anger take over as I looked at him through glaring eyes, "Yesterday. And you should know, I realized something…" I was about to say everything that was on my mind that would hurt him: that Jeremiah and I had kissed, about the fire I felt for Jeremiah in a way that had never happened with Leon, or about how I knew in my heart that Jeremiah was the person I would've been with had Galen not changed our futures… but I realized I didn't want to hurt him the way he had hurt me. I pulled myself together, pushing the anger back in its place.

"What did you realize?"

I took in a deep breath, "That I absolutely loved you, even when Jeremiah had come and confused me in that moment—I still loved you most of all. But you spit on my love, and now you will not get me back…. I hope you can live with your mistake." I said, pushing past him to continue going down the next row of stairs. Leon stayed still for a moment before following again. Though he had been right, this was not the proper time to talk about us, I was glad I knew the truth. I needed to know we were done completely to fully move on in my heart.

We heard movement outside one of the doors leading to the B-7 floor. We stopped moving, fearing we would be caught. Though Jeremiah had told me the guards would be out, I suddenly realized he never said the Dangerous Ones would be out as well… "Kayd, where are we going? We'll never get of here at this point!" Leon whispered harshly.

I pushed my back against the wall, letting my head hit gently on the hard-plastered walls, "I don't know where to go…" I whispered sadly.

He surprised me by pulling me into a hug, "It's going to be ok, Kayd. We will find him… don't worry." I was thankful for the confidence, even if it was just a lie to get me moving. I needed his embrace, even if I wouldn't admit it. He let out a calm breath, "Kayd, maybe if we walk in there and act like we belong, no one would know the difference? I've seen the Dangerous Ones a few times since our parting, and they are always dressed casually. You and I both look cleaned up enough that I think it could work." Suddenly I could see the professional, strong leader I remembered.

I nodded, offering a friendly smile, "That sounds like a plan." We both closed our eyes for a moment before entering the B-7 floor. The floor was surprisingly active, men and women lounging about, drinking fizzy drinks, eating pre-made sandwiches, and laughing as if they were at a party.

As we entered, a few people near the door looked at us with brief confusion before going back to talking. One girl actually came over to us, and I recognized her instantly—Darcy, the girl who was kissing Jeremiah. I was terrified, sure that she would instantly recognize me and imprison me.

"Hi there!" she said in her high-pitched voice with a friendly tone, offering her hand to us both, "My name is Darcy... you must be the new recruits General Lion had told us were coming. What are your Gifts?" she continued in a spunky voice.

"I'm Kendra, and this is Liam." I said with a smile, "We are both Speakers." She smirked back at me.

"Speakers huh? General Lion has been recruiting more and more of you guys." She said with a laugh. "Hey Jeremiah, come check out the new Speakers!" she called out, and my face instantly went pink as I looked back to Leon. We both had the same expression of concern and terror. Jeremiah walked over, still conversing with someone else before finally turning to us.

I could see his eyes trying to adjust, and the instant recognition. He quickly hid it, "Well hey there. I'm Jeremiah, and you are?" He said to Leon first. Leon forced a happy smile and shook his hand,

"I'm Liam."

And then Jeremiah looked back at me, and though I could tell he tried, he couldn't help a genuinely pleased grin from covering his face. "And who are you, lovely lady." He said with a wink, kissing my hand. I blushed heavily, partly because Leon was watching, and partly because having Jeremiah kiss even my hand had me wishing he would kiss my lips again. I could see Darcy fuming as she quickly pushed her way between us. She must have been about 18 years old, and this close she was even more beautiful.

"Now that we are all introduced... maybe you two lovebirds should join the party." She said pointedly at Leon and I, obviously trying to remind Jeremiah that he didn't have a chance with me. My cheeks began to hurt as I realized I was still smiling like a fool at Jeremiah. Leon was watching us quietly, and I could see his worry.

Jeremiah touched her hand, "Darcy, how about I show them around the different floors. You know General Lion hates when we show new recruits around during his time." Darcy nodded reluctantly.

"I could come with you." She urged, but he shook his head before gently kissing her lips. I found myself looking away again, not wanting to see him kissing someone else. Leon caught my gaze, and I saw the instant understanding wipe across his entire face. He was not stupid.

"No Darcy, it will only take an hour. I'll be yours again soon enough." He finished, kissing her much more passionately. I tried not to let my feelings show in my expression as I smiled at them gently,

"You are a beautiful couple."

Darcy smiled excitedly as she pulled Jeremiah close, "I know, aren't we? It's a shame it took him so long to finally realize he was in love with me too!" she said with a laugh.

Jeremiah joined her before peeling her hands off of him, "I'll be back soon—enjoy the party." With that he took us back into the stairwell. He went down two flights of stairs before stopping and turning to us, "You guys are so lucky we were expecting two new recruits... otherwise you would be in a cell next to your brother!" he urged in a commanding whisper.

I sighed harshly, "I know... alright? I just got a feeling, and Leon mentioned that we could blend in."

Jeremiah stared back at me with a gentler expression, letting out his own tense breath, "Well... at least it worked out." He says, squeezing my arm with affection. It shot an electric hit of desire through me.

"You kissed her, didn't you?" Leon asked bitterly, forcing both mine and Jeremiah's eyes at him.

Jeremiah looked at Leon in confusion, "You saw me kiss Darcy."

Leon shook his head charging towards him, "No... you kissed Kayd!" He said furiously as he pushed himself closer to Jeremiah as if he were ready to strike at any moment.

Jeremiah considered him with care before answering, "Yes, I did. But if anyone deserves to be punched, which I can tell you'd love to do to me, it would be you. You are the one that broke Kayd's heart instead of standing by her side!" Jeremiah countered angrily.

Leon flinched back then, the pain of those words clearly punching through his chest, "You don't know the whole story!"

Jeremiah shook his head with a frustrated chuckle, "I wouldn't need to. I would *never* have left Kayd. And considering the fact that you are her *husband*, you shouldn't have either. So yes, I kissed her, but it was after you had left her alone. And from the feeling I got when you two were standing side by side, you are not back with her—right?" Leon locked his jaw in pure fury as he glared at Jeremiah. Jeremiah smiled, "That's what I thought. Now can we go save Kayd's brother?" He nodded to both of us, waiting, and we nodded back, "Great, let's go." He said, leading us further and further down the steps. We came to B-15 before Jeremiah finally stopped, "Ok, so your brother is in G-5." He said, opening the door for us.

I looked at him carefully, "You aren't coming with us?"

He shook his head, "I can't. I need them to think I'm still on their side... I'm sorry but no one can know I helped you." He said before we all walked through the doors.

As we began passing the cells, my heart cried out for each of the prisoners—men, women, children—all sitting or lying in their beds with no will left in them. That block was so quiet that it felt as though you could hear a tree fall in the forest outside of the fortress. Everyone looked the same even though they were all different. When we stopped in front of Galen's cell, I worried that I would find a shell of my brother... but instead it was empty. Leon's expression was one of complete horror.

"Oh my God... it's a trap." Leon growled out with regret, wiping his face with his hand, "We need to get out of here right now!" he said hurriedly.

"Oh, I'm sorry—are you looking for *him*?" said General Lion, the same man I had met only a day before, as we walked a few steps forward. When my black-haired character had been murdered, he must have realized who I was.

I stared on at him with frustration, Galen looking at the ground through tired eyes that had already given up hope. "Galen... please look at me." I called to him. He looked up at me, and I could see the sparkle come back to his eye for a moment. His eyes then scanned the room, landing on Leon. His happy expression wilted.

"Not this one..." he whispered in a strangled voice. General Lion quickly pulled out his paralyzing gun, shooting it towards me. I used the Shockie gift to tell the electricity to go away, and before it touched my skin, the blue waves disappeared, though the small blade on top still found its way into my leg. I cried out in pain. Leon ran at him, making the man throw my brother to the floor. Galen lay helplessly in the center of the hallway just watching us.

"Galen, get out of the way!" I could hear footsteps from down the hallway moving towards us. Galen just watched me as the man came at me once more with a new weapon I'd never seen. Leon grabbed a knife from the general's belt, but the General pushed Leon into one of the electrified cell's bars. Leon fell to the ground, momentarily paralyzed. I could see a few curious faces come to the edge of their cells to watch what was happening. The General quickly came for me, his bright blue sword gleaming in the low lights,

"I don't care if the President wanted you... it's time for you to die, Decider!" he said with a smug look on his face. Leon threw the knife in his hand at the General. The blade caught his left hand, but it kept moving, continuing to fly past him. General Lion fell to the ground in surprise as he looked at his amputated finger on the ground.

He cried out just as Jeremiah found us. He looked at all of us in confusion, "Help me, boy!" General Lion said to Jeremiah. Jeremiah looked at me and then at the General's blade. I picked up the blade and knocked him in the head as powerfully as I could muster. He fell to the ground instantly.

Jeremiah raised his hands at us as if begging not to be killed, "I'm so sorry... General Lion is never here..." he said with deep sorrow.

"Oh sure, it was a total coincidence!" Leon said, moving towards Jeremiah once more, ready to hit him. That's when I realized Galen had not spoken yet. I scanned the area to find him lying on the ground with a puddle of blood around him.

"No..." I cried as I fell beside him, placing his head in my lap, "Galen... stay with me."

He smiled softly, "So it was this one..." he laughed, and bits of blood sprayed from his wound where the blade had caught him next to his heart over an untouched bit of his shirt.

"Galen... I love you. I'm so sorry I couldn't save you. I just..."

He shook his head, "You were the best sister, Kayd. You made my life so much better... even though we had to run for years... I wouldn't change a moment of it." He said as a tear leaked down his cheek. "I love you Kayd..." he whispered with finality.

"You aren't supposed to die, Galen! You should live! You are good..." I focused my Speaker Gift on him as his last breath faded, "Breathe!" I shouted, pounding his chest. "Breathe!" He didn't. I shouted through my tears, but still no more breath came from his lips. My head fell on his chest, "Live... please live, Galen... I need you. I need you..." I sobbed over my brother.

Jeremiah and Leon knelt beside me, but neither touched me, I think they could tell this was mine and Galen's moment. After a few minutes of holding Galen in my arms with my eyes closed, whispering, "He'll wake up... he'll wake up..." We could hear multiple feet clomping down the hallway towards us. Jeremiah looked and I could feel his panic.

Leon finally put his hands on my shoulder, "Kayd... we need to go now." He said softly.

I nodded, trying to pick up Galen, "Ok... we need to bury him." Leon and Jeremiah exchanged a concerned look, "What?"

"Kayd, the vent is too small for you to carry Galen through..."

"I can't leave him!" I shouted.

Jeremiah gave a sad expression, "I'll take care of him, Kayd... I promise. I will bury him properly. But I don't want to have to bury you too. I'll find you someday and tell you where he is." I wilted at the thought as Leon pulled me to my feet forcing me away, the footsteps too close for comfort now.

"Thank you..." I whispered, though my eyes didn't leave my brother's closed eyelids. Leon pushed me forward,

"I'm sorry Kayd, but we have to go right now..." He urged. We managed to get into the vent, crawling through as quickly as we could. By the time we got out the vent door, the new morning was just beginning, though the sun was still waiting on the other side of the mountain. As we entered the fresh air, in a new world where my brother no longer lived, I felt my true pain erupt. I looked back into the vent, knowing we had only crawled for 10 minutes, knowing I could easily get back and somehow prove my brother did not die...

but he did die. In a single moment, a moment filled with chaos and confusion, Galen, sweet Galen, had been hit with the final blow. I was the one meant to die in this situation... not him.

I fell to my knees as I stared back into the vent, trying to pretend none of this was real. I would soon wake up from my nightmare as Galen and I walked through the forest. He would still be beside me, telling me about his silly visions that I was so sure would never happen. Galen would still be smiling with his bright eyes and melodic laughter. He would live...

I found myself sobbing and screaming, screaming and sobbing as I pushed my face to the ground. "I have to go back!" I cried to Leon.

"You can't, Kayd. We would have been captured... then Galen's death would've meant nothing."

I turned on him, jumping to my feet as I ran at him, pointing my finger harshly in his face, "He might've been alive if you had not thrown that knife! You saw him standing there behind Lion! How could you have thrown it when you didn't know if it would even hit the general? It's your fault Galen is dead!" I screamed, pounding on his chest, slapping his face. He pulled me close as I wept into his shoulder.

"I'm so sorry Kayd... I was just thinking of saving you. All I saw was General Lion... I never even saw Galen standing behind him..." I felt his tears gently falling onto my cheek. "I'm so sorry..."

"I can go back and save him, Leon... I could use one of my Gifts," I said, looking up into his eyes, "I'm sure one of my Gifts could bring him back..." suddenly this moment seemed familiar.

"Kayd, there is nothing you can do."

I felt the anger that would compel me to storm off in conceit, and then I remembered the vision. That vision was what alerted me to Galen's death... So, what was I supposed to do in this moment? Galen had expressly told me not to act in anger, but it was so hard not to. I looked into Leon's eyes, the man who just a month ago I had trusted and loved completely, but now I had grown apart from. In his arms now he felt only as a comforter rather than a former lover. Perhaps it was the pain he had caused me before, but I just could not look at Leon now and see a husband. I knew Galen's only real wish was for Leon and I to be together, but was that enough anymore?

I looked back toward the building, "Leon I love you..."

He smiled softly through his tears, "I love you too, Kayd... I could never stop, no matter what we went through."

I didn't look back at him, "I know... but I think we both know it is time to stop living the life Galen tried to make us live..." I finally met his gaze again, pulling away from his embrace, making his face fall, "Like you said before, maybe we just aren't good for each other? We don't seem to bring out the best in each other... and I'm tired of seeing you as the miserable version of yourself that I made you to be."

He watched me with deep sorrow, "Kayd, maybe Jeremiah was right, and we should just support each other right now..." I felt myself flinch at Jeremiah's name, and I know Leon caught it. Hurt came to his eyes as he pulled back, "You really do love him now, don't you...?"

I wanted to lie, but my heart had no strength to do it, "I think I might."

He let out a heartbroken breath, "Kayd... this is the time we need to stay close. I'm sorry how I hurt you, but I need you, and I think deep down you need me too. I don't care what happened between you and Jeremiah... I just want you back."

I shook my head with a sad smile, "Of course you do... not that you believed that before seeing me and Jeremiah an hour ago. You weren't even considering me then..." I force out, my eyes closed so I can block out the mournful gaze I know he was giving me, "You don't get to suddenly change your mind now that Galen is gone... he isn't here anymore to remind me why I am supposed to be with you!" I shouted, my face getting warm as I looked into his eyes.

He flinched at my harshness, but his gentleness remained, "Kayd we can mourn him together... you don't have to do this alone..." he said, looking more like his old self again. I knew he was being sincere, but what if he changed his mind again? I would not go through this again to be hurt. I needed to look out for myself... I felt my emotions close off as I looked at Leon through a new set of eyes.

He looked like my past. I touched his cheek softly, and hope returned to his eyes,

"Goodbye Leon. Maybe someday I will see you again." I saw the agony consume him as my hand fell from his cheek. He didn't say anything else, or try to stop me, as I walked away from him. I didn't know where exactly I was headed at that moment, or how I would survive on my own... all I knew was that I wanted revenge. The President would pay for all those who I had lost, and who Leon had lost. Leon had once told me that I could change everything with my Gift... maybe he was right.

All I knew for sure as I walked away from Leon, and walked away from the path leading to my brother's body, was that this was not the last anyone would hear of Kaydence Harrow. I am the Decider, and it is only the beginning.

Epilogue

Jeremiah watched Kayd and Leon run to the vent in the nick of time, but as Darcy and a few Soldiers came into his sight, all he could think about was what Galen had told him only a few days earlier.

Whenever the guards would take their break from 2-5 am, Jeremiah would come down to B-15 and sit outside of Galen's cell. Jeremiah was constantly amazed by the joy and sincerity that Galen had even when the Soldiers were breaking him down daily. Jeremiah slowly watched Galen's innocence wearing thin after being at the Fortress for two-and-a-half weeks, and his heart broke for the boy. Though he had only just met Galen, this little boy seemed to be the first person in thousands to be brought to the Fortress that truly made him think about getting away from it all.

"Jeremiah…" Galen called out that day.

"Yes, Galen?" Jeremiah said gently as he moved closer to Galen's cell.

Galen scowled as he forced himself to his feet, scuttling slowly towards the edge of the cell as if in pain. *They must be to the physical tortures now…* Jeremiah thought sadly. "I feel bad…" Galen whispered.

Jeremiah offered a forced smile in hopes of encouraging him, "I know this is hard, but kid, I've never seen someone stay so strong when the Soldiers begin their torture methods..."

Galen shook his head, not meeting the Freezer's eyes, "I might have made a mistake..."

Jeremiah looks back at him in surprise, "What kind of mistake, Galen?"

Galen looked up then, tears streaming down his cheeks. His lip quivered as he spoke, "Kayd... she was going to be with you, but I forced her on the path to Leon instead. I thought they would be better for each other..." Jeremiah watched him in shock. Was that why he and Kayd had such a strong connection? He hadn't been able to stop thinking about her since he left her and Leon's home. There were moments he even swore he was seeing their future together through his dreams the farther apart they seemed to be.

"No one can make someone go a certain way that they don't want to go, Galen. She just loved Leon. There's nothing you could have done to change that."

Galen shook his head, his tears stronger now, "No... she was never going to meet Leon, but with my Gift I looked at all the different paths and possibilities... and I saw the unlikely path of getting to Leon. She had no idea I was leading her to him... and then they fell in love. Had I allowed her to take the path she would've taken on her own, she would already be with you..." Galen shook his head.

Jeremiah stared back with wide, unblinking eyes. He felt as if something was pressing down on him, perhaps it was the weight of a future he never got to live? "Why would you do that?" Jeremiah asked, truly baffled.

Galen sighed tiredly, "Because… I knew you were a Freezer, and that you were with the Authority. I was convinced you were going to change her for the worst… but you turned out to be really nice…" Galen let out a depressed chuckle, "And now Kayd and Leon hate each other. He left her…"

Jeremiah shook his head, "Galen, I saw the love she had for him, and the love he had for her only a month ago… he wouldn't have left her."

"She will be here in two days." Galen said like it was old news.

Jeremiah considered the young boy in confusion, "Let me get you out of here, Galen… if you really think your sister and Leon will be here in a few days, then I can get you somewhere safe for her to find you."

Galen sighed, looking at his cell wall, "No… I tried that path before—it didn't work. I will have to stay here until she comes for me." He said miserably.

Jeremiah furrowed his brow, "Galen… if she is coming for you, maybe I could help her get to you? I can get you all out safely."

Galen nodded lightly, "Yes, that will be the safest way for Kayd. But you have to leave her and Leon at the door to this floor. Do not come down the hall unless you hear a scream."

Jeremiah shook his head, stunned by the certainty in Galen's tone, "Galen, what are you..."

Galen raised his hand, "This is important, Jeremiah! For the cameras you need to pretend that you had no idea who she really is, or why she came here."

"Ok, I will..."

Darcy's voice called out for Jeremiah, and he looked in her direction for only a moment.

"And Jeremiah..."

"Yes, Galen?"

"When I die, I need you to get Kayd out of here as quickly as possible... don't let her get caught." Galen said with fresh tears caressing his cheek. Jeremiah's eyes widened, but no more words could be spoken as Darcy pulled him away from the cell.

Jeremiah thought back to that moment now as he looked at Galen's dead body—the only one to realize what had happened to the sweet boy he had grown to call friend so quickly. He made sure to get Kayd and Leon out of the hallway as quickly as possible, but he was still not prepared for the grief that would hit him as he looked at Galen's still form. As soon as Kayd and Leon were out of sight, he fell to his knees beside his friend and pulled his lifeless hand into his own.

"You really did know everything... didn't you, kid?" He said, tears filling his eyes. Darcy and a few of the largest Soldiers swarmed into the hallway, guns raised.

Darcy looked terrified and furious as she came to Jeremiah's side, "Jeremiah, there was an alarm raised... apparently that guy and girl who came to our floor were intruders!" She looked to the ground to see General Lion lying on the ground, "Why are you sitting next to the kid? Shouldn't you be tending to General Lion instead?" she asked, truly confused.

The Soldiers began scanning the perimeter, running towards the very vent Kayd had escaped through. Everything seemed surreal for Jeremiah as he continued to hold Galen's hand, "I checked on the General first... he just got hit in the head. The kid is dead though..." he said, trying to hide the pain in his voice, "I felt that the kid needed a final prayer."

Darcy rolled her eyes, "Oh Jeremiah, you always care too much about people," she said with a scoff.

The Soldiers came back to the scene and two of the larger Soldiers each took one end of General Lion's body to carry. Another Soldier went to pick up Galen too, but Jeremiah stopped them, "Please, I'll carry this one." The Soldiers and Darcy considered him with confused concern, "I got to know the kid, ok? I know what you guys do with the bodies of the Gifted who die around here... I want to make sure he gets a real burial." Darcy's eyes showed brief compassion even if the idea confounded her.

Darcy looked back to the Soldiers, "It doesn't hurt to let him bury one of them." She said with authority. The Soldiers shrugged and nodded before carrying the General to the elevator. Darcy and Jeremiah were left alone, Galen tucked safely in Jeremiah's arms. "What was it about this kid?" she asked

Jeremiah looked at Galen's somber face and remembered back to what Galen had said about the future he had changed concerning Kayd. If Galen had been right about everything else, could he really have been lying about Kayd and Jeremiah being meant for each other?

Jeremiah smiled softly, "He just feels like family..."

Jeremiah took Galen outside, telling Darcy that he wanted time to himself to mourn. He brought a shovel to dig a small grave in the most beautiful part of the forest next to a little waterfall. He set Galen down gently on the ground and began digging. Tears were finally allowed to pour down his cheeks as he thought about the sweet boy he could've known longer if only things had been different. But maybe that was part of why Galen wanted a different future for his sister? He didn't want her to be stuck as a goon for the Authority like Jeremiah was.

"Damn it! Why did he have to die, though?" he shouted to the sky. Suddenly a small voice whined. Jeremiah turned around to find the source of the voice, and then he saw movement out of the corner of his eye next to Galen. His eyes widened as he looked at the young boy again, "Galen...?"

The End

Note from the Author

Thank you so much for reading! I hope you enjoyed Kayd's story! This is just the first book in the series, and I can't wait for you to hear the rest of the story. I started writing this book when I was 23-years-old, the year my daughter was born. This book has been so incredibly special to me, and to know that it is finally going out into the world is both exciting and terrifying.

~ Mycheille Norvell ~

Made in the USA
Middletown, DE
14 December 2020